WESTERN ISLES LIBRARIES

Readers are requested to take great care of the item while in their possession, and to point out any defects that they may notice in them to the Librarian.

This item should be returned on or before the latest date stamped below, but an extension of the period of loan may be granted when desired.

DATE OF RETURN	DATE OF RETURN	DATE OF RETURN
0.9. MAR 2015 SY		
2 6 MAY 201 TT		
LtM 13/7/2,		
28 /09/21		
UM 28/09/21		
1 1 NOV 2021		
2 5 FEB 2022		
LT 26/6/22		

CIRCULATING

WITHDRAWN

ALSO BY MAGGIE SHIPSTEAD
FROM CLIPPER LARGE PRINT

Seating Arrangements

Astonish Me

Maggie Shipstead

W F HOWES LTD

This large print edition published in 2014 by
W F Howes Ltd
Unit 4, Rearsby Business Park, Gaddesby Lane,
Rearsby, Leicester LE7 4YH

1 3 5 7 9 10 8 6 4 2

First published in the United Kingdom in 2014
by Blue Door

A CIP catalogue record for this book is available
from the British Library

ISBN 978 1 47126 761 1

Typeset by Palimpsest Book Production Limited,
Falkirk, Stirlingshire

Printed and bound in Great Britain
by TJ International Ltd, Padstow, Cornwall

For two beloved friends:

NICHOLAS,
who knows about the place where art
and life meet, and

MICHELLE,
who goes to the ballet with me

PART I

SEPTEMBER 1977 – NEW YORK CITY

In the wings, behind a metal rack crowded with bundles of cable and silk flower garlands and the stringless lutes from act 1, two black dachshunds lie in a basket. They are awake but motionless, their small, uneasy eyes fixed on the dancers who come smiling and leaping offstage and give themselves over to violent exhaustion, standing stooped, hands on hips, heaving like racehorses. The dancers grab fistfuls of tissues from boxes mounted to the light rigs with gaffing tape and swab their faces and chests. Sweat patters on the floor. A stagehand pushes an ammonia-smelling mop around. The pas de deux begins. Two Russian stars are out alone in the light, both defectors. The surface of the stage has the dull shine of black ice; rosin dusts it like snow.

Ordinarily, members of the corps do not dare acknowledge the dogs, but Joan Joyce crouches and strokes their long backs. She fingers their velvety ears and smooth little skulls. The creatures shrink away into their basket, but she persists. In the shadows, other corps girls stand waiting in a clump, tutus overlapping like a mat of stiff lavender blossoms.

'What are you doing?' one of them whispers. 'You can't touch those.'

Joan's roommate Elaine Costas, a soloist, is sitting against the wall and stretching. Her pointe shoes are pressed together at the soles like hands in prayer, her face bent to their arches. Her costume is yellow, the bodice embroidered with gold. 'If Ludmilla were going to murder Joan,' she says, looking up, 'she would have done it already.'

One of the dogs sets a paw against Joan's wrist and braces away, his hard ebony nails digging into her skin. She kisses at him. He lifts his ears, then remembers himself and flattens them, recanting his interest. Joan has never danced as well as tonight. She is of the corps but also entirely herself, both part and whole. The tiny ball of cells clinging to her uterine wall is a secret, but she feels as translucent and luminous as a firefly.

Arslan Rusakov and Ludmilla Yedemskaya appear in the bright channel between the black stage drapes and stop, glazed with sweat and white light. He turns her waist between his palms, his face set in an ardent mask. Love in a ballet is something that does not exist and then suddenly does, its beginning marked by pantomime, faces fixed in rapture, a dance. After, when they are hidden in the wings or behind the curtain, the dancers will grimace like goblins, letting the pain show.

At home in their apartment, Elaine sometimes

4

does an unkind imitation of Arslan's love face, dancing pompously and then turning to answer herself with a parody of Ludmilla's smile: bared teeth beneath flinty eyes. Joan laughs and asks for more, but the mockery stings. Arslan had been her lover. She had been the one to help him defect.

He and Ludmilla had been a couple when they were both in the Kirov, and now they are getting married. They had announced their engagement after a performance of *Swan Lake* with champagne for the whole company. Ludmilla's head was swathed in a crown of white feathers. Joan and Arslan were done before Ludmilla arrived, but still the tiny yellow-haired Russian provokes Joan's sense of having been taunted and robbed, deprived.

Applause, and Ludmilla sweeps into the wings. The music for Arslan's variation begins. Joan keeps petting the dogs, but the animals crane their long necks for a glimpse of their mistress. 'They are not nice,' Ludmilla says after a moment, her accent flat and heavy like a stone in the back of her throat. 'You should not touch.'

Before curtain, the dachshunds had moped around Ludmilla's feet while she warmed up, narrowly avoiding being kicked. She never seems to pay them any attention, but she brings them to every class, every rehearsal, every fitting, every performance, every gala. They were a gift from Arslan when she arrived in New York after her defection, replacements for dachshunds left behind in Leningrad. Their bony, penitent faces are always turned, like so many others, toward her. They would never think of barking, not even when cymbals crash or when stagehands pump out chilly clouds of fog from a machine to make an enchanted haze or suggest the surface of a lake.

'They seem sweet,' Joan says.

Ludmilla, dabbing her cheeks with a tissue, gazes at her with amused malevolence. 'They bite.'

'I don't think so.'

'They are my dogs, not your dogs, but if you want get bite, suit yourself.'

Suit yourself is something Arslan says because it is something Joan says. She taught him, and now he has taught Ludmilla. Joan gives the dachshunds a final rub – one bares a set of tiny, sharp ivory teeth at her, as dainty and menacing as his mistress – and stands up. Ludmilla turns away to watch Arslan pirouette at center stage (he is a prince! it is his wedding day!) as the music accelerates and sweat flies from his hair. Arslan is racing the conductor, trying to squeeze in more turns. When he is done, the audience will let loose the huge, docile roar of amazement they always do. The ovation is a given, but he will still earn it. He is extraordinary. The audience loves him for being extraordinary and also for having been born to the enemy, for coming to dance for them instead.

The end of the music. His last turn squeaks around a beat late. The roar explodes from the belly of the theater, blasts out to the back of the house. Arslan bows, bows again, gives a modest flick of his head. Ludmilla draws herself up, raises her arms over her head, and steps briskly out from the wings. Her variation begins, but Joan does not watch.

Joan has known plenty of pregnant dancers but only a handful who stayed that way and only one who then returned to the company – a principal famous enough to be forgiven for the months of leave, her slow battle back into shape. For most of the women Joan knows, a child is unthinkable. The body has already been offered up; the body is spoken for. She is only eight weeks or so and still not showing, but she is surprised she hasn't been found out. The dancers keep close surveillance on one another, report suspicions of weakness. Elaine might have guessed, Joan thinks, but it's not her nature to interrogate or tattle. Usually they share a banana in the morning before class, but Joan, both nauseated and famished, has a new compulsion to toast frozen waffles and spread them with peanut butter. Elaine, eating her banana half, watches the passage of the sticky knife, says nothing. Mercifully, magically, Joan's nausea tends to dissipate during morning class. She hasn't betrayed herself by puking.

In July, after the blackout, she had faked a

7

slight sprain and gone to visit Jacob in Chicago. He is not her boyfriend. In high school, they had explained themselves as best friends, proud of their status as a bonded but platonic pair, a relationship that seemed modern and cosmopolitan to them, worlds away from the short-lived, sweaty-palmed hormonal couplings happening around them. But Joan had known Jacob wanted more. For so long, he was too timid – and too proud – to try anything.

He had kissed her once, just before he left for college. It had been the kind of kiss that asks for something enormous. When she pushed him away, he was angry, and she had turned his anger around and punished him with it and hidden behind it. Then he left, and they wrote letters, which seemed safer.

She supposes Jacob still is her best friend, although during the time she was with Arslan and then recovering from being with Arslan, she had allowed their friendship to lie fallow. She prefers to think that way – her bond with Jacob was resting, regathering itself – instead of admitting she had neglected him. But Jacob is the forgiving type, the comforting type, the patient type.

In Chicago, at first he had affected a breezy version of their high school intimacy, taking her to a loud and smelly bar, alluding to the latest woman he was seeing, letting her buy the drinks. 'What's the latest with Arslan the Terrible?' he'd asked in a brotherly tone. But shifting the

8

momentum had not been difficult. She'd touched his arm as they drank, leaned into him, bumped against his side as they walked to his apartment, and, over a nightcap, told him she'd missed him. 'I've been considering,' she said. 'Like you asked me to.'

'Yeah?' he said, guarded. They were sitting on his sway-backed sofa.

'I think maybe.'

'Maybe what?'

She was too afraid to look at him. 'Just, you know, maybe.'

She had anticipated a long nocturnal conversation full of hesitation, negotiation, reminiscence, and uncertainty. But instead he had taken off his glasses and set them carefully on his junky coffee table and then lunged at her the way he had before, when they were teenagers. In spite of herself, she laughed.

'What?' he said.

'Nothing,' she said. 'Sorry. Just nerves.'

There had been no discussion of pills or condoms. She had the sense he was afraid to raise any impediment to what was finally about to happen.

Ludmilla is turning rapidly across the diagonal as the music builds toward the end of her variation. The corps girls in their lavender tutus shake out their legs, prepare. Joan can feel how impatient the audience is to applaud. Their hands are held apart like straining magnets. Ludmilla wraps the tension around herself as she turns.

9

When Joan begins to show, when she is found out, she knows she will feel regret, sorrow, panic – but now the sensation of purpose soars over her like the hunting bugle from act 2. She is surprised by the strength of it, the way it unfurls.

Applause. She falls into line with the others and is pulled out into the light.

The summer has been long, hot, chaotic. Civilization seems fragile. When the lights went out for a night in July, thousands of people looted and marauded and set fires. David Berkowitz has been arrested, but the specter of random death lingers. Elaine knows all the bouncers in the city and has enticed Joan to nightclubs and parties where glittering people loom out of the smoke and flashing lights, sometimes in costume – Cleopatras, unicorns, Dionysuses – slip-sliding and pivoting, not caring *how* they dance, just that they are dancing. Hot spots. Joan thinks of thermal vents, volcanic fissures. She dislikes crowds and jostling, but she has seen the smiling cokehead crescent moon at Studio 54 and peeked through the doorway to the orgy room at Plato's Retreat and been guided by more than one guy who knows a guy who knows a guy through downtown deadlands and up secret stairs to illegal parties in cavernous lofts. Elaine doesn't look like a ballerina when she's out – she turns slinky and loose on the dance floor, matching the steps of whatever man materializes in front of her – but Joan is too precise, too reserved, too square. She has tried drugs, but they leave her clinging to a banquette or crouched in a bathroom stall, immobilized by anxiety.

Elaine ingests a steady but restricted diet of cocaine without apparent consequence. The key, she has said to Joan, is control. Control is the key to everything. Elaine has a strict limit for coke, a regimen. She will do a bump before a performance for confidence and maybe another at intermission if she's dragging. She will do a line or two – never more than two – once or twice (no more than twice) a week when she's out, and she will substitute coke for lunch when she wants to drop a few pounds. She's not greedy about the high, doesn't want it all the time, just wants the boost of it. If she's short on money and doesn't have a man who's supplying her, she will cut it out entirely. No problem. That way it is a routine, something already managed, and the drug will not interfere with what's important, which is dance.

Elaine always has men but is never in love, except with Mr K, the artistic director, who also believes in regimens. Their love can be managed, must be managed. Joan had been surprised by how kind Elaine was during the tumultuous futility of her affair with Arslan, how patiently she listened as Joan plotted with a conspirator's intensity the hypothetical events, realizations, and declarations that, if they occurred, would ensure Arslan's lasting devotion. Arslan! A man who had

11

never been faithful to anyone and did not seem to love her. Maybe Elaine enjoyed the proximity to unmanageable love, the whoosh of it brushing by, the spectacle of someone else losing control. She must crave those things or else she wouldn't have such an appetite for nightlife. Joan wonders what she will think – possibly already thinks – about the pregnancy.

The sweepers are moving through the theater, clacking their dustpans. The audience has gushed, marveling, out onto Columbus Avenue. Arslan and Ludmilla have slipped away through the stage door. Tomorrow will start with company class. Almost every day starts with class, and those that don't are shapeless and problematic. Only what's left of the night separates Joan from more stretching, more dancing, from the genteel swoop and clatter of the piano, everyone at the barres while Mr K patrols, sweater tied over his shoulders, saying, *And open, and two, and again, lengthen your leg and UP, stay, stay, stay. No, girl. Like this.*

Joan should sleep while she can, but she isn't ready to go back to the apartment. She sleeps in a twin bed against the far wall of their small living room. For privacy, she tacked a sheet of printed Indian cotton high to the wall and draped it down over her bed to form a kind of tent, but the sheet only makes the room seem squalid and ramshackle. Which it is, in a way. The apartment is a crash pad, somewhere to go between classes and

12

performances, between men, somewhere to recover from the hot spots.

She finds Elaine in the soloists' dressing room.

'Do you want to go out?' she asks, peering around the door.

Elaine, wrapped in a towel, is brushing her smooth black curtain of hair and studying herself in the mirror of the long makeup table. A plastic cup of wine sits on the counter, surrounded by colorful tiles of eye shadow, rounds of blush, tubs of pancake, fake lashes fanned out in their plastic cases. The wine helps her come down at night. No more than two glasses. 'Sure. Where?'

'I don't know. I thought you'd know.'

Elaine waves her in. 'Come in already.'

A few other soloists are still around. One is wiping her eyelids with a cotton ball. Another stands naked, blow-drying her hair. Another lifts her dance bag to her shoulder and walks out, giving Joan's shoulder a friendly pat as she passes. A wardrobe assistant moves through the room, collecting tights to be washed, straightening costumes on hangers, putting the hangers on a rolling rack. Joan sidles in and perches on the table.

'Do you have anything else to wear?' Elaine asks.

Joan looks down at her jeans and platform sandals, her striped tank top. 'No.'

'We should go home first, then.'

'No, Elaine, please, I'll lose momentum. It doesn't have to be a big thing. Just a drink out somewhere. I don't want to go right home.'

'Well. Okay.' Elaine pulls her dance bag out from under the table and paws through it. She thrusts a bundle of purple cloth at Joan. 'Here.' Joan unfurls a loose, filmy blouse with a low neck. She strips off her tank top and pulls the blouse on over her bare chest.

'Can you see my nipples though this?' As soon as she has spoken, she regrets drawing attention to her breasts, which are swollen.

Elaine's eyes are sharp and green and set close against her long, narrow nose, pinning it in place. No change registers in them. 'Not really,' she says. She turns to the naked dancer with the blow dryer. 'Yvette, do you have anything I could borrow to wear out?'

'I have a little dress,' the girl says.

It is a very little dress, and yellow, but it suits Elaine, as most things do. 'Do you want to come to a party?' Elaine asks Yvette.

The girl, who is zipping up another little dress, blinks as slowly and mechanically as a doll as she considers. 'Yes,' she says. 'That would be very nice.' Joan is disappointed even though she likes Yvette, finds her dippy and harmless. Yvette was born in France and retains traces of an accent and of continental diffidence even though she has lived in New York since kindergarten. But Joan is becoming nostalgic in anticipation of the end of her ballet life and had imagined the night as belonging to her and Elaine, a memory just for the two of them, although Elaine will probably vanish as soon as they get wherever they're going. She has a way of vaporizing at parties, being immediately absorbed into the revelry.

Outside, the three of them find a taxi heading downtown. The city's summer breath rushes forcefully in through the windows, smelling of garbage and gasoline, and they recline in the warm air, saying little, worn out but also energized, their blood circulating smoothly, as though the performance had swept their veins clean. Joan is already too hot in her jeans and borrowed top. She envies the others' little dresses even though their bare legs must be sticking to the grimy vinyl seat cover. The driver peeks in the mirror, the silver rim of his glasses catching red and green sparks from the traffic lights. He handles the wheel gently, cautiously, with his plump hands. Most cabbies flirt a bit when the dancers are out together, make some suggestion about where they should go, comment on how nice they all look, but he doesn't. He takes his glances in the mirror, like someone peeping over a fence.

The party is near Astor Place, in a brick building with peeling yellow paint and a fire escape made out of rust. It is not Elaine's usual sort of glitzy, careening, pill-popping party but something else, just a party, a humid crowd of languid people gathered in a smoky apartment. Edith Piaf warbles from the stereo. Joan didn't need to have worried about Yvette. The girl takes the French music as

15

a sign of welcome and sets off for the table of bottles in the far corner, greeting strangers as she goes with little sideways *bonjours*.

'Drink?' Elaine says.

'No, I need to drop weight.'

Elaine takes a pack of cigarettes from her purse. 'Want one?'

'No, thanks.'

A knowingness hovers around Elaine's pursed lips and raised eyebrows as she lights up.

About Yvette, Joan says, 'I don't know why she still does this French act.'

'She's just French enough to pretend to be French. I don't know – look at her. It works. I should think it's obnoxious, but I don't.'

They look together through the people. At the makeshift bar, Yvette is smiling up at a tall and gorgeous black man. She cuts her eyes to the side, murmurs something out the corner of her mouth, making him lean in.

'I'm going to get a drink,' Elaine says. 'And hopefully a very tall man.'

Joan grabs her arm. 'No, don't. I'll never see you again. You'll disappear.'

'This place is tiny.'

'You have a way.'

'Come with, then. Five steps that way. We can rope ourselves together first if you want.'

Joan follows. 'How did you know about this party?'

'I went home with the guy whose apartment

16

this is a couple months ago, and then I ran into him the other night. He said he was having a thing. I wasn't going to come, but then you . . . he's – where is he? – oh, he's that one.' She points through the crowd to a pale head with full pale lips and small pale eyes. The head, partially obscured by a woman's red curls, nods in a courtly way, smiles slyly. It is the smile of a man who knows women like to think they are being amusing.

'He's handsome.'

'Isn't he? I thought so.' Elaine pours bourbon into a mug and offers the bottle. 'You sure?'

Joan shakes her head. 'All your men are handsome.'

'I would *not* call this guy one of my men. I would call him . . . Christopher? I'm not sure. I should have asked when I saw him again, but it seemed impolite. Maybe we can delicately find out from someone here.'

'Except Mr K. He's not handsome.'

'Mr K doesn't have to be handsome. He's a genius. You should know. Arslan doesn't have to be handsome either.'

'Arslan is handsome.'

'No, Arslan's sexy. Anyway, he's not a genius the way Mr K is. Mr K *creates*. Mr K has changed everything.'

'Please, tell me more about your boyfriend, your old, gay boyfriend.'

Elaine taps her cigarette into an empty wine

bottle, unflappable. 'Labels are a waste of time. So is possessiveness. I know what he is.'

'God,' Joan says on a long breath. 'I can't believe how liberating it is not to care anymore. I watched Arslan walk out the stage door with Ludmilla tonight and didn't want to kill myself. Finally. I'm cured. It's heaven.'

'Hmm.' Elaine drags on her cigarette, drops it into the wine bottle. 'I think you're pregnant.'

Joan smiles at the linoleum floor. She draws her toe across it in an arc. 'Because of the waffles?'

'Lately you seem like you're saying good-bye all the time, like you're about to go catch a bus.' Elaine studies her. 'Have you told Jacob?'

'No.' Joan watches the tentatively identified Christopher as he walks around with a jug of red wine, filling people's glasses and mugs. This is the first time she has spoken about the pregnancy except with the doctor who gave her prenatal vitamins, and Jacob's name is loaded with a heavy, sudden future.

In high school, she had decided her mild sexual curiosity about Jacob was nothing more than a generic offshoot of her general sexual curiosity. He was younger, which was not sexy, and wore little wire-rimmed glasses, which had seemed to signify something important then, and he was transparently devoted to her, which was not sexy, and he was academically brilliant and a little insecure (not sexy, not sexy). Joan, however, had the mystique of ballet to trade on, her tininess and her suppleness, the grace that had been drilled into her until she was physically unable to be awkward. Lots of boys wanted to date her, and dating them was simple, while dating Jacob would not have been.

But when they were sitting side by side at the movies or watching TV on the couch when her mother was out, not speaking and not looking at each other, he would stay so still that she sensed he was restraining himself, wary of any movement that would betray what he wanted, and some hidden sensory organ in her would rotate toward him, probing, considering.

'Did you do it on purpose?' Elaine asks.

'Of course not.'

'You can't do this if it's only about running away from Arslan.'

Since she got pregnant, the cattle prod jolt of Arslan's name has worn off, become only a faint zap, two weak wires touched together. 'It's not. It's really not. I might be running from everything else, but I have to go. I have to find something else. You'll make it. I was never going to.'

'You did it on purpose.'

'I didn't!'

'It doesn't matter. It's done. But you don't have to . . . you could, you know, just quit the company. Not have a baby. Get a job. Do something else.'

Solemnly, Joan shakes her head. 'I couldn't just decide to stop. I thought about it. But I'm too much of a coward. I can't stay in the city if I'm not dancing, and I wouldn't know where else to go. Or what to do, generally.'

'So you're counting on Jacob to figure all that out for you. This all seems really elaborate, Joan. I feel sorry for Jacob. He's walking around Chicago right now with no idea he's a marked man.'

'He's getting what he wants.'

'Oh yeah?' Elaine takes another cigarette from her pack. 'Well then. You're a Good Samaritan.'

'Give me a cigarette, please.'

'You shouldn't smoke.'

'I know. This one and then I'm quitting. I'm quitting everything. Everything is going to be different.'

'Inevitably.'

Finding nothing else to say, they pretend to be interested in the party that drifts around them as lightly as fog. Joan makes eye contact with a series of men. They are the kind of men who look over shoulders while they chatter, searching for the people they will chatter at next. The crowd shifts, revealing the host's pale head inclined attentively toward the fast-moving mouth of a blond woman in a paisley jumpsuit.

Joan says, 'Will you introduce me to Christopher?'

Joan lies awake. Beside her, the man sleeps. Even his snores are polite and well formed. His name is Tom, not Christopher. Probably some other Christopher had swum through Elaine's nocturnal world, crossing bubble trails with this handsome

Tom, an assistant professor of Old and Middle English at NYU. His bed is surprisingly clean and nice smelling for a single man with bohemian tastes. Joan wonders if he will be the second-to-last man she ever sleeps with.

The yellow night drops a window-square on the pale sheet. Tom makes a rough sound in his sleep that might be Old or Middle English. The cells continue to multiply. Joan rests her palm against her belly, trying to divine the exact spot where life has been planted like a tulip bulb. Usually when she is in bed with a strange man – there haven't been so many – she has trouble sleeping because she is preoccupied by the nearness of the unfamiliar body that has been recently and intimately explored and is now remote, locked away in sleep. But Tom holds no curiosity for her. She strokes her own skin, wonders what time it is. His wrist with his watch is under his pillow, and she doesn't see a clock in the room. When the sun rises she will make her way home and then, later, to class. She wonders how many more times she will go to class. When she stops dancing, class will continue on without her, every day except Sunday, part of the earth's rotation. The piano will swoop and clatter, and Mr K will say *No, girl, like this* to dancers who are not her. Her empty spot at the barre will heal over at once. But she wants a few more days, a week or two. She wants the cells to grow in time to the piano, to Mr K's clapping hands, his *one pa pa pa, two pa pa pa, and UP pa pa pa,* to the rhythm of her battements. Until now, even when surrounded by twenty women dressed just like her, moving in unison with her, she has always been lonely, but the cells give her a feeling of companionship. For the first time she can remember, she is not afraid of failing, and the relief feels like joy.

NOVEMBER 1978 – CHICAGO

As Jacob crosses the quad, shuffling home through new snow, he is seized by a rebellious impulse to stop at a bar. Not that he doesn't want to see Joan and the baby, and not that having a quiet beer by himself would be a crime, but the enormous obligations that have arrived abruptly (and, one could argue, prematurely) with his new status as a family man have recalibrated his sense of himself, made him ashamed of his moments of selfishness and guilt stricken whenever he feels a twinge of resentment. He wants so badly to satisfy and delight Joan in all possible ways and to be a good father to Harry that he is not certain there should be space left over for wanting a beer. Or solitude. Or freedom, which is unmistakably a thing of the past.

He has never been one to fetishize freedom, though. Since he can remember, he has pursued obligation and commitment, which is why, at twenty-four, he is already into the fourth year of his doctorate. That he is, at twenty-four, also already the father of an infant son and already married to a woman he has coveted since it first occurred to him to covet women, might not have been part of his original plan, but he can't claim he hadn't been an enthusiastic participant in Harry's conception or that he hadn't wanted to marry Joan, at least as far as he was capable of imagining marriage, since he was a high school kid desperately playing it cool.

The snow is the first serious one of the year. It settles in strips on naked tree branches, builds white doilies on the stone traceries of Gothic windows. In the summer, the façade of Green Hall is bearded with Boston ivy, and a wreath of leaves surrounds Jacob's office window, giving the light a pleasantly verdant quality, like the inside of a tree house. But now, in late November, the vine is a withered caul of twigs, tapping and scratching at the walls. Jacob changes trajectory, heading for a dank subterranean bar he likes and away from the tiny apartment where Joan and Harry are waiting. The apartment has a demonic radiator that shrieks in defiance when Jacob tries to turn it off and incubates all the fetid baby smells and makes his hair brittle and his skin itchy. Joan, who is always cold, likes the radiator and will not let him call the super. She takes a reptilian solace in its heat, perching neatly sideways atop the flaking silver coils.

The mug of Old Style the bartender coaxes from the tap is mostly foam but is delivered with a look that discourages Jacob from complaining. He is happy, anyway, to be sitting on a stool with a ripped vinyl cover, resting his elbows on sticky Formica, gazing at pocked dartboards and a jumble of Bears and Cubs ephemera. There is a TV behind the bar, but it's angled so only the bartender can watch. Light flickers over the ranks of bottles.

The woman Jacob was dating before – and, truthfully, during and for some time after – Joan paid her fateful visit had introduced him to this place. Liesel, a Ph.D. student in chemistry. There is one other guy at the bar: thirtyish, with a mustache, on the beefy side, sipping whiskey.

'Great place, isn't it?' Jacob remarks. His stolen hour, now that he has committed to it, is making him expansive and giddy.

'Yeah,' the guy says, 'a real hidden gem.' He has a strong Chicago accent and a plump face that suggests, in a friendly way, that bullshit would be unwelcome.

'I used to come here with an ex,' Jacob says.

'Yeah?'

'It was kind of her spot. I haven't been here since we broke up.'

'Bad breakup?'

'It wasn't great.' Then, wanting to clarify, Jacob adds, 'I married a ballet dancer.'

At *ballet dancer,* the guy's smile seems to snag on something. 'Yeah?' the guy says. 'Like a professional?'

Jacob nods. 'Yeah.'

The fact that Joan is a dancer impresses most

men and rankles most women. *Was* a dancer, although he has no plans to tell this stranger she is retired. When Joan was pregnant, Jacob had thought she might try to go back to ballet after the baby, but she said flatly that she couldn't. Her career had run its course. She will teach, but she will not perform. Elaine sent them tickets to the Joffrey not long before Harry was born. On the way home, Joan had cried on the El, clasping her thin arms around her belly, but she only shook her head when Jacob said it didn't have to be over for her. He didn't understand, she said. She had never been that good, anyway, she said, and to keep trying would be pathetic.

There is, in this decision, a loss for Jacob he would never admit to her. For as long as he has known Joan, since they were almost children, she has lived a double life, as a dancer and as a civilian, and her retirement means she has been reduced in some essential way. He will miss seeing her onstage, displayed so beautifully at the front of all that darkness, and he will miss the mystery of her hours of class and rehearsal, her proximity to other beautiful women and to the hands of other men. He finds low-level jealously to be enlivening, pleasantly astringent.

He has his limits, though. During the months Joan was involved with Arslan Rusakov, Jacob had been in agony. Her other boyfriends, beginning in high school, had irritated and disgruntled but not tortured him; Joan had not appeared to

26

be very attached to the others, had certainly not loved any of them. Then Rusakov came along and swallowed her up, and Jacob's belief that they would end up together one day, after they'd exhausted the dubious pleasures of trying out people they didn't love, had begun to dwindle. His mother, who has never liked Joan, made a point of phoning him long-distance when she showed up in magazines or newspapers with Rusakov, and he would go out to the newsstand to see for himself, flipping clumsily through the pages and then staring down at the photos until the guy said, *Library's down the street, buddy.* Joan's letters dwindled to a trickle, and the few she did write only made things worse.

The mustache guy signals the bartender for another drink, and the bartender, surprisingly, hops to it. 'Where'd you meet?'

'High school. In Virginia.'

Jacob and his two older sisters had high IQs, and their father, a naval officer, was frequently reposted, allowing their ambitious, unmaternal mother to skip her children forward in school until they were high school freshmen at twelve and college students at sixteen. The great mercy of Jacob's life was that he grew early (but then stopped – he is not tall) and was a reasonably handsome, affable kid, good enough at baseball and track to avoid classification as an irredeemable nerd. Joan's locker had been across from his when they were freshmen, and she was so small, so knobby and tentative like a fawn, that at first he had hoped she was young, too.

'Excuse me,' she had said, appearing beside him on the first day while he fussed with his books and notebooks. 'Do you know where room three-nineteen is?' She wore a red and blue plaid dress with a collar and a red belt and peered at him with anxious earnestness, like a tourist asking for directions in a dicey neighborhood.

'Yeah,' he said. 'It's on my way. I'll show you.'

'Are you a sophomore?' she asked as they walked. 'How do you know where things are already?'

'I took a class here last year,' he said, trying to project proprietary confidence. 'I got the lay of the land.'

'Lucky.' She flinched away from a group of older students. 'I thought about coming down on a weekend and making sure I knew where to go, but then I thought someone would see me and think I was nuts. You probably think I'm nuts. It's just, I have a feeling I'm going to do this wrong.'

'Do what wrong?'

'Everything. High school.'

'You'll be fine. Just act like you're sure you belong.' He was echoing what his sister Marion had said to him that morning. 'Nobody knows any better.' He let a beat go by. 'How old are you?'

'I'll be fourteen in October. I'm a little young. When's your birthday?'

'March,' he said, neglecting to mention that his next birthday would be his thirteenth.

'Why did you ask?'

'I was just wondering. You look young.'

'I hope I always do,' she said with unexpected vehemence. 'I do ballet. I can't be big or old.'

Jacob, who wouldn't have minded being either of those things, said, 'It might be hard to avoid getting older.'

'I know that,' she said, sharply again. She was not as meek as she had first appeared, and he liked her more for it. 'It only matters how you *look*.'

'That's not true,' he ventured after a moment, 'in the big picture.'

He was afraid he might have offended her, or that she would think he was an annoying goody-goody, but she made a wry face. 'I mean in ballet,' she said. 'Which is my big picture.'

They fell into separate groups of friends – Joan's smallness and prettiness and docility made her popular – but they chatted by their lockers and greeted each other in the halls. Their houses were not far apart, and sometimes they walked together. The ballet studio was on the way to Jacob's house, and when he didn't have baseball, he escorted her there, carrying her dance bag. He never went inside, and, in his imagination, the unassuming little storefront was a cloistered place of rites and mysteries. Sheer white curtains covered its front windows, and through them he caught vague, gauzy glimpses of girls in black leotards.

'Is that your brother?' Jacob heard one of Joan's friends ask in the lunchroom.

'Basically,' Joan replied, and he felt both honored and insulted.

Her nerviness and discipline appealed to him, and he felt protective of her in a way that seemed adult and masculine and new. As the younger brother of two bossy sisters, he was used to being clucked over by girls, but Joan seemed to trust that he could take care of himself and also, as needed, her. He understood that this was a role worth cultivating. Her mother was single and worked and didn't understand ballet or Joan. Joan's dance teacher, Madame Tchishkoff, was of the formidable, exacting variety and offered little beyond unyielding rigor and the motivational power of perpetual, implacable disappointment. Joan's school friends were the kind of pretty girls who clumped together to assert their collective prettiness. They were companions and accessories, not confidantes.

When Joan was lonely or distressed, it was Jacob she called, and he would take the phone from his scowling mother and retreat into the pantry, closing the flimsy door over the cord, gazing idly at the cans of soup and boxes of crackers while he listened. On the rare afternoons she didn't have ballet, she summoned him to watch TV and help her with her homework at her house, which was always too dark and didn't seem to have enough furniture and so felt like a hideout. Jacob's mother would not allow a television in the house, nor did she approve of Joan's lack of supervision or of friendships between boys and girls, and so he told her he was staying late at school.

Joan trusted him with her darkest secret, which was that she had not only found her mother's diaphragm but become obsessed with checking its presence in the bathroom drawer against what her mother *said* she was doing on a given night and the sometimes contradictory information offered by her Filofax.

'See?' she said to Jacob once, having dragged him into the bathroom and opened a drawer with great portentousness, as though revealing the entrance to an Egyptian tomb. He saw cotton balls and shiny makeup compacts, emery boards, nail scissors with handles in the shape of a bird. 'It's gone.'

'Okay,' he said, baffled by both her emotions and the workings of a diaphragm.

'She's *doing* it!' Joan told him, near tears. 'With that *man*! His name is *Rick*! He works in her *office*.'

To Jacob, this was not information to be cried over but rather to be filed away for later consideration. Joan's mother was a thin, brusque woman who wore neat suits and pinned her hair in elaborate updos, the mechanics of which eluded him.

'Don't worry,' he said. He closed the drawer. Joan stared desolately at its white-painted face, its little ceramic knob in the shape of a rosebud. 'It doesn't have to bother you.'

He wished he could think of something less dumb to say, less helpless, but she nodded and

31

folded her arms over her chest. 'It feels better just to show you,' she said. 'But promise you won't tell anyone.'

He realized, with a flush of gratitude, that her standards for wisdom were pathetically low. He patted her shoulder. 'I won't.'

He liked her delicate, feline face, her long, wispy hair, her narrow hips, her duck-footed walk, the gap between the tops of her thighs when she was in tights, her small, bony hands. If his sister Marion would drive him and not tell their mother, he went to Joan's recitals, and he liked the way she was willing to stand onstage and be looked at. Eventually, March of sophomore year, when he finally actually turned fourteen, he confessed his age, and by then they were too close for her to make much of a fuss, although he thought he detected a new and faintly patronizing undertone in the way she spoke to him, especially about her dates, which were as frequent as her ballet schedule would allow and, he gathered, relatively chaste. She seemed more interested in the public victory of securing the attention of popular and athletic boys than the private encounters that might follow.

'I can tell you anything,' she told Jacob often, which, to him, sounded less like a compliment than a command, the way his father said, *You'll make this family proud.* Her confessional openness struck him, sometimes, less as a sign of intimacy between them than a smoke screen meant to keep him at a distance. She would chatter on, telling him how Barry Sauerland had offended her at the winter formal by implying that she was not his first-choice date or how Floyd Bishop had called her an icicle. She never seemed to notice that Jacob did not reciprocate her confidences, or not exactly. He confided in her about his father's distant rigidity and his mother's suffocating rigidity and about their clockwork marriage that, on rare occasions of malfunction, caused both to go wild with rage. But he did not talk to Joan about girls, even though he took dates to dances and some-times to the movies, disguising his lack of a driver's license as a lack of a car.

Just before graduation, Joan tore a ligament in her foot. She had been slated to dance in a student performance in New York, where she would be seen by the directors of companies there and from San Francisco and Chicago and *everywhere*, she said, but now she could only lie around her house with her foot in a cast, paralyzed with fear that she would not heal, that she would miss her chance.

'Let's go to the beach,' Jacob said on a hot Saturday. Joan was lying on the couch with her cast propped up on a pillow, and he was sitting on the floor beside her, absently digging his fingers into the jungley olive-green pile of the carpet while they watched *American Bandstand*. 'This is getting depressing.'

Track was over; he was officially going to Georgetown, was officially the valedictorian, could

33

relax for the first time in his life, and his big reward was to be pressed into constant service as Joan's footman in her mother's austere, gloomy den. At first, he had been eager to spend long, unsupervised hours indoors with Joan, but she was so morose that it seemed inappropriate to persist in the hope that they would finally make out, if only to dispel the boredom. Instead he made sandwiches for her that she didn't eat, poured Tab over ice, changed the channel at her bidding, and waited for the unseen filaments of her ligament to knit themselves back together. Even Joan's mother, off for the weekend with one of Rick's successors, was having more fun.

'I can't go to the beach,' she snapped, pointing at her cast. 'Remember?'

'You don't have to go in the water. Let's just get out of here. My mom will let me take the car. She's so happy I'm leaving soon.'

'I'll get sand in my cast.'

'We'll put a bag over it.' An idea struck him. 'I'll carry you.'

She looked skeptical.

'I'll put you down on a towel, and you can just lie there. It'll be almost as good as lying on the couch all day. You'll love it.'

'You're not that strong.'

'You don't weigh anything.' He was not entirely certain he *could* carry her all the way from the car to the beach, but he was willing to try. Her injury made her more approachable, somehow.

Not that he was afraid of her. He was just aware of her boundaries, of the prickly force field around her. Standing over her, though, while she lay hobbled and clutching her plastic cup of soda, he decided to be daring. 'Stand up,' he said.

His authoritative tone seemed to surprise her. She set her drink on the carpet, swung her legs around, and, taking his outstretched hands, stood unevenly on her bare foot and her cast. He put one arm under her knees and one around her back, and then he straightened up, cradling her. The easy way she lay in his arms reminded him that she was no stranger to being carried. Jacob had met her pas de deux partner, the only boy at her studio, Gregory, son of Russian immigrant scientists, a sallow, pimply creature who was educated by private tutors to avoid the brutalizing influence of high school. Gregory, for all his apparent wimpiness, could lift Joan over his head with ease. Jacob had wondered what it would be like to lift her, to grasp her by her thighs or her waist and move her body through space as he pleased. She looked at him. Their faces were very close. 'Okay, fine,' she said. 'Let's go to the beach.'

Jacob's mother handed over the keys to her Rambler wagon with minimal admonitions. The front seat stretched out long between him and Joan, its scratchy cream upholstery radiating early summer warmth. Joan sprawled in the sun: wiry legs poking out of short shorts, bikini ties in a tantalizing bow at her nape, her face turned to her

35

open window. The Rambler, with its big windows and long bench seats and vast carpeted launchpad of a cargo space in back, did not seem, as it usually did, like a blocky symbol of maternity but was transformed into a terrarium of sexual possibility. For weeks, Jacob had been gearing up to try something with Joan. Not because he didn't care about their friendship but because he felt like his participation in that friendship, as it was, had become disingenuous. He wasn't a saint or a child. He wasn't the palace eunuch. He wasn't her cousin, as he knew she had told one of her boyfriends. She might reject him – probably would reject him – but he needed to come clean. High school was, for all intents and purposes, over, and he needed to slough off its context. He wasn't eager to be separated from Joan, but he was curious what would be in store for him at Georgetown, who he would be there.

They turned off the main road and bounced along a sandy lane to their usual spot, some way down the shore from the popular swimming beach. Before they'd left, Joan had rallied enough to stump around the kitchen filling a thermos with fruit punch and her mother's vodka, and after he parked, Jacob took the towels and the ice chest and crossed the low, sharp-grassed dunes. He spread the towels out on dry sand, and then he went back to get Joan. She was standing on her good foot, leaning against the Rambler.

'I think it would make the most sense for me to

ride piggyback,' she announced when he drew near. 'For long-distance transport.'

He considered. He had already held her in his arms, and having her cling to his back sounded like a new and interesting variation. 'Okay,' he said. 'You're the boss.' He turned around and crouched down. Nimbly for someone in a cast, she hopped aboard. As he started across the sand, he kept his eyes on the terrain in front of him, but his nerves were busily mapping her body. His hands were wrapped around the backs of her thighs. He could feel her ropy muscles under his fingers and a film of sweat. The rough plaster of her cast occasionally scraped the outside of his left calf. Her arms were around his neck, her sharp chin on his shoulder, the soft points of her small breasts against his back. The spot where the crotch of her shorts pressed against his waist was almost too potent to think about. His glasses slid down his nose, and he kept having to toss his head like a horse to keep them from sliding off. They didn't speak until he stooped to let her dismount onto the blue-and-white-striped towel.

'Such service,' she said, sitting and smiling up at him uncertainly. She felt the pull, too. He knew she did.

He sat. She looked away, out at the surf, which was breaking sluggishly, the waves plumping up in gelatinous heaps before collapsing into exhausted white frills. He was alive with fear and need. Then she said, as though everything were normal, 'The worst part about being injured is how smug my mom is about the whole thing.'

He closed his eyes against the glare of the sun. 'Yeah?'

Joan nodded. 'The other day she circled an ad for a typing course and left it on my pillow. I wanted to hit her.'

'You can't do that.' He dug in the ice chest and busied himself pouring out cups of vodka punch.

'Hit her?'

'Type.'

She smiled ruefully. 'With my mom, it's like she's missed the whole point of my entire life. I work myself to death at something that's really actually important, and all she wants is for me to be a secretary. It's not like I know if ballet's going to work out, but I have to believe or else there's no point.'

'At least,' Jacob said, trying to focus on the problem at hand, to be, in spite of everything, a good friend, 'you know that what you want was your idea in the first place. My parents brainwashed me into the fine citizen I am today.'

'What do you mean? You don't want to go to Georgetown?'

'No, I do. But I'm not sure I wanted to be skipped ahead and put in extra classes and all that. I don't know. It's done. I get to leave home early, so I should be grateful.'

'Sometimes I wonder,' Joan said, her mouth red from the punch, 'how you're supposed to know

38

if you're really feeling what you think you're feeling. Like how do we know everybody sees colors the same way, you know? Do we all feel "happy" the same way?'

Jacob shrugged.

'In ballet,' she went on, 'when something's really beautiful, I feel a lot, but not happy or sad, really. Just a feeling. With goose bumps. I like it.' After a moment, she sighed and rolled onto her stomach, resting her forehead on her arms. 'If I can't dance, I know I won't die, but it feels like I will.'

He rolled over onto his stomach, too. 'It'll work out.'

She turned her head so they were looking at each other. 'You're the only person who takes care of me. You think I don't notice, but I do.' Her punch-stained mouth was as inviting as red velvet.

Later he would not believe that he had simply scooted across his towel and put his mouth on her red one, lunged at her, really. The desire was so pure it set his teeth on edge. He pushed her over onto her back with an insistence he didn't know he was capable of. Her arms went up around his neck; her hands clasped the back of his head; he sprawled across her. Some seconds passed before he became aware that her hands had dropped to his chest and were pushing at him. He lifted his face slowly, unwillingly.

She looked stricken, panicked. 'I can't,' she said.

His frustration produced an abrupt and furious certainty that he had been cruelly wronged. 'What do you mean you can't?' he demanded. 'Of course you can.'

She shook her head, opened her mouth, but said nothing.

He couldn't stop himself from saying, 'You're a selfish tease, and I'm sick of it.'

She sat up. Her small face was hard, knowing. 'Oh, I see. You're not really my friend. You were just hoping to get some all this time. Didn't you have anything better to do? Isn't there someone else you could follow around? You're such a *kid*.'

'No one cares about you like I do,' he said. The core of his anger had gone cool, and he felt an appalling flicker of the remorse that would follow. '*I'm* the one who takes care of you. You said so yourself. But what does that get me? Nothing.'

'What does that *get* you?' she repeated. 'What do you *think* it should *get* you, Jacob?' She flopped flat onto her back, limp, legs apart. 'Here you go. Here's the grand prize. Buffet's open. Help yourself. Go ahead.'

He looked down at her and couldn't help but consider kissing her again. Instead, he wrapped his arms over his head and pulled his knees to his chest. In the past, when he had imagined kissing her, his worst-case scenario – also his most likely scenario – had ended with humiliation. He would plant an exploratory kiss; she would balk, embarrassed; he would be humiliated. He had not anticipated the lunge, the greedy engine driving him through the kiss toward more and more. 'What's wrong with me?' She didn't say anything. He looked at her. 'Really. What's wrong with *me*? You go out with other guys. I know you like me more than them, but you let them kiss you.'

'Nothing's wrong with you,' she said. 'Usually.' Whatever debt might have been between them had been erased, or reversed, by the word *tease*. She owed him no explanation for why she didn't love him the way he wanted her to. 'Let's just forget about this. Let's go home.'

'I'm sorry,' he said. 'I'm so sorry.'

'I know,' she said. 'Let's forget about it.' But when he extended his hand to help her up, she waved him off.

'You'll get sand in your cast.'

'You're the one who wanted to go to the beach,' she said and set off over the dunes.

They saw each other that summer but not often. Jacob was scrupulously respectful. Joan made a show of joking about all the girls he would get in college. Georgetown had gone coed the previous year. There was malice to the way she showered him with affectionate mockery, but he endured it, thinking about how he would leave in August and get some perspective. That would be a relief. Their friendship was no longer a thing in itself. They were warily circling a different thing, something that might exist or might not.

Then he left and heard nothing from her, and for a time he thought their relationship, whatever

41

it was, might have run its course. He missed her, but he also felt a self-congratulatory satisfaction in having outgrown her. He learned to play racquetball. He drank beer. He decided on psychology, much to the disappointment of his mother, who had been pushing for medicine. He dated a girl named Sarah and lost his virginity to her. Everything was fine, and then, late one night, drunk, he wrote his first letter to Joan.

The door opens and a woman comes into the bar on a burst of cold air. She is bundled in a sheepskin jacket with epaulettes of snow and a purple scarf. An ear-flapped lumberjack hat is pulled low on her brow. She stops short. 'You've got to be kidding me,' she says, staring at Jacob from between hat and scarf like a knight peering out of a suit of armor.

'Liesel?' he says. 'Is that you under there?'

In answer, she unwraps her scarf from around her broad, shrewd milkmaid's face. 'Ta da,' she says. Before he can process what is happening, she goes and kisses the mustache guy on the lips. The guy raises his glass at Jacob.

Liesel pats the guy on his beefy pectoral. 'This is my boyfriend, Ray.'

'Hey,' Jacob says.

'Ray, this is my ex-boyfriend, Jacob.'

'Yeah,' Ray says, 'I'd guessed.'

'Really?' Liesel looks between them. 'How?'

'He said he was married to a ballet dancer.'

'Do you tell everyone?' Liesel asks Jacob with scorn and amusement. 'You should get cards printed up and go around tossing them in people's laps on the El. Anyway, I thought I got custody of this place.'

'I wanted a beer,' he said. 'It's too cold to walk anywhere else.'

They have not spoken much for a year, not since he dumped her, which he had only done because, perplexingly, she had not dumped *him* after he told her about Joan's pregnancy. She takes off her jacket and turns it inside out over a barstool; snow drips off it onto the floor. The bartender sets a beer in front of her.

Her wispy blond hair, recently and unwisely cut to chin length, lies limp against her head, but the cold has flushed her cheeks and lips in a way that makes him think of sex. He chides himself for being so predictably horny, like a lab subject responding to stimuli. Since Harry's birth, Joan has not been interested in sex, but, for Jacob, the relentlessness and insistence of the baby's physical being draws constant attention to bodies and skin and nakedness and his own maturity and virility. He finds himself getting turned on in the most inappropriate situations, such as by a pissed-off ex, in front of her boyfriend.

Liesel doesn't attract him as strongly as Joan, but he likes her looks, which are ruddy and earthy. She had tried to couch their breakup as a rejection of her appearance. *Sorry I'm not a ballerina,* she'd said, bending the last word into a long, sarcastic sine wave.

'What do you do, Ray?' he asks.

'I'm a cop.' Ray smiles.

Liesel leans against him, and he wraps an arm around her waist and tucks his fingers into her pocket. 'No more academics for me,' she says. 'I can't take all the narcissism and insecurity.'

'Fair enough,' Jacob says.

'Really, though, what are you doing out drinking all by yourself?' Liesel asks.

He has no answer, of course, beyond his simple desire to be drinking and by himself and not at home. But to say this would suggest discontentment. One of Jacob's greatest fears is that his life will not appear intentional. Had he subconsciously wanted to run into Liesel? Maybe. But only to use her as a reminder that he is happy. 'I was supposed to meet a colleague, but I'm afraid I'm being stood up.'

'A colleague,' Liesel says, imitating his haughty tone. 'How unfortunate.'

It is, Jacob realizes, time to leave. 'I should go.'

'Great running into you.' Liesel smiles. 'Here in my favorite bar. What a coincidence.'

When he opens the door, piled-up snow falls inside. 'Nice move!' calls the bartender. But there is nothing Jacob can do. He clambers out into the cold, wedging the door closed behind him as best he can. The stairs are buried under a ramp of powder, and he climbs carefully, clinging to the

44

frigid handrail, probing for each step. At the top, in a streetlamp's soft orange circle, he pauses, enjoying the cold, which settles on his body like a weight. He turns for home.

A blast of heat strikes him when he opens the door, and he strips off his coat before he even takes the key out of the lock. Joan is sitting on the floor with her back against the hissing radiator and her legs open in a wide V around the blanket where Harry is sitting upright, unsupported, in a diaper and a University of Chicago T-shirt, studying an assortment of rattles strewn around his plump legs. They turn to look at Jacob, Joan with the absorbed, private smile she gets around the baby, Harry with grave hesitation that turns to open-mouthed delight, showing his gums and two bottom teeth.

'Hello, sweethearts,' Jacob says, tugging his sweater over his head and stepping on the heels of his boots to pry them off.

When he stoops to kiss Joan's cheek, he slides his hand down the neck of her shirt. She gave up on breast-feeding as abruptly and conclusively as she had quit dancing, even when the doctor said she should keep trying. Jacob suspects she had simply disliked it. Her breasts are bigger than they were before Harry but still no more than gentle hillocks on her chest, self-supporting, nothing pendulous. She looks up at him, not lusty, mildly amused. He tweaks her nipple. 'Knock it off, they're sore.'

'Do you know how many times we've had sex?' he asks her. 'Ever?'

'I'm not keeping a tally.'

'Thirty-six. Eight when you came to visit. Twenty-one when you were pregnant. Seven since the baby.' He lies down on the floor, curved on his side, his body closing the wedge of her legs, penning Harry in, who cranes around to look at him and tips over.

'Oops,' Joan says to the baby. Harry sweeps his limbs like four oars.

Jacob smoothes Harry's spider silk over his scalp. 'It's not that many, is all I'm saying.'

'There's no hurry. You'll have plenty of time to get bored with me.'

'I won't get bored.'

'Also,' Joan says, 'I still feel – I don't know – off. I mean in my body. I did when I was pregnant, too. I don't feel like myself. I don't feel sexy. I feel strange.'

Jacob does ordinary, utilitarian things with his body: eat, drink, sleep, walk, jog, swim occasionally, have sex if the opportunity presents itself. He doesn't do any of these things with unusual finesse or grace or stringency. Joan talks about her body as though it were her primary stake in the living world, an entity capable of moods separate from her own. Jacob wants her to say that both she and her body want him, that she is looking forward to a lifetime of sex with only him. But begging for reassurance is unattractive, unmanly, something

46

he can permit himself only in tiny, rationed bursts. Joan's father left when she was a baby and never came back, and Jacob thinks, psychoanalytically speaking, she should be the one to worry about *him* leaving. It's worrisome that she doesn't seem to worry. In fact, in all the time he's known her, he can't remember her ever seeming as relaxed as she does when she's home with the baby.

Harry curls his toes and claps his feet together like two scoops.

'I like how he gestures with his feet,' Jacob comments, giving up the subject of sex. 'I should start doing that. Just wave them around when I want to make a point.'

Harry pushes out his legs and, rolling sideways, swivels up to a sitting position. He flaps in celebration. Gently, Joan grasps his hands, and Harry pumps his torso and bows his legs and is suddenly, startlingly upright, balanced on those gesticulating feet. His diaper hulas for balance. He has been doing this for a week. Seven months is early for a baby to stand – Jacob knows this even though infancy isn't his field. His dissertation is on the identification of gifted children, but he is wary of getting attached to the idea of Harry being gifted, of inadvertently pushing the boy or making him feel like a disappointment.

'Do you want to show Daddy?' Joan asks Harry. 'Do you want to show him what you can do?' She releases the baby's hands, and for a breathless moment he balances on his own, feet spread wide like a surfer's. Then he flexes at the waist and falls onto his padded butt.

Jacob picks Harry up under the arms, turns him around, and looks into his face. 'You,' he says. 'We're going to have to watch you.' Joan had asked him to name the baby, bestowed complete power on him to do so, and he had chosen Harold after his grandfather who died early in Joan's pregnancy.

Joan stands and goes to their tiny kitchen nook to warm up some formula. She is wearing poufy harem pants, thick socks, and that thin, soft shirt he wants to put his hands in. 'Is there anything to eat?' he asks.

'Formula, bananas, and cereal.'

'You didn't go to the store?'

'It was too cold.'

Jacob eases down on his back, bringing Harry with him to lie on his chest. 'Mommy thinks because she can live on bananas, so can everyone else,' he tells the baby. Harry grasps his shirt with both hands and squints drowsily, coming down from the thrill of standing. The old chestnut is true: Jacob has always liked babies, but the love he feels for his own is an epiphany, shocking in its irreversibility. Even so, as he watches Harry's tiny fingers crab at his shirt, he can't help but wistfully consider, again, the early end to his bachelor-hood. When Joan had come to see him the previous summer and hopped so briskly into his bed, it had seemed to vindicate his long-held conviction that his stock would rise steadily the further he got from high school. Finally holding Joan's naked body, he had felt tenderness and love, but he had also, distinctly, felt the primal triumph of the sower of wild oats.

'Guess who I ran into?' Jacob says in a low voice, not wanting to interfere with Harry's wind-down.

'Who?'

'Liesel.'

Joan appears from the kitchen, dribbling formula from a baby bottle onto the inside of her wrist and licking it off. 'Really?'

'Yeah.'

She picks Harry up, uncovering a baby-sized patch of sweat on Jacob's shirt. 'It's a thousand degrees in here,' he says.

'Mmm.' She settles cross-legged on the couch with a towel over her shoulder and the baby reclining against her arm. Idly, Jacob turns a rattle over in his fingers, watching her, wanting her to look at him. Her contentment is wrapped so tightly around Harry that he can never be certain it extends to him, too.

He gets up and goes, without much optimism, to search for dinner. As he does most nights, he pours out a bowl of cornflakes. The last of the milk is not quite enough to cover them. 'Do you think you'd be able to make a grocery run tomorrow?' he says, sitting beside her on the couch and wiping a dirty spoon on his shirt. 'I'm not asking for a steak dinner. Just soup or something. Something I can heat up.'

'Sure.' She raises her eyebrows at Harry and makes her lips into an O, mirroring his face as he suckles the bottle.

'You know, never mind. I'll go myself.'

'Suit yourself.'

He wants to pinch her, to hide Harry behind his back, to say something that will amaze her. Instead, he says, casually, 'I think Liesel still has a thing for me.'

'Really? Why?'

'Is it such a mystery? I'm a catch. Was a catch.'

'No, I meant why do you think that?'

'Oh. I don't know – I could just tell.'

Finally she looks at him, perplexed. 'Jacob, are you trying to make me jealous?'

He watches Harry work at the bottle, his small hands coming up to caress it as Joan holds it. 'Yes. I am. I'm sorry. It's stupid.'

'It's not *stupid*,' she says. 'It's just not necessary.'

'Here, give him to me.'

She passes Harry and the bottle to him without disconnecting one from the other and drapes the towel over his shoulder. He wants her to watch the two of them at the same time, to see that they are part of the same picture. 'Maybe,' he says, 'it's just that when you want someone for so long, and then you get that person magically out of nowhere, you have trouble believing it's for real.'

She smiles at him, brightly, the way she does

when she is nervous, and the creeping in of her old skittishness reassures him more than anything she could say. 'I think you miss the crush,' she says. 'I'm probably a letdown because life is still life. Just with less suspense, and a baby.'

'You're not a letdown,' he says, brushing Harry's powdery cheek with a finger. 'I'd rather have you than wish for you.'

The exact mechanism by which Joan became pregnant is something that bothers him from time to time. She had said she was on the pill, and then, later, when he'd asked how this could have happened, she said something about having had a stomach flu right before she came to see him, and maybe the pill doesn't work when you throw it up. He can't think of a reason why she would have done it on purpose.

He says, 'But I worry that you're not happy. Sometimes it feels like you're a fugitive hiding out here, like you're in the witness protection program. I keep thinking I'm going to come home and find a note. That's the new suspense.'

Her feet burrow under his thigh, always seeking warmth. 'I'm happy.'

He is not sure he believes her. 'Good,' he says, patting the tops of her feet. 'I'm glad.'

December 10, 1970

Dear Joan,

Well, I've been drinking. I should say that right away. I was at a party with the girl I've

51

been seeing (yes, I've been seeing a girl), and we walked along the river, and then I told her I was feeling sick, which is true but really I wanted to come back here to my room and write you a letter. I wonder if I'll see you when I'm home for Christmas. Where are you? I'm sending this to your mom's house, but I don't even know if you're there. I hope you're dancing, wherever you are. If you're taking a typing class, please quit immediately.

Joan. About the day at the beach. I'm sorry. I was a jackass. I'm sorry for what I said and for acting like I had earned some sort of right to kiss you. My friendship isn't contingent on kissing, I promise. But I'm not sorry for the actual kiss. I have always wanted to kiss you. Maybe you knew that. Maybe I should have told you sooner and not let it build up.

I think we might end up together, Joan. Do you think I'm insane? Does the idea horrify you? You kissed me back at first, for a second. You didn't say why you stopped. Then I was a jackass. That day, before, I said you were lucky because you'd decided for yourself what you wanted out of life and I hadn't. But that wasn't true. I realized later I'd decided for myself that I want you. Will you please just consider that I'm the right one? Just consider it. Don't decide now. Consider it, I don't know, forever. Or at least until it happens.

I am going to have one more little bit of whiskey, and then I am going to mail this. And in the morning I'll probably regret everything, but it'll be too late.

Love,

Jacob

January 20, 1971

Dear Jacob,

I'm sorry I didn't write sooner. As you probably realized, I didn't go home for Christmas. I've been in San Francisco – did my mother tell you? Madame Tchishkoff helped me get a spot as an apprentice here. I'm so relieved. My foot is basically better, and the city is beautiful. My dancing has improved a lot, I think. I hope. Anyway, I didn't get your letter for a while, and then I didn't know how to write back. I still don't, but I am. The long and short of it is that I adore you. I told you I know you took care of me. I don't know if I said that I was grateful, but I am. I've never really had romantic feelings for you, exactly, though. I knew you felt a little differently. Maybe it was selfish of me to just let things go on. I was afraid of you bringing it up or trying something, and when you did, I didn't know what to do. You'd think I would have decided in advance, but I couldn't decide. Then when it happened, it felt like too much. I think you want too much from me. Does that make sense? I can't put things into words the way you can. Is it enough to say that I'm confused? Maybe things will change. Some people seem to know themselves. I don't feel that I do.

But I would like us to write, even if it's (still) selfish of me. I miss you. You are my best friend by miles and miles. Is that okay? I wish there were some way for people not to want things from each other. But now you have my address. Write me back and tell me about how brilliant everyone at Georgetown thinks you are. (Tell me about the girl, too.)

Much love,
Joan

JUNE 1982 – SOUTHERN CALIFORNIA

As the plane descends, Joan holds the curtain to one side and peers out. Desert crinkles up into scrubby mountains topped with antennae; those drop away into low hills fringed with a terraced reef of neighborhoods. Then parking lots, electric blue swimming pools, golf courses, highways, and, just beyond the plane's falling arc, the ocean. She fidgets, flipping the armrest ashtray open and closed. The smell of stale ash and sweet mint gum reminds her of touring with the company, everybody sleeping and stretching and getting up to smoke in the back, circulating up and down the aisle as though at a cocktail party.

Jacob is already down there somewhere. A school district, flush with state money, has hired him to expand a program for gifted children. First the children are identified, then they are placed in small classes with specially trained teachers, and then they are tracked and studied over the long term. Jacob is enthusiastic, pleased to be regarded as a young hotshot, an innovator. He can build something here, he says. The system shouldn't neglect the most promising individuals. He flew out before Joan and Harry and bought a house in a place called Valle de los Toros, one of those California towns that melt invisibly into the next, forming a continuous, hundred-mile-long patch-work of coastal domesticity.

'Really,' Jacob says to Joan as they unpack the kitchen things, 'what they've done is taken suburbia to the next level, cut out the middleman.' He has emptied a box of newspaper-wrapped dishes, and now he makes a precarious stack of mugs in a cupboard, not bothering to rinse off the ink and dust. 'People like to live in places with specific names, so they chopped the sprawl into tiny little pieces and gave each piece some fakey Spanish label. This way, we can all tell ourselves we actually live somewhere – like we have a *hometown*, like we're living the wholesome small town life, when really each of us is just one fleck of pig snout in the biggest hunk of real estate sausage ever made.'

'Appetizing.'

'You'll like it. Don't think too much about it. It's easy not to think when the weather's so nice.'

Joan shuts the cupboard on the dusty mugs. 'What do I have to think about anyway? Thinking's not my thing.'

'Come on. You know I didn't mean *you* specific-ally. I was making fun of the whole California *thing*.'

'Maybe you're right. I don't dance anymore. I should try thinking.'

'What is this? Why are you jumping on me?'

She shouldn't trap him, poke at him. He hasn't done anything wrong. 'Sorry,' she says. She searches the kitchen for a way to change the subject. 'We don't have nearly enough stuff to fill these cupboards. It looks like we're pretending to live here.'

He takes off his glasses, polishes them on his shirt, and puts them back on. 'Sometimes you act like a child.'

'I said I was sorry.' She sounds more petulant than she intends. She hates to disappoint him. She fears the slow, corrosive trickle of reality into his adulation. There is a silence. 'I don't know what I'm supposed to do here.' She gestures out the window at their patio, their overgrown lawn, Harry playing in the grass.

'Do whatever you want. Teach ballet, maybe. Or don't. Do nothing if you want.'

Joan stares out the window.

Jacob goes on. 'I don't know how much more supportive I can be. Literally. I can't think of anything else I can do for you. Just tell me what you want.'

'I don't know. Nothing.' She watches Harry. 'It's the new context. I tell myself I'm making a fresh start, and then I stay the same.'

'It's fine to stay the same. I just want you to be content. That's really it. I don't have a secret agenda.' He hesitates, plunges. 'Most of the time now you're here with me – really here, invested;

57

it's not like it was at first – and I think, good, she's letting me know her, really *know* her the way people do when they're *married*. And then other times you're so distant it's like someone's swapped you out for a forgery. You seem like you're going through the motions.'

Joan looks out the window. Harry is collecting dandelion puffs, gathering four or five in his small fist before he puffs out his cheeks and blows them into smithereens. *The motions.* She has been trained to believe that the motions are enough. Each motion is to be perfected, repeated endlessly and without variation, strung in a sequence with other motions like words in a sentence, numbers in a code. 'I'm trying,' she says. She is crying.

He comes to her and puts his arms around her. 'I know. But I wish you didn't have to try so hard.'

She rests her face against his shoulder, relieved the conversation is over, that they have moved on to comforting. She knows he wants her to say she loves him. He always wants her to after he has expressed any frustration or dissatisfaction. He is afraid and wants her to soothe him. She doesn't want to say it. She wants to grasp a barre and to go through the battements.

Sandy Wheelock picks kumquats from the tree in her backyard, dropping the tiny orange fruit into one of her daughter's sand pails. Really she is outside because Chloe came running into the kitchen proclaiming, 'The lady is doing tricks on the patio!'

'What lady?'

'Next door.'

'What tricks?'

'Belly tricks!'

Chloe had been unable to clarify ('With her feet!'), and so Sandy went out to see for herself. From the shelter of the kumquat tree, sneaking glances over the fence, she sees a slender young woman in ballet shoes, a T-shirt, and odd black overalls made of a thin, billowy material. Her hair is in a ponytail, and she is standing on a rubber mat and using the back of a metal chair as a barre, resting her heel on it and pressing her forehead against her knee. Then she briefly stands flat on both feet with her heels together before rising onto her toes and lifting one leg out and up so her pink satin shoe is well above her head. In the shaggy grass, a little boy about Chloe's age plays absorbedly with dandelions and pinecones.

Chloe is leaping and spinning around the yard. Sandy gestures at her to calm down, but the child is lost in her game and begins to accompany herself loudly in the funny, guttural voice she uses for singing and for making her toys speak to one another. Across the fence, the ballet woman and the little boy look up.

'Hi there!' Sandy says.

The woman's leg descends slowly, less like a leg

than a settling wing, and her gaze is curious, wary, divorced from the contortions of her body. Her smile, showing small teeth, is bright and jittery. She bends to untie the pink ribbons and leaves her shoes on the rubber mat as she walks barefoot across the grass, her toes wrapped in white tape. The stranger introduces herself as Joan Bintz, and her little boy is Harry.

'I didn't realize a family had moved in,' Sandy says. 'I only saw a man.' On several evenings, she had spotted him sitting out in the late sun and reading in the same chair Joan was using as a barre. He is handsome in a bookish way, trim and dark, with a narrow face and wire-rimmed glasses, and Sandy is annoyed to discover he is married to someone so lithe, a woman who does ballet alfresco and has a son content to play with pine-cones. Sandy is still dogged by the weight she gained with Chloe. Hidden by the fence, she runs a hand over her stomach, checking on it. From a distance she guessed Joan would be in her early twenties, but, up close, she looks closer to thirty, a few years younger than Sandy. She is pretty in the way someone so thin can't help but be pretty, with a jaw both dainty and square, a sharp nose, and eyes that are large, dark, and cautious. Sandy has the impression she has been crying.

'Jacob came out first to find the house,' Joan says. 'Harry and I came later. Everything's still a mess in there. I'm having trouble making myself unpack.' She smiles again, abruptly, quavering.

60

'I hear you. I still have boxes in the garage, and we moved in four years ago.' Sandy lifts the pail of kumquats over the fence. 'Would you like these? This tree hasn't gotten the memo that the season's over.'

Gingerly, Joan ventures two fingers into the bucket and extracts one of the little fruit. 'Do I peel it?'

'No, you eat it whole.'

Joan holds the kumquat between thumb and forefinger as if it were a quail egg and examines it before opening her mouth and resting it on her tongue. She chews pensively. Sandy wonders if eating is always such a production with her.

'Interesting,' she says when the tiny mouthful has finally made its way down her gullet. 'Like a dollhouse orange.'

'Here, take the whole bucket.' Sandy does not care for kumquats. The tangy burst of juice does not make up for the waxiness and bitter oil of their rinds. Gary likes them and plucks them like jujubes from a bowl she keeps on the kitchen counter. 'We've got a million.'

Joan smiles – unforced for the first time – and reaches for the pail. 'That's so nice.'

Though she would never say so, Sandy holds the opinion that mothers who keep their figures have sacrificed less than mothers who have widened and softened. Furthermore, though the idea is only half formed and well buried beneath her good nature, she suspects thin, maidenlike mothers, who

61

might more easily find new men, of being less committed to their children than she is. Joan is a very thin mother to be sure – and, at first appraisal, maybe too tightly wound – but her gratitude for the kumquats softens Sandy, who says, 'It's none of my business, but are you okay?'

Joan's eyes well up. She bends her head, hiding behind the fence. Sandy observes that her forehead is perhaps higher and rounder than ideal and is gratified by the imperfection. 'I'm a little homesick,' she says.

'For where?'

'Nowhere, really. I just feel uprooted. It's fine. I'll settle in.'

'Moving is very stressful,' Sandy says. 'You're stressed – you'd be a freak if you weren't. Do you want to come in for a cup of tea or something? Shot of tequila?'

But Joan has noticed Chloe, who is still dancing. 'How old is your little girl?'

Chloe stands on one foot and hops in a circle, arms straight up over her head like she is riding a roller coaster. Sandy studies her, trying to see what has interested Joan, but only sees a child at play. 'She just turned four.'

'Harry is four, too. Does she take dance?'

'No. She does tumbling.'

Joan fingers her ponytail, frowning. Sandy doesn't want to have to talk about Joan's ballet shoes, the exercises at the chair, the flexibility that the husband must enjoy. 'What does your husband do?' she asks.

And Joan's answer sends a thrill through Sandy because she and Gary know Chloe is gifted. There can be no doubt, Gary says. Their daughter observes more keenly and learns more rapidly than any child he has ever met. Gary should know, too – he was a gifted child and an excellent student until he got bored in high school and stopped trying. He's always wished someone had challenged him. 'Aren't teachers supposed to inspire you?' he says. 'None of mine could have inspired paint to dry.' And his dad had been a dud, and his baseball coach hadn't liked him. With a little encouragement, a little recognition, who knows how high he might have risen? Admittedly, he's great at his job, but, given half a chance, he might have done something more significant than managing the leasing office at the mall. He might have made the big leagues or been a professor or a doctor or something. Sandy was never very studious, and she worried when she was pregnant that her genes would drag down Gary's. But even when Chloe was a baby, Gary could see all the smart things Chloe did, and now Sandy just wants to get her tested already, stamped as gifted, so they can relax.

'Come inside,' she tries again. 'Have something to drink. Bring your son.'

Joan looks back at her house, her discarded ballet shoes. 'I should finish.'

'Oh, come on,' Sandy says. 'Live a little.'

In a few minutes, Joan is at her front door, her

white-taped toes and battered feet in a pair of rubber sandals, a cardigan over the billowy overalls even though it is eighty degrees out, her son hanging from her hand. This, Sandy knows, ushering them inside, is the beginning of something. They will live the next part of their lives side by side, their children growing up in tandem. Even though she doesn't quite like this thin, wary woman yet, she will try to be her friend. They are neighbors.

'Welcome!' Jacob says, opening the door for the Wheelocks. 'Come in before you blow away.' It is October, and the Santa Anas are in full force – dry, prickly autumn winds that whip trees around and howl at windows and rattle leaves along the gutters and pile them in the corners of yards. Driving home from school, Jacob had seen an actual tumbleweed blow through an intersection. Californians treat the winds as a weather event of grave importance. On Santa Ana days, his colleagues discuss them in knowing, respectful tones, squinting at the horizon like Bedouins crossing the Sahara. Somewhere up north in LA County, a brushfire has started, and the evening sky is a hazy orange grey.

The Wheelocks have a posed, formal look on the doorstep, and they don't lose it as they come inside and go through the greeting routine. Jacob can't blame them for being uncomfortable; he hasn't been able to establish a rhythm with either

Sandy or Gary, but he is glad Joan has a friend and that the kids get along. Harry leans against Jacob's leg and Chloe against Gary's. The children regard each other with serious faces, full of solemnity and apprehension about their impending playtime. Chloe, Jacob fears, is the reason Sandy and Gary are tense around him. According to Joan, Sandy talks a lot about how gifted the child is, and indeed every time Jacob goes next door to pick up Harry or runs into Gary taking out the trash, he is regaled with another overblown story about this little girl he strongly suspects falls within the normal range of intelligence. Jacob has already decided that he can't be the one to test Chloe next year.

Sandy is carrying a rectangular pan covered in foil, a cake for Joan's thirtieth birthday. 'Double fudge!' she says.

Probably with a lard center, Jacob thinks. Joan's main complaint about Sandy, reluctantly confided, is that she gets after her to eat more, and now that he's started paying attention, Jacob has noticed Sandy pushing food on Joan like she's planning to turn her into foie gras. Gary holds out a bottle of wine by its neck, showing the label. 'Thought we'd have a nice little cabernet.'

Jacob leans in to look it over and nods, sure the other man knows his appreciation is feigned. 'Joan says you're a connoisseur.'

Gary waves the word away. 'Barely.'

He is tall, an advantage he emphasizes by

affecting a slight stoop whenever Jacob speaks, as though otherwise Jacob's words might not find their way all the way up to the lofty altitude of his ears. He has a small head and a fox's triangular face and narrow, sly eyes. On weekends and in the evenings he is devoted to his road bike and cycles for hours, crouched head down over the handlebars that curl like rams' horns, decked out in a stretchy neon green outfit that displays his lean, if borderline stringy, physique. His hair is always side parted and combed in a careful fluffy swoop over his forehead, and he dresses for work as though he were heading off to some trading floor and not the leasing office at the mall, favoring striped suspenders and blue shirts with white collars and cuffs. For Joan's birthday dinner, he has opted for yachting attire: a white Izod shirt with the collar turned up, chinos, and loafers with no socks. Jacob, in jeans, longs to tease him, but the man is humorless.

Jacob takes the wine. 'Birthday girl's in the kitchen,' he says, leading them down the carpeted hallway that connects the living room with the rest of the house. The Wheelocks' house is a mirror image to the Bintzes', and Jacob always feels unnerved in their same-but-different rooms, oddly violated by the sight of another family living in a box the same size and shape as the box that contains his family and their unique life. The children scramble away upstairs to play. Jacob walks slowly so that Sandy and Gary have a chance to admire a wall of enlarged photos of Joan onstage, midleap in a tutu or striking a modern, angular pose in a leotard. He picked them out himself and had them framed. In the only photo Joan chose, she arches backward over Arslan Rusakov's arm. Rusakov's face is turned away. Her throat is taut and exposed, and her eyes bore into the lens. Jacob dislikes the photo and the pulse of anxiety it causes in him, but Joan said the others were pointless without it.

Sandy bustles ahead in a hurry to deliver her cake while Gary pauses and leans close to one photo and then another, scrutinizing. Even though this is what Jacob wanted, he doesn't like the man's silence or his nose just inches from Joan's leotard. 'Come on into the kitchen,' he says. 'We'll open the bottle.'

The wine has turned. As soon as they clink a toast to Joan, Gary sips and then barks so loudly everyone jumps, 'Spit it out! Just spit it out. It's piss.'

Sandy and Jacob swallow – after all, the wine is only a little sour, not too terrible, not poison – but Joan is startled into letting hers splash out of her mouth and back into her glass.

'You try to give people a nice bottle,' Gary says, 'and look what happens.'

'No big deal,' says Jacob. 'We have wine here.'

'No, the fun's gone out of it. I'll just have beer.'

Gary crosses to the sink and upends the bottle. The purple liquid glugs away down the drain.

When they sit down to dinner, Gary fixes Jacob with a hard stare meant to suggest he won't be easily fooled and asks how anyone can really be sure which kids are gifted and which aren't. 'No offense to your profession,' he says, 'but how can a test really prove anything? What if some kids are so gifted they resent tests? Some kids don't like structure, you know, they get bored easily. It seems to me like those kids might be some of the ones you're looking for.'

Harry and Chloe are under the table pretending to be dogs – they are going to be dogs for Halloween – and Jacob slips one of them a bit of chicken, uncertain if fingers or teeth take the scrap. 'Well,' he says, 'with five-year-olds, boredom and rebellion don't tend to be big problems. If you have a five-year-old who's too disillusioned to take a standardized test, that kid's probably not a good match for the program anyway. You make a fair point though, Gary, because it's true that people test differently on different days and over the course of their lives. And there are different forms of intelligence – Howard Gardner's idea. People think IQ is the be-all and end-all, but it's not.'

'But IQ's what counts, isn't it? For your program?'

'For the purpose of grouping children into special day classes, psychometrics are the best tool we have right now,' Jacob says.

Beside him, Joan sits watching the Wheelocks eat, her own plate untouched, tensely monitoring the trajectory of each forkful. She has already apologized for her cooking, which no number of compliments will ever convince her has gotten pretty good. No number of compliments will convince her of anything, and one of Jacob's projects in their marriage is to wean her off perfectionism. After Harry turned two, some private impulse had driven her, finally, to learn how to prepare something other than hard-boiled eggs and yogurt. He had played it cool, being careful not to overpraise her first mangled meals – Joan has no patience for flattery – but even now, two years and immense gains in skill later, even the simplest recipes tie her in knots, and she murmurs the instructions to herself as through incanting over a dangerous potion.

'Joan, you eat like a bird on a hunger strike,' Sandy says. Obediently, Joan takes a bite of salad.

'Don't hassle her,' Gary scolds. He gives Joan a brisk, apologetic nod, and she looks back at him, stymied. Her knife and fork hover over her plate. Jacob has wondered if Gary has the hots for Joan, but that doesn't seem quite right. More likely Gary just appreciates her as a physical template, a more refined model of wife than his own. Something about dancers' bodies, the obviousness of their manufactured perfection, makes people brazen about looking and commenting.

Flustered, Sandy redirects her attention to Jacob.

'What do you mean, people can be gifted in other ways?'

'The gist is that someone who might not do well with traditional academic tasks could still have other aptitudes. Like for music or spatial relations. Or someone might have interpersonal gifts.'

'That's you, honey,' Gary puts in, conciliatory.

'Or someone might be physically gifted – Gardner calls it bodily-kinesthetic intelligence – and be an excellent athlete or a dancer like Joan.' Jacob strokes his wife's leg under the table, then remembers the children and stops.

Gary says, 'I aced an IQ test when I was a kid. Off the charts, I guess.'

Jacob nods politely, as though it were possible to 'ace' an IQ test. All people want to do is tell him about their IQs, which are either off the charts or, in the case of a certain breed of red-faced men on airplanes, *so low they almost put me out with the cattle, but, sure enough, a few years down the road I started my own business, and now you wouldn't believe what I'm worth, so just goes to show you IQ tests don't amount to a pile of beans.*

'What I'm afraid of with Chloe,' Gary goes on, 'is that she won't get the support she deserves.'

'That happened to Gary,' says Sandy. 'No one challenged him.'

'I'm not complaining, but I want Chloe to have every opportunity.' Gary wipes his mouth, drops his napkin back into his lap, shakes his head. 'Every opportunity.'

'In my experience,' Jacob says, hearing and regretting the preachy note in his voice, 'the key is to allow children to discover what they're passionate about.'

'How old are you?' Gary asks.

'Twenty-eight.' Before he can stop himself, he adds, 'And a half.'

Gary's smile is controlled and contemptuous. 'Robbing the cradle,' he says to Joan.

A yipping comes from under the table. 'Do I hear a puppy?' Sandy says. 'Is there a puppy under this table?'

The yipping turns to a howl and then trails off.

Sandy leans to one side and lifts the tablecloth, peering underneath. 'What kind of puppy is it?'

'Two puppies!' Harry announces. 'And one's a bitch!'

Gary dives under the table like a sea lion after a fish. 'Excuse me, young man? What did you say?'

Jacob feels his son's small hand on his knee. He bends and peers into the dim space, at the small curled bodies of the children and the large staring faces of Sandy and Gary. 'Dad,' whispers Harry. 'A bitch is a girl dog. Chloe's a girl. We're playing dogs.'

'You're right,' Jacob tells him, 'but it's also a bad name people call each other to be mean. Probably you should just avoid saying it.' He sits back up, and the Wheelocks surface too.

Joan is fighting the giggles and losing. For a long minute she turns away, shielding her face while

71

the others watch in silence. It's the tension, Jacob knows. In high school she would laugh when someone got yelled at in class. When she looks up, her eyes are red and watering. 'Sorry,' she says to Gary and Sandy, her face crimping with the effort of seriousness. 'I didn't even know he knew that word.'

'He owes Chloe an apology,' Gary says.

'As far as he knew, he was being factual,' says Jacob. 'If we make a big deal out of it, we only draw attention to it.'

Joan trembles in her chair, tears rolling down her cheeks. He can't look at her or he'll laugh too.

Gary runs his tongue over his incisors, close mouthed, making a gorilla face. 'Thanks for the parenting lesson, but Chloe needs to know she's respected.'

'He's not being a misogynist. They're playing puppies.'

'I don't see what's funny.'

Joan plunks her elbows down on the table, making the china rattle, and presses her face into her hands. Jacob feels himself being pulled after her as though by a tether. As he tries not to laugh, he makes an accidental strangled sound, which sends him shooting off the edge. He lists toward her and presses his face into her shoulder. She leans back against him, shaking, and rests one hand on top of his head, lightly gripping his hair. 'I'm sorry,' he wheezes. 'I'm sorry. It's contagious.'

Whether it is a blessing or curse that the contagion spreads to Sandy, Jacob doesn't know. Probably a blessing for him and a curse for her, as Gary singles her out as the target of his most stern and outraged glaring. The children are laughing too, under the table. They are all in it together until, inevitably and abruptly, control filters back, and they pull themselves upright, hot faced, spent, vaguely ashamed.

'Got that out of your systems?' Gary asks. He has an air of beleaguered dignity, like the only sober one in a room full of drunks.

'I'm sorry,' Joan says. 'I just *lost* it.'

Sandy waves her hands. 'It feels so good to laugh like that.'

Gary's narrow eyes cut to her, and the woman cringes. In his agitated state, Jacob is acutely aware of the guilty, animal way Sandy's back hunches and she flashes a grimace, exposing her teeth.

'What were you saying before?' she asks Jacob. 'I was interested.'

'I don't remember.' Jacob gropes for the lost thread of his thoughts, his euphoria draining away.

'Something about passion.'

'Oh. Right. Well. My basic point was that people tend to make opportunities for themselves when they love something. Look at Joan. She saw a picture of Margot Fonteyn in a magazine when she was four and said, "I want to do that."'

With the air of scoring a point, Gary asks, 'Did

you want to be a psychologist when you were four?'

Joan dabs her eyes one last time with her napkin, rises, and begins clearing their plates. Jacob has noticed their ongoing refusal to acknowledge her dancing. When he mentioned it to Joan, she brushed him off, saying she's not a dancer anymore, she doesn't need anyone to make a big deal about it. 'No,' Jacob says, resisting the urge to ask if Gary had played Mall Leasing Office as a kid, 'but I was always interested in people and the way their minds work.' He twists in his chair, watching his wife. Everything she does is elegant, including carrying dirty dishes for a pair of boors. 'Joan, tell them how you remember feeling when you saw that picture.'

'I was so little.'

He holds out his hand, beckoning her back from the kitchen. 'Tell them.'

She comes closer, uncertain, like a fawn, her cheeks flushed from laughing. Even those few steps betray her as a dancer. She hasn't lost her turned-out, precise walk. She is so upright, so deliberate; her head is supported so regally by her long neck.

'It's silly,' she says, 'but I just loved her. I loved this woman I'd never met. I didn't even know what to call her or why she was up on her toes. I wanted an explanation. I had to find out what that picture meant.'

The Wheelocks look at each other. Gary raises

his eyebrows slightly, skeptically. 'Well,' he says, 'it's getting late.'

Sandy puts a hand on his arm. 'No, Joan has to have cake.'

'Did you ask her if she wants cake?'

'It looks delicious,' Joan says.

'Joan was the one who helped Arslan Rusakov defect,' Jacob persists, avoiding his wife's eyes so as not to see her surprise that he would bring up Rusakov. 'Did she tell you that? She drove the getaway car. Have you heard of him?'

'I read the newspaper every day,' Gary says. 'Of course I've heard of him.'

Sandy is staring after Joan, who has retreated to the kitchen. 'Joan, you never said.'

'It's ancient history.' Joan's voice floats back from the kitchen. 'It could have been anyone. I just did what some strangers told me to do. Should I light these candles?'

'You can't light your own birthday candles,' Sandy says.

'Every family has a mythology,' Jacob says in bed, lying on his side with his arms folded across his chest. His pillow pushes his glasses away from his face at a funny angle. Joan has always found his postures of relaxation to be odd and stiff, and this one is no exception. He looks like a tipped-over mummy.

'How so?'

'You know, everyone has a role and an epithet

and a story about how they came to be who they are.'

'Epithet?'

'Like, "Unappreciated-Genius Gary."'

'Hmm.' Joan considers. She has always liked it when Jacob comes up with these theories. They become games to play, puzzles to solve. Lying on her back, she stretches her arms up and eyes them critically, letting her elbows and wrists curve out so she is holding an oval of air, her fingertips almost touching. Her arms are still thin enough, but she is losing tone. She drops them. 'Perfectionist Joan.' She points a finger at him before he can protest. 'It's what you think.'

'Then what am I?'

They stare at each other, and Joan senses they are both trying to gauge how truthful the game should be. 'Gentle Jacob,' she offers.

'Jacob the Nerd.'

'Jacob the Gentle Nerd?'

He smiles, and she can see that he will not offer up one of the labels they know would be more accurate: Jacob the Proud, Jacob Who Does Not Make Mistakes. It must have cost him to mention Arslan to Gary. He says, '*Perfectionist* isn't the first word I think of when I think of you.' His tone is mild, but the game has turned dangerous.

'No? What is?'

He rolls onto his back, looks at the ceiling. She likes his profile: his strong chin with its dense, clipped beard, his long nose with a bump just below the bridge. 'Unobtainable.'

'Oh, Jacob. I have been obtained.'

Behind his glasses, his eyes briefly close. 'You know what I mean. It's vestigial.'

She considers climbing on top of him, kissing him, but he will recognize the cheapness. She could tell him there is no one she would rather be married to, that her love is growing, but slowly, accumulating imperceptibly the way trace minerals in dripping water build rock structures in caves, and it would all be true. But what he wants is impossible – he wants to change the past, for everything to happen in the right order. He wants them to love each other equally, but he is afraid of what it would be like if they did.

'I haven't laughed like that in a long time,' she says. 'I used to lose it in high school when someone would get in trouble. Remember? It was the same at ballet. If Tchishkoff really tore into someone, I'd get the giggles. I felt like a monster. Some poor girl would get ripped apart, and I'd have to leave because I was laughing so hard. What *is* that?'

'You're what's known as a sociopath. You have no empathy.'

'Oh, okay. Glad to have a diagnosis.' After a moment, she says, 'You know, if I had loved you right away, like I should have, when I was fourteen, you would have gotten tired of me, and I wouldn't have you now. I had a whole plan, you see. You fell for it.'

He turns to look at her. 'I am such a dupe.'

She slides across the sheets, hooks one leg over him, and sits up so she is straddling his belly. She rests both her hands on his chest and looks down at him. *The beauty of sex,* Elaine said once, *is that you don't have to talk.* Jacob's hands come up to clasp her thighs. His chin lifts; his eyelids droop. Desire looks like something going away at first, an ebbing. Sex is something they do well together. With Arslan, fear had made her ravenous. Even his laziest, most perfunctory touches had thrilled her because they meant he was not yet gone. She had clambered around doing his bidding, neither of them considering what she wanted. There is no thrill with Jacob, but there is comfort and pleasure and the freedom that comes from trust.

He shifts. His hands move to her hips. 'Why don't we ever talk about having another baby?'

He must feel her unease because his hands stop moving, and his eyes lose their dreaminess. 'We do,' she says.

'Not really. I hint, and you dodge.'

Sitting on him has become awkward, but she is afraid he will take it as a rejection if she moves away. 'No, I don't.'

'You do. Look, if you don't want another one, you should at least say so.'

'How can you be sure *you* want another one?'

He nudges her off him, not roughly but with an apologetic grimace. 'You're sitting on Sandy's cake. I just am. I see us with another. I liked having sisters.'

'God, a girl.' Joan sits cross-legged, one of her knees against his thigh, and picks at her fingernails. 'I don't know. I don't know if I want to risk all the things that can go wrong. Everything would be different if we had another. Why take the chance? Why mess with something that's working?'

'No,' Jacob says, excited, lifting onto his elbows. 'No, you have to be biologically brave. It's in our nature to take that chance. I understand the fear, but I don't think fear should be enough to stop us.'

'You're not the one who has to be pregnant and give birth. *You* don't have to push another person out of yourself. I hear women say they forget all about birth as soon as it's over, but I didn't. I don't know why nobody seems to take birth into account when they think about having a baby.'

'A few stretch marks aren't the end of the world, Joan.'

'I'm not ready.'

After a moment, he pulls her down beside him, her head on his shoulder. 'I wish you wanted one.'

'I know.'

After another silence, he sets his glasses on the nightstand and switches off the light. In the dark, lying against his body as though it were a gently respiring bolster, she imagines she can feel his thoughts coming through his skin like a fever. She feels his disappointment, his accusatory argument that she had been willing to trick him into conceiving a baby when he was young and unprepared but now that he has spent five years proving himself as a husband and father, she is unmoved by his desire for another. She feels him criticizing her vanity, rejecting her concern for her body as unjustified, even pathetic, now that she doesn't perform. She feels his sadness that the family he imagined isn't to be. She feels his love grow less dense around her, like fog lifting.

But, really, all she can feel is his breathing. It strikes her as strange that two people lying quietly in the dark, remote in their thoughts, locked away in their bodies, have everything necessary to make a third person who will, barring tragedy, lie quietly through darknesses long after they are dead. She had excused herself from Jacob's love when they were teenagers because *she* was young and unprepared, a luxury she hadn't granted him. But now she is his, they are each other's, and for him to be unhappy, to love her less, is intolerable.

'There's still time,' she says. 'I need a little more time.'

Under her ear, she feels a pulse in his shoulder. That his heart has begun to pound with hope makes hers pound with fear. She should give him what he wants. She will, just not quite yet.

'When?' he says.

'Soon.'

He shifts to lie squarely on her. She touches his face. In the early days, his weight had felt oppressive, suffocating, but now the burden of him is comforting. 'I can live with soon,' he says.

She doesn't want to have to say anything else. She pulls his head down and meets his mouth with hers.

AUGUST 1984 – DISNEYLAND

Merlin tilts a long finger over the heads of children and parents, over mouse ears and Peter Pan hats, through the strings of their balloons, and, in his booming wizard voice, bids Tim approach the stone and remove the sword. All the children raising their hands, straining to show their worthiness, subside in disappointment that a grown-up has been chosen. Tim squeezes through the ranks of families and goes to stand beside Merlin. He strikes a silly body-builder pose.

'Valiant knight,' says Merlin, opening his arms to show off his robe's voluminous purple sleeves, 'are you the one we seek? Do you possess the strength to free this mighty blade from yonder stone? Are you destined to become ruler of the realm?'

'You bet!' says Tim.

Tim's daughter Amber, who has rejected Sandy's offer to hold her up so she can see better, stands on tiptoe and whispers, 'My dad is really strong.'

Sandy suspects she's right. She had met Tim the previous afternoon on the artificial white sand beach by one of the pools at the hotel, the pool that Chloe and Harry love because it has water-slides made out of big, fake rocks. Except for his ponytail, he reminds her pleasantly of the frat boys she used to date: burly, soft in spots, sunburned. Tim is a carpenter, divorced and in the middle of a weekend-long attempt to bribe Amber into forgetting she has anything to be unhappy about. Chloe, barely deigning to watch as Tim makes a show of pushing up his sleeves and pretending to spit on his palms, says, 'He's not going to do it. I've seen this before.'

'He can do it,' Amber says desperately. Her father braces one foot on the stone, grasps the sword's hilt, and pulls. Nothing happens. Tim crosses his eyes and sticks out his tongue. Most children in the audience laugh but not Amber.

'Your dad's being funny,' Joan tells her.

Sandy and Joan planned this trip months ago. They envisioned it as part girls' getaway and part last hurrah before the kids start first grade – two nights in a hotel, two days split between the park and the pool, no husbands. They had planned so well and so far in advance that when Sandy decided she was tired of Joan and didn't want to go anymore, it was too late. Chloe would have been crushed, and Gary wouldn't let her lose the cost of the hotel room, which was already paid for. 'Plus,' he said, 'Joan's a good friend for you to have.' She had not asked what he meant because she knew he imagined this weekend would be a good chance for her to observe how Joan stayed so thin (Sandy already knew: no food, surreptitious cigarettes) and that she would come home twenty pounds lighter, as though from a summer at fat camp.

Amber folds her arms over her small chest. She is a chubby, demanding child with small, suspicious blue eyes and a bushy crown of tight black ringlets. 'No, he isn't. He's pretending he can't do it, but then he's going to.'

'They need to get a little kid,' Chloe says sagely. 'Only kids can do it.'

'Why?' Harry wants to know.

Chloe tsks with irritation. 'Because. That's the joke.'

Tim finally lets go of the sword and wipes his brow, shaking his head. Merlin pats him on the back. 'Valiant knight,' he announces, 'you have tried nobly, but you are not meant to be ruler of the realm. Perchance there is another who wishes to try?'

As Tim makes his way back through the crowd, Merlin chooses a Japanese boy in shorts and a pirate hat. Tim lifts Amber onto his hip, and when the boy draws the long blade from the stone, his mouth falling open in astonished joy, Amber begins to cry. 'It's not fair,' she says. 'He cheated.'

'I bet you would have been able to pull out the sword,' Tim tells her, tucking her curls behind her ears.

Her mouth and eyes have all but disappeared into her plump cheeks. 'I wanted you to do it.'

'I told you,' Chloe says. 'Only kids can do it.'

'Zounds!' says Merlin. 'Good knight, you have proven yourself worthy to wear the crown. I hereby proclaim you ruler of the realm!' Instead of a crown, he takes a small medal on a blue ribbon from his robe pocket and hangs it around the boy's neck, sweeping into a deep bow. The boy clutches the medal and gazes down at it. Gently, Merlin grasps him by the shoulders and gives him a light push, sending him stumbling back to his family.

Amber squirms in Tim's arms like an unhappy cat while he juggles her twisting limbs, trying not to drop her. 'Amber! It's *okay*!' He grimaces at Joan, of course, not Sandy, even though Sandy was the one to invite him along. Joan is being her usual boring self, never letting loose, smiling on delay, hesitating too long before saying yes to anything: a ride, a soda, a rest on a bench, a bathroom visit, a spin through a gift shop. Even the way she sneaks off to smoke so Harry won't see seems self-righteous and prissy. 'It was just pretend!' Tim says. 'It's just a game. Just for fun!'

Abruptly, Amber stops wriggling. 'I want an ice-cream sandwich,' she says, 'and I want to go on Dumbo.'

Tim's sunburned face creases with crestfallen exhaustion. Sandy feels for him. His divorce, from what he told her on the beach beside the pool, was an ugly one. 'Okay, you bet,' he says.

They turn as a group to look for the nearest

ice-cream cart, and Joan says, 'It's early for ice cream, isn't it? We haven't even had lunch yet.'

'Having fun isn't exactly Joan's strong suit,' Sandy says to Tim. 'I love her anyway.'

'Joan,' says Tim, 'I'll buy you an ice cream. Let's go crazy. You too, Sandy. My treat.'

'It's early for ice cream,' Chloe pipes up, parroting Joan. 'I don't want any.'

'Party pooper,' Sandy says.

Joan drops a curtsy for Tim, her feet in an impossible position. 'Valiant knight, I accept your ice cream.'

'Now do you want some?' Sandy asks Chloe, but Chloe shakes her head. For a child, she is strangely indifferent to pleasant temptation.

They walk past the shiny elephants in circus hats flying on steel arms around a colorful mechanical globe, past the line of people waiting to board Peter Pan's pirate ships, past the many brick chimneys of Toad Hall. Near the Pinocchio boats, a grey-haired black man in a white paper hat is selling ice-cream from a canopied cart. The air smells like sugar and chlorine and sun-warmed concrete, and from a distance comes the sound of a brass band and the clatter of toboggan cars descending the Matterhorn. As Tim hands Joan an ice-cream sandwich with great ceremony, Sandy regrets ever suggesting that he spend the day with them. With a sudden ferocity, she hates what she's wearing. The blameless shorts and sleeveless white blouse feel constrictive, malicious.

If she were alone with Joan, she would be irked by her spoilsport habits – the way she won't drink fun cocktails, the way she gets Harry to settle down at night by letting him cling to her neck like an orangutan while she hums and sways and murmurs, the way she gets up at the crack of dawn without an alarm clock and stretches and exercises in the room, holding on to the back of a chair the way she had when Sandy first saw her, her twiggy arms and legs going up and out, forward and back, and so on into an infinity of the dullest kind – but Tim had to come along and prove how much more desirable Joan is than Sandy, even though Sandy is the one who knows how to have a good time. Not that Sandy would cheat on Gary, but to flirt, to play pretend in this world of smooth, perfect, colorful moving surfaces, is to breathe deeply, to relax back into the shape of the person she once was.

She has asked herself if Joan's body and Gary's admiration of it – everyone's admiration of it – is the only reason she is losing patience with their friendship. But there's more: she doesn't trust Joan. She suspects if she could see herself through Joan's eyes, she would not like what she saw. The roots of her suspicion are obscure: Joan has never been anything but nice, never allowed judgment to show through. But maybe that's part of the problem. Joan's controlled exterior makes her seem like she's hiding something. It didn't help that Harry was identified as gifted and Chloe wasn't. Gary sees a conspiracy. Surely the son of the young, self-styled star psychologist in charge of the whole charade would never be declared average. Surely someone had his thumb on the scales. Surely Chloe could not be allowed to take her place among the chosen children. Gary might like Joan okay, but he loathes Jacob. Sandy stops short of imagining some nefarious plot to keep Chloe down, but, looking at her child and Joan's as they sit with ice-cream-smeared Amber between them and avidly monitor the approach of a person in a fuzzy yellow Pluto suit, she can't see how one is smarter than the other. Harry is so quiet, such a mama's boy, while Chloe is opinionated and confident.

Pluto stops, waves a big-mitted hand, and crouches down, inviting a hug. The children rise and move toward him, opening their arms, drawn into the embrace by the irresistible gravity these suited characters hold for them. Chloe buries her face in the dog's shoulder while Harry presses his palm against its smooth red tongue and Amber reaches to stroke its muzzle. Chloe has been shy around the princesses and the other characters who are recognizably human, but she hugs the animals fearlessly, emotionally. All three children engage with their whole bodies, allow their backs to be rubbed and patted by the big stuffed paws. Often, dazed and pleased, they have to be gently peeled off by the characters themselves.

'What I want to know,' Tim says quietly, 'is who

these people are who want to go around hugging kids all day.'

Sandy is disappointed he wants to ruin the moment with a joke, but she plays along. 'I've heard,' she says, 'that the people inside don't even get to wear their own underwear. Apparently there have been issues with crabs.'

'No shit!' Tim says and then covers his mouth, looking to see if the children heard. But Amber, Chloe, and Harry are lost in the afterglow, arms slack, staring after Pluto's skinny tail.

'Dad,' says Amber, squinting, 'I want a Pluto doll.'

'Maybe later, okay?'

'*Dad.*'

'Later, baby.' The ice cream and the hug have appeased her, and she does not persist.

Joan is playing reflective. 'I thought the kids might be scared of the characters, but they act like they've always known these people – or mice or dogs or whatever.'

Tim looks at her like she's a genius. 'I never thought of it that way.'

'I was just thinking the same thing,' Sandy says. 'They're really having fun. It's great.' But nobody says anything, except Chloe, who says she has to pee. Sandy says okay, she'll take her, and then they should all be brave and go on the Matterhorn.

Amber has no intention of riding any roller coasters, but she wants Tim to go so he can tell her about it, and it is decided, mostly by Sandy, that Joan will take Amber on the teacups and then on Alice in Wonderland while Harry and Chloe and Tim and Sandy ride the roller coaster.

'It'll be a good chance for you to . . .' Sandy mimes a cigarette at Joan.

Joan ignores the gesture. 'Does that sound okay, Harry?' she asks. 'Do you want to go on the Matterhorn?'

'Okay,' the child says.

Sandy suspects Harry is afraid but doesn't want to be shown up by Chloe. She wishes everyone would go away for a while, let her and Tim be alone in little cars in dark places, get rattled around and pushed into each other.

Yodeling music is piped through speakers along the line for the Matterhorn, which is very long, wrapping partway around the mountain before a series of switchbacks inside an open structure meant to suggest a Swiss train station or chalet or something, not that Sandy's ever been to Europe. Gary promised to take her, but now he says it's too expensive. Hearing Joan casually mention her time in Paris and all the other places she went on tour with the company doesn't help. Sandy once confessed her dream of seeing Big Ben and the Tower of London, and Joan only said the food was bad in England. Sandy asked her how she would know, since she never eats, and Joan had not laughed. She wishes she could be nicer to Joan; she wishes she liked her more.

The Matterhorn is a craggy cement sculpture of

a miniature mountain with a white-painted over-hanging peak. Speeding toboggans flash through the caves that perforate its sides. A waterfall cascades behind an arched stone bridge. Passengers shout and scream; every minute or so the abominable snowman who lives inside gives a loud roar. Tim offers Sandy a sip of his soda, and she drinks coquettishly from the straw. Harry clutches his stomach and complains of butterflies. 'After this,' Sandy tells him, 'when you're a roller coaster pro, we can go on the space ride. You go really fast past stars and planets. There's a chocolate chip cookie in the sky, but only for a second. You have to watch for it.'

'My mom might want me to wait with her,' says Harry.

'You've been on it?' Chloe asks Sandy.

'Yes,' Sandy says.

'Daddy was probably with you. That's probably why you weren't afraid.'

'No,' Sandy says, 'I wasn't afraid because I wasn't afraid. It was fun.'

'Your mother is very brave,' Tim tells Chloe. 'Fearless.'

'How do you know?'

He winks at Sandy. 'I can just tell. She's that kind of lady.'

'You have no idea,' Sandy says, feeling cheerful again. Tim starts to yodel along with the music. The children fall all over themselves laughing. She wonders if he'd been making her jealous on purpose, as a tactic, or if Joan is simply out of sight and out of mind. She sidles closer to him, leaning against the railing, and while the children reach through a low fence to pluck white and purple petals from the flowers planted around the mountain's base, he puts his arm behind her, around her, his fingers brushing her side. When the children look up, he swings away as though stretching.

'How's the single life?' she asks in a low, confidential voice.

'Fine most of the time, but I get lonely. I don't do so great with being lonely.'

'Fat chance.'

'What do you mean?'

'I bet you're never lonely. I bet you're a ladykiller.'

'Me?' He twinkles. 'Nope, crying into my can of soup every night.'

'Right.'

Chloe lolls against the railing, watching them, her fists full of petals. 'Sweetie,' says Sandy, 'don't stare. What is it?'

'Why are you talking to him?'

'He's my friend. My new friend Tim.'

Glowering, Chloe goes back to the flowers. Tim leans close to Sandy's ear and says, 'I do like those ladies, though.'

'Big surprise.'

He undoes his ponytail and combs his hair with his fingers, making a new one. There are damp spots in the armpits of his red T-shirt. 'How's married life?' he asks.

'Could be worse.'

'Sorry.'

'You know how it is.'

The tip of Tim's thumb rubs the side of her hand. 'This is a great day,' he says. 'My girl is happy. Not a cloud in the sky. Got a gorgeous new friend. Life seems pretty good.'

'I agree,' Sandy says. The pressure of his thumb increases.

By the time they board their toboggan, which, Harry rightly points out, looks more like a spaceship than a sled, Sandy is officially keyed up. Sex saturates the world, blurring it. Tim climbs in first and pats the blue plastic between his legs. Sandy sits, nesting in his groin. Chloe hesitates, wanting to sit with them, but Sandy tells her to get in the front compartment with Harry. The children are loose in the space, small and jittery. As the ride jerks out of the station, Sandy leans back against Tim's chest. Chloe twists around. 'Mom, I don't want to fly out.'

'Did you fasten the belt?'

'Yes.'

'Then you won't fly out.'

'We can fly out?' Harry cries, also turning around.

'No,' Tim says. 'You're safe. Look straight ahead so you don't hurt your neck.' The toboggan rattles down through a cave and then clanks slowly up through a steep darkness, flattening

Sandy against Tim. His breathing lifts and lowers her. Boldly, he slips a hand under her arm and squeezes her breast, too hard really, but she lifts her arm, giving him better access. The air turns cold and damp; tape-recorded wind howls; the abominable snowman's two red eyes appear in the darkness with a roar; the children shriek. Tim's hand goes away and comes back, snaking around her stomach, grabbing the inside of her leg through her shorts. Gary has told her he doesn't want to have sex until she loses some weight, and in response she has defiantly gained a few pounds. She has started sleeping naked, knowing she is turning him on but also that he won't yield out of principle. *Don't your pajamas fit?* he asks. *This is more comfortable,* she says. Not everyone has to look like Joan. Joan would look like Sandy if she weren't anorexic.

The toboggan makes a sharp turn, gathering speed, and they pass through a blue ice cave and out into the rushing air. The bright buckets of the Skyway float past. Tim's thighs clamp Sandy in place; his fingers creep inside her shorts. His aggressiveness and her own furtiveness remind her of being young. They spiral down, cutting through the mountain and changing direction. Sandy doesn't want the ride to end. She can't get out of this toboggan. Tim's mouth is against the bare skin of her neck, his teeth and tongue rattling along with the ride. She lets her head fall back against his shoulder, her eyes close. His mouth jerks away; wind cools the wet spot left behind. Opening her eyes, Sandy sees Chloe staring at her. The tracks dip into a pool of green water and the toboggan sails through, sending up sheets of spray.

OCTOBER 1985 – SOUTHERN CALIFORNIA

Elaine begins her day with a very hot shower, instant coffee, a brisk walk from the hotel to the theater, and company class on the stage. Rehearsals will be later, after the sets are loaded in. Since she is one of the first to arrive, she helps drag the barres out from the wings. The airplane has left her tight – she can gauge her muscles' moods perfectly; today they pull at her bones like recalcitrant children – so she leaves her sweatshirt on over her leotard and adds a pair of vinyl shorts, rolling the waist down around her hips. By the time the last dancers arrive and Mr K claps his hands to begin class, her muscles have begun to relent, and she has a sweat going.

She is thirty-one now, her body already less tolerant and cooperative than it was. The days when she could party through the night and survive class are long gone. She doesn't smoke, drinks less, eats well, has cut out drugs except for coke, just a tiny bit before performances and at intermission. Sometimes a bump in the afternoon if she's having a long day. She travels; she meets people, has lovers but loves only Mr K; she is applauded. But all of that happens around the periphery of the narrow range of activities – class, yoga, massage, sleep – that will help her remain a dancer. She scrabbles against her inevitable decline, works to retain her strength, stave off injury. She has had stress fractures, torn ligaments, surgery on her left knee. Never in her life, not once, has she danced the way she wishes to, but futility has become an accepted companion. The ideal that lives beyond the mirror makes teasing, flickering appearances but never quite shows itself, never solidifies into something that can be looked at and not just glimpsed. She might surprise it as she whips her head around, spotting during pirouettes, or catch it flitting through one hand or foot. But it never stays.

The only redemption she finds in age is that she understands so much more than she did when she was twenty and tireless and reckless and resilient. She can express more now; she knows what to express. The critics have noticed. They say she has become a better actress, but she believes the improvement isn't in her acting but in her ability to feel. Even in Mr K's more conceptual works where she is less a character than a kinetic idea, she can convey experience, humanity, emotion. 'Less feeling,' he tells her sometimes. 'Stop feeling. You won't die if you don't feel for a little while. Just dance. It's only about the steps.' Sad, really, how ballet has such limited use for wisdom. When she's fifty, she might be the witch in *Sleeping Beauty*, the nurse in *Romeo and Juliet*, roles that call for pantomime and heavy makeup, presence more than technique. Margot Fonteyn danced into her fifties, but Elaine is no Fonteyn. Even if she were, she would not choose to carry on for quite so long. A woman old enough to be a grandmother has no business prancing around in a tutu, pretending to be a virginal peasant or princess.

Onstage, Elaine misses the mirror. Without it she is halved, uncertain of her existence; the dark maw of the theater is a poor substitute. She looks at her shadow on the floor until Mr K catches her and adjusts her chin with a long, cool finger, saying, 'All you will see is a hunchback.' So she watches the rows of arms lifting, the heads swiveling. A ribbon of music unspools from the piano. Slippers brush against the floor. Knees and hips crack. 'One,' says Mr K. 'And up, and three, and out, and just the upper body, good, and out, and fifth, and out, and fifth, yes, and turn.'

During class or rehearsal, he never treats her differently from the others, but in the nighttime quiet, lying side by side in his bed, his hand resting companionably on her stomach, he has told her she is his true muse, she has become his idea of a woman. Idea, not ideal, which she would recognize as a lie. It is the idea of her – the idea of women in general – that obsesses him: their capacity as vessels, their aesthetics, their otherness. He eroticizes them, desires them in a way, but does not lust for them. He lusts for men, she knows, but she has never seen him be lecherous toward the boys in the company. She suspects he feels demeaned by lust. That part of his life is walled off, invisible, underground, nocturnal, private.

Elaine and Mr K sleep together often; they have sex rarely, usually only when he is drunk or riding the high of a new ballet. She calls him Mstislav when they are alone, but she still thinks of him as Mr K. He has suggested that she move in with him, and she supposes she will. They have mossed together. To think she could extricate herself at this point would be delusional. When she was younger, she had been tormented by his indifference in bed, had thought it meant he was always on the verge of abandoning her, and she had tried to hack herself loose from him. She told him she wanted normal love, a husband, monogamy, something she could explain to other people, but then, after a year, when normal turned out to be a disappointment, he made a ballet on her: *Catherine the Great*. It was her best role, the closest she had come to dancing the way she wanted. Her destiny is to serve a greater artist. They will share a life inside his apartment, but he will venture out into the city for his adventures. She will be free to do the same.

The girl on the other side of the barre, a dancer in the corps, murmurs, 'Did you hear? Franny kicked me out of our room last night, and then

I passed Mr K in the hall, on his way. He gave her perfume last week, too. Guerlain. She's getting promoted.'

'Well,' Elaine whispers without turning her head, 'she's very good.'

Together they rise up on demi-pointe. The girl says, 'She said they didn't fuck – he just wanted to get naked and lie in bed and pet her like she was a dog.'

'Great story.'

'He wasn't even hard.'

One of Elaine's distinctions as a dancer is the measured, deliberate quality of her movements, which is the product of her cool, orderly mind. She is both annoyed and impressed that a dancer in the corps would speak to her, a principal, this way. They sweep down into grands pliés, and from under the barre, Elaine says, 'Not something you're ever going to have to worry about.'

'Especially since I'm not a boy.'

Rising, Elaine says, 'Or talented.'

She has found ways to put aside the indignities of her situation with Mr K. That is what she does: she sets them aside, moves them to a place outside herself. Still, sometimes she wishes he would vary his routine. A girl piques his interest, inspires some bit of choreography, and then he selects the perfume, a different one for each girl. The gift is not a token of affection but a mark of ownership. He will decide how they should smell. He will decide more and more about them, make dances on them, and, in service of his genius, they will do anything for him. Like the perfume, the sex (or whatever version of physical intimacy he demands now) is a gesture of possession, not passion. He wants to see and know their bodies as thoroughly as possible. Elaine could have slept with him only once, after she received her bottle of Jean Patou, but she kept coming back, needing to know she could. When he made his first dance on her, he rearranged the cells of her body according to his own specifications, rewired her nerves, possessed her. Her civilian boyfriends could not understand her that way. They treated her like a fragile possession of exotic provenance, when she is really a tool, an invention, a weapon. Mr K is the only person who loves ballet as much as she does. Love for ballet is necessary to survive it, but she doesn't know if she survives because she loves to dance or if the love comes from a need to survive.

'Breathe, breathe, breathe with it,' Mr K says, walking around the stage. He pauses in front of the newly baptized Franny. 'Dear, with your arm. No. Like this.' In his grey flannel pants, checked shirt, and black dress shoes, he demonstrates. Franny mimics him well. The good ones see what he wants; they are his mirror.

The company does more pliés, then ronds de jambe, tendus and the rest of the battements: dégagés, fondus, frappés, développés, and grands. To Elaine, the movements are less exercise than a

101

process of organization. With each beat of a leg and sweep of an arm, she creates order, winding gears that will tick the rest of the day away.

After class, she strikes off down the freeway in a rental car, the whoosh of traffic making her feel timid and provincial, even though she is the one who lives in a real city, who should be accustomed to density and rush. It is warmer than she expected and dry. Joan is not a frequent or prolific correspondent, but when she writes, she says she likes California. She enjoys its warmth and convenience, its newness. Following Jacob's directions, Elaine exits the freeway, skirts a mall's vast parking lot and the grassy shores of a man-made lake, and pulls into an office park of low white buildings with reflective blue windows. She could never live in this benign suburban dreamland.

As she pulls open the door to the ballet school, she sees Joan through a studio's big window, facing the mirror, leading a class of adult women, moms looking for exercise and for some trace of girlhood dreams. They are ungainly in their leotards, wearing slippers, not pointe shoes, and not turned out. But the sight of them is touching, triggers a gloating pride in Elaine that these women wish to do what she does. She had wondered if she would feel jealous of Joan with her family and easy life, but she feels only pleasure in her own existence, her freedom from the ordinary. In front of the big window, she strikes a silly

Fosse pose, waits for Joan to catch sight of her in the mirror.

'I was hoping you'd bring Harry,' Elaine says. 'I've been so curious to meet him.'

They are sitting at a table with a striped umbrella outside a donut shop near the studio. Elaine sips coffee and fiddles with a packet of Sweet'N Low. Joan sets her cigarette in a black plastic ashtray and digs her thumbnail into an orange, stripping the rind away in a ragged coil. 'He's at school. It's Wednesday.'

'Oh. Of course. Stupid.'

Joan can't tell whether Elaine had really forgotten about the existence of school. 'Second grade.'

'I kept asking you to send a picture, and you never did.'

'Didn't I? I'm sorry – I meant to. I can be so spacey.' This is not strictly true, and they both know it.

'Don't you have a picture in your wallet or something? Isn't that what you're supposed to do?'

Joan purses her lips, conceding, and takes her wallet from her tote bag. She opens to a plastic sleeve of photos. Harry's is on top, gap toothed in his first grade portrait, his dark bangs falling straight across his forehead.

'God,' says Elaine. She takes the wallet from Joan's hands, examines it, and then abruptly hands it back. 'He's different than I imagined.'

'Not a great haircut,' Joan says.

'I thought he would look more like you.'

'He looks like Jacob,' Joan says, fishing in her bag again. 'Do you want a smoke?'

'I'm on a health kick, but okay. For old times' sake.' They light up and smile at each other, feeling young.

'Are you still doing blow?'

'No, not really. Just in emergencies.'

When Joan first joined the company, someone had told her Elaine was looking for a roommate, and they had become compatible cohabitants, then friends. They were bonded by their constant fatigue and the endless ministrations their bodies required. They liked to sit side by side on the edge of the bathtub, drinking tea and soaking their feet. Each was grateful to have an ally. From the beginning, there was no question that Elaine was by far the better dancer. Elaine was waiting to be promoted; Joan was praying to stay.

'I'm bringing Harry to the matinee,' Joan says. 'You'll meet him then.'

'Does he dance?'

'No.'

'You should make him try it. He might like it.'

'He doesn't seem interested.'

'We need boys.'

'You sound like an army recruiter.'

'They are an army – the young ones. Waves of them. Mostly girls, though. I like the boys, not the girls. I'm afraid for them, too. We're losing boys.'

'I've heard.'

'Is Harry gay?'

'He's seven.'

'So?'

Elaine has grown harder. Her voice, her eyes, her bones. Her sternum is like a turtle shell with skin stretched over it. They are all thin, dancers, but Joan can discern infinitesimal variations in thinness, and Elaine's is the minimalist body of the survivor. She has reduced herself to the most essential pistons and gears. Nothing extra can be allowed to create strain or cause wear. She is a witty dancer with clockwork timing, best suited to comic heroines and the demanding tempos of Mr K's ballets. On Sunday, when Joan takes Harry to *Don Quixote,* Elaine will dance Kitri in red and black lace, a perfect curl of hair glued to each of her cheeks. She will prance and snap her fan, do the flamboyant sissonne leap where she nearly kicks the back of her own head. Now that Elaine is a principal and has danced the major roles, she has become an object of curiosity for Joan, like someone who has experienced space travel. If Joan had not had Harry, she would still not be dancing Kitri, but Elaine, stacking packets of sweetener with bony fingers at the end of bony arms, caught in a small eddy of leisure between class and rehearsal, seems like an apparition, a ghost of what might have been.

But it would not have been, Joan reminds herself. She reminds herself, too, that she doesn't miss the feeling of living at an accelerated pace, each year counting for more than an ordinary fraction of life, like dog years. Her childhood was dominated by discipline, fear, repetition – her small self in an endless, tearful hurry to get better, to get *good* in time to have a career. Her childhood bled seamlessly into her adulthood, each contaminated by the other. She had not felt grown-up until Harry.

'I'm dying to see you dance,' Joan says.

'Don't be. I'm the same, just older, with all the same bad habits.'

'No, you were always wonderful.'

Joan has lined up the slices of her orange end to end like a train, and Elaine takes one from the middle and bites it in half. 'I'm a workhorse.'

'You're a star.' Joan doesn't know if she wants her to be a star or not, fulfilled or not. She doesn't know if Elaine thinks she is jealous, if that is why she is downplaying the miracle of becoming a principal.

'No. I don't have that dazzle. I think I thought I could learn it. You watch dancers who have it, and you know it's magic, but then when it comes to your own dancing, you tell yourself you just need to work harder. And then you work and work, and you're still just you, and then one day you realize you're not getting better, only older.'

'We're all getting older.'

'Being older doesn't matter as much for most people. It really doesn't.'

Joan, wishing to reassure but also to needle, says, 'You're Mr K's muse. That's important.'

Elaine flares slightly. 'Yes, I got on the right bandwagon. I believe in him enough to serve him. I'm his biggest project. He's made a life on me. And in return, every time he gets written about – and he will forever – I'll get written about too. After we're dead, people will still be wondering if we had sex. I'll live on as an ambiguous appendage to a genius. I think there's a blankness about me he likes. He projects onto me. He likes the idea of a vessel. It's an honor and an insult. I don't want to sound bitter. I'm not bitter. Sometimes I'm afraid he just couldn't find anyone else so willing to be subsumed. So. There it is.'

'No,' Joan says, not knowing if she means to agree or disagree, surprised to feel some distaste about Elaine's arrangement with Mr K. She had not noticed herself becoming conventional, but, undeniably, she is out of practice deciphering relationships like theirs – or the way hers had been with Arslan – that are part love and part self-imposed misery and part ballet experiment. Her impulse is to tell Elaine to find a nice man to marry, but Elaine never will. Joan would not like it if she did. She prefers Elaine to remain fixed in her old life like an obsolete weather instrument gathering data no one ever sees.

Elaine stubs out her cigarette and says, 'Do you ever hear from Arslan?'

'God, no.' Joan flicks her fingers the way Arslan would, shooing the idea away.

'Will you ever write to him?'

'No. I don't know what I would say. What good would it do? He probably doesn't even read his own mail. Some intern would send me a signed photo.'

'I don't know. Maybe you'd put some demons to rest or something.'

'I don't have any demons. I'm happy.' Elaine's face betrays no skepticism, but Joan knows it's there. 'I love Jacob,' she says firmly. 'Of course.'

'Not of course. He was an escape hatch.'

'But I must have known it would be okay. On some level. I think I wasn't open to loving him until I needed to be.'

'Like arranged marriages that turn out to be love marriages. Except it was always a love marriage for him.'

'Yes,' Joan says simply.

'And for you now too?'

'Yes.' Joan looks away, embarrassed. That she has finally fallen in love with Jacob is good luck for both of them, but to say so would demean it.

With an air of declassifying information, Elaine says, 'I'm probably moving in with Mr K. Do you think it's a mistake?'

'I don't know. What would qualify it as a mistake? Is he still . . . does he have boyfriends?'

'I assume so. I never ask. What *would* qualify it as a mistake? I don't know what my threshold is for mistakes anymore. I used to make them all the time. I adjusted for them. Now I only do safe things. This doesn't feel safe, though. It's committing to something that people find strange. Maybe I'm worried we won't be able to stand each other, and it'll be over, and I'll have nothing.' She restores the packets of sweetener to their ceramic box. 'He doesn't even screw the new girls anymore. This girl this morning told me – Never mind. It's not important, only gross.'

'I want to hear.'

'No, I can't say it out loud. It'll make me feel sick. Forget it. We're going to his dacha up the Hudson more. He's different there. Nicer. The butterflies and wildflowers mellow him out. I keep expecting him to start wearing belted shirts like Tolstoy. He says he'll marry me when I retire. I think he just wants to feel like less of an old queen.'

'God. Do you want to marry him?'

'I don't want to marry anyone else. Maybe that's half the battle. And I don't want children. They deform the body.'

Joan adjusts her cardigan. 'No kidding.'

'At least you've grown titties. Does Jacob want more?'

'Titties or children? No to boobs, I think, but yes to kids. We've been trying, but nothing.'

'How long?'

'A year and a half.'

'You want more, too?'

Jacob wants to go to a fertility doctor – just to *see*, he says. Joan won't. She tells him they should be grateful for what they have. She doesn't want to know. Reprieved from the burden of another baby, she has mourned the lost possibility more than she would have expected. 'I do and I don't. I can live with either.'

Elaine eyes her. Her shrewdness is more on the surface than it used to be. She seems shrewd and also weary, like a dictator who has weathered more than one coup and anticipates more. 'Did you know that Arslan and Ludmilla split?' Elaine says.

'No.' Joan sits back. She feels a sour satisfaction and an odd disappointment. 'I'm impressed they made it as long as they did.'

'I don't think they've been together much the past few years.'

Joan lights another cigarette, offers the pack to Elaine. They angle their streams of smoke away from each other. 'When did you fall in love with him?' Elaine asks.

'Arslan?'

'Jacob.'

'I saw him across the village square, and we did a big dance for all the peasants.' She hopes Elaine will be bought off by the joke, but Elaine waits without smiling. Joan looks away, says, 'Little by little. It's an accumulation of ordinary things.'

'Romantic.'

Joan bristles. 'It is, in a way.'

'Romance is irrelevant, anyway.' Elaine smokes. 'At least for me. I prefer collaboration. Speaking of, did you see Arslan's special on PBS? *Rusakov and Friends* or whatever it was?'

'I saw the beginning,' Joan says, irritated that

110

Elaine keeps bringing up Arslan, irritated at herself for being irritated. For a moment she is nostalgic for her failed friendship with Sandy, Sandy's lack of interest in her past. 'Cheesy. That top hat. Do you think he'll ever come back to the company?'

'I doubt it. I've heard he's happy in Europe. They throw money at him. They can't get enough of the weird ballets he's making. I saw one in Milan – it was just him and a huge red rubber ball and a white ramp. It was actually fantastic.' Elaine looks up at the sky. 'It's so hot out.'

'You should have come in February.'

'But what else?' Elaine asks after a pause. She sits straight in her chair, arms square on the rests like a brooding empress. 'What else is there?'

'Nothing really.' Joan smiles, melancholy, thinking that friendships go through cycles of extinction, that perhaps she and Elaine won't be able to evolve quickly enough. 'I'm boring.'

'No,' Elaine says without conviction.

'I am.'

'You have Harry. Harry's not boring.'

Joan stubs out her cigarette and allows herself a half smile. She has made Harry, and Elaine will never have anything like him. 'He's just a little boy.'

'But maybe he'll be a dancer.'

'Maybe,' Joan says. 'Who knows. He doesn't have to be.'

'Won't you mind if he never tries?'

'Not at all.'

'Not true. But what else?'

There is too much to tell. Explaining themselves would be impossible, even an attempt would be exhausting, and Elaine has to go to rehearsal. Joan has to pick Harry up at school.

'Merde,' they say to each other upon parting, the way members of the corps do for luck just before going onstage.

PART II

FEBRUARY 1973 – PARIS

Joan kneels in a dark box in the third loge of the Palais Garnier, the Opéra, peeping over the red velvet railing. Six rickety chairs stand close around her, but she knows they creak and is careful not to disturb them. The houselights are down, but the glow from the stage picks out a profusion of gilded plasterwork: serene deities, trumpeting angels, lyres, garlands, flowers, oak leaves, masks, Corinthian columns, all deeply shadowed, piling up around the proscenium and among the boxes like the walls of a craggy gold cave, climbing to Chagall's painted round ceiling of naked angels and voluptuous ballerinas and goats and chickens and lovers and blue Eiffel Tower and red-splotched rendering of the Palais itself. From the center of this hangs the great sleeping chandelier: an enormous gold and glass thistle hung upside down to dry, darkly gleaming.

The Kirov's orchestra noodles around in the pit, waiting. At stage left, just in from the wings, the young star who has been the subject of so much hubbub stands in a heavy grey sweater, white tights, and thick army-green leg warmers pulled up to his thighs. Joan's angle is not ideal – she is looking steeply down on him – but he seems too delicate and too boyish to be impressive. Most of the corps girls milling around in black leotards and white practice tutus are taller than he is. The ballerina who is his partner, however, is tiny, like a fairy, and she stands facing away from him, smoking a cigarette in a long white holder and absently blowing rings of smoke. Her head is wrapped in a printed scarf. Rusakov makes one smooth turn around her and plucks the holder from her fingers. He skips backward, puffing and making faces at her. Not taking the bait, she watches impassively, then pivots and disappears into the wings. He tires of his own game at once and presses the cigarette in its holder into the hand of one of the corps girls. She appears terrified by the gift and passes it off to her neighbor, who rushes into the wings after its owner.

Joan is not supposed to be watching the rehearsal, but she can always claim she did not understand the remonstrations of the ballet master. Still, to be safe, she had crept in a back door and made her way higher and higher through the gloomy backstage passages and stairways until she emerged into the third loge, which was quiet and a little musty without crowds of gossiping, mingling Parisians. Its balconies overlook the bronze and marble excess of the *grand escalier*. There is a curved wall of closed doors, each with a round porthole and leading to a box. She had used an usher's key, purloined in advance, to open the door of box 11.

Some invisible cue makes the dancers flee the stage and the orchestra collect itself. The conductor lifts his baton, slices downward. After a few bars, Rusakov launches out from the wings. He has shed the leg warmers and sweater, and his body, in tights and T-shirt, is perfectly proportioned, muscled but not bulky. His legs appear longer than they are; his ass is round and high. Rumor has it that the Kirov won't cast him as a romantic lead because he is small, preferring to use him as Ali the slave boy or the Bluebird or the Golden Idol, but his stage presence is aggressive and masculine, arrogant. He has arched, almost pointed eyebrows and very dark eyes that bounce imperiously off the empty theater. At first the raked French stages had given Joan trouble. She would migrate toward the pit on her turns, earning a few kicks from the next girl in line. But the stages in Russia are raked, too, and Rusakov shows no discomfort as he flutters downstage, hooking his body from side to side in a series of brisés volés. Another rumor is that he bleaches his hair to look more Russian, less Tatar, and the contrast of his feathered blond mop against his olive skin and black, restless eyes is striking.

The choreography is old-fashioned, but as Rusakov circles the stage doing high, perfect coupés jetés en tournant, his technique is not fusty but pure. His movements are quick but unhurried, impossible in their clarity and difficulty and extraordinary in how they seem to burst from nowhere, without any apparent effort or preparation. But the beauty of Arslan's dancing is not what moves Joan to cry in her red velvet aerie: it is a dream of perfection blowing through the theater. She has been dancing since before her fifth birthday, and she realizes that the beauty radiating from him is what she has been chasing all along, what she has been trying to wring out of her own inadequate body. Forgetting herself, she leans out over the railing, wanting to get closer. *Étonnez-moi,* Diaghilev had said to his dancers in the Ballets Russes. Astonish me.

As Rusakov executes a final leap offstage and the music abruptly ends, the silence that follows is an injustice. Someone starts shouting in Russian. It is the artistic director. He leaps from his seat and charges up the aisle, bellowing. Rusakov reappears, his face blank. He listens to the harangue but does not nod, only stares at his slippers. Without waiting for the other man to finish, he stalks to the back of the stage, and with no music except the lone, rising, furious voice, comes whirling forward in the fastest chain of steps Joan has ever seen. Each step leads inexorably and precisely into the next. Nearly in the pit, he stops and holds an arabesque, all his momentum falling away, leaving a flawless statue. Then he spits and walks offstage. A deeper silence than before follows. Joan looks up at Chagall's angels. Their fleshy wings are like those of penguins, more like fins than tools of flight. As she gets to her feet, she bumps into the chairs, making a clatter, but she doesn't look back to see if anyone has heard.

Behind a curtain, the box has a small antechamber with crimson damask walls, coat hooks, a mirror with a wooden shelf beneath it, and a small velvet fainting couch, also red. She sits on this couch in the dark and snuffles, wiping her face with her hands. After two years in San Francisco, she had come to Europe to dance in a new competition in Switzerland and was spotted there by the director of the Paris Opéra Ballet, who offered to take her on as a *quadrille,* the lowest rank in the company. There was something about her he liked, he told her. Not everything, but something. He can make her better, if she will work. And so she had come to Paris and rented a room in Montmartre from a sullen girl in the company who does not speak to her. She had a short affair with a violinist who liked to hold her feet, tracing his fingers over the bloody patches and rough calluses. Then she had a slightly longer fling with a dancer, a *sujet,* as they call soloists, and she has learned enough French to get by. Every morning she goes to the opera house for class in the huge, round studio that hangs like an unpopped bubble between the auditorium and the Opéra's green dome. Instructions come to her mostly as the names of steps, which she only knows in French anyway, and as eight counts and clapping and singing – *bum BA BA, bum BA BA* – and rapid bursts of elaborate description she can't follow and, sometimes, to her, *comme ça, comme ça* with a demonstration she imitates as best she can. If she succeeds, she earns a *voilà, simple, voilà, c'est tout.* If she fails, there is a small grimace, a twitch of the head, a resigned smile, a retreat.

For Joan, Paris has the feeling of waiting. All the elegance, the light and water and stone and refined bits of greenery, must be *for* something, something more than simple habitation and aggressive driving of Renaults and exuberant besmearing with dog shit. The city seems like an offering that has not been claimed. Its beauty is suspenseful. Joan has walked the boulevards and bridges and embankments, sat in the uncomfortable green metal chairs in the Tuileries, puttered down the Seine on a tourist barge, been to the top of the Eiffel Tower, stared politely at countless paintings, been leered at and kissed at by so many men, stood in patches of harlequin light in a dozen chilly naves, bought a scarf she couldn't afford, surreptitiously stroked the neatly stacked skulls in the catacombs, listened to jazz, gotten drunk on wine, ridden on the back of scooters, done everything she thinks she should in Paris, and still there has always been the feeling of something still to come, a purpose as yet unmet, an expectation.

But, now, in the dark, on the red velvet couch where fashionable Parisian ladies used to retire from the scrutiny of the opera house, Joan finds herself unexpectedly atop a moment that feels significant. Her life, unbeknownst to her, was narrowing around this point, funneling her toward it. The city was never waiting. *She* was waiting. For Arslan. Already she has started to think of him by his first name. If the beauty of Paris is suspenseful, the beauty of his dancing is almost terrible. It harrows her. Her throat is tight with fear. She is afraid of how this man, this stranger, has already changed the sensation of being alive. She is afraid he will slip away. All the things she has felt for months – the mundane loneliness, the frustration with language, the nagging anxiety, the gratitude for the opportunity to dance – all that is gone, replaced with brutal need. She should leave. She should go home and then to class tomorrow and the next day and the day after that. But her need is too powerful to ignore. She must see it through.

Carefully, she eases the door of the box shut behind her. The loge and *escalier* are deserted. The orchestra kicks up again, muted and distant. She has left the door to the back staircase propped open, and she passes into the convoluted innards of the Palais, making a few navigational flourishes to avoid spots where she might encounter Opéra

121

stage crew or where the Kirov would be likely to have stationed security guards. She goes up through a stairwell and along a catwalk through the fly tower, where the painted backdrops fall silently through space like huge blades, and then she descends and descends. He will not be in the best dressing room; she guesses he will be in one of the second best, and she must cross the width of the theater to get there, something most covertly done through one of the basements. Her loneliness within the company has made her an expert in the geography of the opera house. Between rehearsals, when the others go out together for espresso or climb to the roof to gaze across the city and smoke with patina-green Apollo and his upraised lyre, she wanders the corridors and staircases, seeks out corners where she can sit invisibly and read a book. Some doors are locked but not as many as should be. The concierge is lazy.

The cryptlike basement is dark, but she finds a switch. Harsh fluorescence lights its stone vaults and the piles of miscellaneous stage junk underneath them. There are plain black cases for delicate things – lights, perhaps – in neat, anonymous stacks, but then there are loose assemblages of props: foam boulders, tables and chairs, floppy velvet stags, crates of fake fruit, canopy beds in pieces, an elaborate tomb, thrones, swords, scepters, a guillotine, carriages, muskets, angels' wings, donkeys' heads, trees, a magnificent rubber boa constrictor, Corinthian columns, and heaps of other jumbled objects under plastic sheeting or canvas tarps from the gas-lamp days. Joan hurries through, pausing only to lift the drape from an oval mirror and look at herself. She sees a flushed face, lank hair, eyes dilated in the gloom, a floral dress too thin for the season, tight in the waist like Parisian women wear. She draws herself up. She tells herself she is ethereal, mysterious. She will simply appear, like the fairy in the window in *La Sylphide*. She reaches under her skirt and pulls off her ratty underwear, dropping the scrap of cloth into an enormous urn, three feet tall, dusty and black, that stands beside a pile of wooden gravestones.

His name is written on a piece of tape stuck on a door. She is waiting when he comes in, his sodden T-shirt already stripped off and balled up in his hand. He pauses and glances back out into the hallway, looking both ways before he shuts the door. For a moment, he studies her. Then he touches her cheek and says, 'Très belle.' He shows her the tears that come away on his fingers. 'Mais pourquoi triste?'

'Je ne suis pas triste. Je suis très heureuse parce que je suis avec le meilleur danseur du monde.'

He does not seem especially flattered or surprised to find a strange girl speaking schoolgirl French in his dressing room, calling him the best dancer in the world. Nor does he appear impressed by how she managed to evade the Kirov security men or confused about what to do with her. Ordinarily, her love affairs are entered into skittishly, sometimes reluctantly. She doesn't dive into bed but flutters in like a wayward moth. But now she strips off Arslan's damp tights almost violently, as though she were skinning an animal. On the floor, his black eyes flick to her – amused, not especially surprised – when he discovers she is naked under her dress. The glance reminds her of how he had looked spotting his turns, arrogant, tapping his gaze briefly, indifferently against the empty theater, needing nothing from it.

Clutching this Russian stranger, smelling his sweat, feeling the oddly remote pressure of him inside her, she wants some piece of the fearsome beauty he has onstage. She wants to take some of his perfection for herself. He buries his face in her neck, as though flattening himself against a bomb blast. Even as his body presses on her, chest to chest, the outsides of his legs against the insides of hers, he seems hidden.

She pries his face up with both hands, makes him look at her. Still she isn't satisfied. She cranes her neck so their faces are as close as they can be without touching. 'Regarde-moi,' she whispers. 'Tu m'étonnes.' He tries to twist his head away, but she holds on. 'Regarde-moi,' she says again.

Something travels through the dark eyes, some obscure disturbance. And then he looks at her the way she wants. He sees her; she knows he does.

She releases his face, but he doesn't look away, not until he is done and closes his eyes.

Before she leaves, she writes her name and her mother's address in Virginia on a slip of paper with a kohl pencil. She does not expect to hear from him.

MARCH 1974 – NEW YORK CITY

Elaine has the mailbox key and so is the one to collect the mail and so notices the new letters coming for Joan. They are exotic interlopers among ordinary white envelopes from Jacob and terse postcards from Joan's mother: thick paper, odd sizes, European stamps, the address written with foreign flourishes by different hands. Elaine leaves the letters on the kitchen table. Joan takes them without comment and retreats behind the Indian cotton curtain that shields her bed. There is the sound of tearing, the rattle of paper, and then silence.

Joan never mentions the letters, and Elaine does not ask, is not curious about them per se but dislikes not knowing things, especially things that go on in her apartment. The silence surrounding the letters irritates her more and more until this night, when Joan is out and Elaine slips behind the curtain and sits on Joan's bed. The small space is pleasant – secretive and cozy like a child's fort. Light filters through the fabric. The rest of the apartment seems muffled, far away. There aren't many places to conceal the letters, and Elaine finds them at once, in a box under the bed, tied together with an old pink ribbon from a pointe shoe, set neatly atop a slew of Jacob's letters, some of which appear unopened. She unties the ribbon. One after another she takes the pages out of their envelopes and arranges them in neat rows on the bed. They are in French, which she can't read, but they all have the same signature: Arslan. Some have accompanying notes from the people in Lyon or Zurich or London or Munich who have forwarded the letters and seem to form a chain of smuggled correspondence: *You must not tell anyone about your letters from Arslan,* they write. *Secrecy is essential. The situation is fragile.*

Elaine is impressed. Both that Arslan Rusakov, who has become famous in the ballet world since he won the gold medal at Varna, writes Joan letters and also that Joan has kept the secret. There was even a bit about him on 60 *Minutes* with a snippet of footage from Varna: him dancing Ali the slave boy's variation from *Le Corsaire.* Everyone in the company is setting odds on whether or not he'll defect, whether he'll have the chance. American dancers have begun to take ownership of him, talking about him as though he were one of their own, trapped behind enemy lines. Elaine had been skeptical. For all they know, the man could be a Communist Party loyalist who only wants to dance in ballets glorifying the Red Army. But that was before she found the letters. Clearly something has him riled up, but what can he want with Joan?

She studies the slanted lines of French, willing them to become clear. The word *danse* appears again and again. Above his signature, he writes *bisous.* Kisses. Suddenly she is desperate to know what Arslan Rusakov has to say about dance, if he and Joan have actually met, why he has chosen Joan for a pen pal. Something about the correspondence feels unfair. Elaine is by far the better dancer; Elaine understands more about dance. Joan probably thinks she is as committed to dance as Elaine, but she can't possibly be. The simple fact of her inferior talent prohibits it.

If Joan and Arslan have met, it must have been in Paris. Joan doesn't bring up her year with the Opéra Ballet very often, although she still wears the loose black overalls favored by dancers there, either out of pride or habit. Before Elaine found Arslan's letters, she'd had the impression that not much had happened to Joan there. The usual cycle of class, rehearsal, and performance was made novel and lonely by the struggle to understand what was being said and the grandeur of the opera house and the brusque Frenchness of the other dancers, and then it all became familiar and became drudgery. Joan's big accomplishment was getting an audition for Mr K that turned into a spot in the company, a ticket back to New York. As far as men, Joan has only mentioned a violinist with a foot fetish and a *sujet* who had, unbeknownst to Joan, previously rejected her Montmartre roommate. The roommate was a dour, silent, door-slamming creature who scrawled

Putain! in lipstick on the bathroom mirror after she found out about Joan and the *sujet. Putain!* Elaine wrote on the bathroom mirror once, early in their cohabitation, when Joan went out on a date and didn't return. The joke was a gamble; at the time she hadn't known Joan well enough to be sure she could be teased, but Joan came home in the early hours and added *'Elaine is a . . .'* above the accusing word, kicking off a practice of lipsticking insults or freestanding dirty words on the mirror. This mirror is not important, not compared to the big ones in the studio, and there is a vindictive pleasure in obscuring it with crass, red, waxy words. They apply their makeup in the mornings one feature at a time, fitting lips or an eye into a clean patch, avoiding the whole.

It is after eight, but Mr K will still be at the theater. Elaine slips one letter into her purse, puts the rest carefully back in their box, shoulders on her coat, and goes out. The neighborhood isn't terrible, just a little seedy, especially at night when gratings are locked over storefronts and trash bags are piled on the sidewalk. She always walks quickly, using speed as a talisman against getting mugged. It is a middle neighborhood, an uneasy tipping point. A few blocks uptown, a more serious unraveling begins. SRO hotels and weary apartment buildings give way to shelters, pawnshops, methadone clinics, empty lots, and boarded-up buildings on which tangles of graffiti grow like ivy. But a few blocks downtown is the theater, a square, luminous building on one side of a broad, sleek plaza. Two other square, luminous buildings, boxes that contain operas and symphonies, face into the plaza. The three stand together with a tolerant, formal intimacy, like heads of state posing for a portrait. The company's offices and practice studios are in a less exalted building across the street. The occasional pedestrian who happens to look up at its windows might see dancers at work, moving silently behind reflected bits of sky.

Elaine canvasses the dark hallways until she finds Mr K in one of the big rehearsal rooms with a principal dancer, Clarissa. She watches them through the narrow window in the door. Mr K is making a dance. He wears a three-piece grey suit and a checked shirt with an open collar. Blue silk blooms from his breast pocket. He steps forward onto one toe, extends an arm, rocks back, talking the whole time. Clarissa stares at him, nodding. Mr K steps away, leans against the mirror, claps his hands once. Clarissa takes a beat to prepare and then goes through a complicated combination. The step forward, extended arm, and rock back are buried in the middle of it, barely perceptible. That is the key, Elaine knows: to be able to give Mr K exactly what he wants, to understand him. He likes her, has begun to pay more attention to her. He gives her corrections in class and calls her by name. Every time he pauses beside her at the barre, she wants to kneel at his feet and have him pour ballet into her, to receive his visions.

She sits on the floor of the hallway and waits. She tries to decide what she will say about the letters, but all she can think of is that he should see them. They are important, and they are about ballet, so he has a right to know about them. After a while, maybe half an hour, Clarissa comes out, a towel over her shoulders. She jumps when she sees Elaine but collects herself and rolls her eyes, holding the door open. Not looking at her, Elaine sweeps past. Mr K is at the baby grand piano. He stares thoughtfully at the ceiling and plays a few bars to himself. At the sound of her footsteps – she is still in street shoes – he frowns and folds his hands in his lap.

'Yes?'

'I'm sorry to intrude,' Elaine says, 'but I have something I need to show you.'

'Show me?' He presses one finger down on middle C. 'What can you have to show me, child?'

She takes folded paper from her bag. 'I found letters, lots of letters, between Joan and Arslan Rusakov. I can't read French, so I don't know what they say, but I thought you should know.'

He purses his lips, plays a short run of scales. 'For heaven's sake, dear, come closer. Don't shout across the room.'

She comes and stands beside the piano like a singer about to give a recital, holding out the letter. She expects him to seize it and pore over it, but instead he continues to play, staring off at nothing, kneading out a slow improvisation, seemingly

131

oblivious to both her presence and the activity of his fingers. Eventually, he resolves his melody and drops his hands into his lap, turning his full attention to her. 'Elaine,' he says. 'Child. What is it you want me to do? You want me to read this letter? Spy on poor little Joan and a man I do not know? Maybe it is a simple love letter.'

'No, they're about dance. There are lots of them.' She unfolds the paper, sets it on the music stand, and taps it to make him look. 'It says *danse* a million times.'

He squints at the paper. 'So it does.'

'What does it say?'

'You are too nosy, my dear. It is, as you surmised, about dance. He is telling little Joan all the things he thinks about dance.' He squints again. 'He has grand ambitions, this young man.'

'That's exactly . . . I came to you because, what if he wants to defect? What if—'

He holds up a hand. 'Indeed. What if? Should I write letters to him myself, posing as Joan, urging him to defect? Should I parachute into Leningrad with a machine gun and break him out? Should I write to the president, request an invasion? No, if this is what Arslan Rusakov will do, he must do it himself. Of course I would be happy to have him here because by all accounts he seems to be extraordinary, but there is nothing for us to do but be patient. It is not a small thing to defect. You must leave a great deal behind. Even if you are someone who has very little, you leave more than you can imagine. People close to you will suffer. They might be punished on your behalf. You must be willing to sacrifice them. You will be a traitor. You probably don't think much about having a country, Elaine, but you would if you were leaving yours and could never return.'

Her embarrassment at being chided emboldens her; she must take a risk or else slink away. 'How did you decide to do it?' she asks. 'When did you know you were going to leave?'

Mr K studies her face, his expression stern, but then he smiles, slides over, and pats the space beside him on the piano bench. She sits, and he puts an arm around her shoulders. His face is close to hers. She has heard he sleeps with the dancers he promotes and has assumed that someday she, too, will sleep with him, but she is unprepared for anything to happen so soon. His thigh presses against hers. The material of his suit is very fine, a light dove grey. She has heard he sleeps with men, too, but only outside the company. Dancers, even the gay ones, talk about that as if it is sleazy, shameful – it's the *secrecy*, they say, the *self-hatred* of it, and why even *bother* with the girls? – but Elaine can't imagine Mr K doing anything that isn't aesthetically perfect. She can't imagine him hating himself, because he is a genius. If he sleeps with men, it must be beautiful.

'It was an impulse,' he says. 'An instinct. What do they say – fight or flight? I prefer flight. Especially then, flight was a relief. I could not fight anymore. Maybe I always knew I wasn't meant to stay in Russia, but I didn't know I was going to do it until I did it. I was in Berlin at the end of the war, in the army, and I . . . I ran away. It was much easier for me than it is for them now. There was so much chaos for me to slip into. I found my way to Paris. After the war, for a while, I wasn't afraid of anything. I felt nothing. That is how I survived. Millions were not going home because they were dead. Why should I go home only because I happened to be alive? I would not see my mother again, but what was that compared to everything else? At the time it seemed like nothing. I threw away my uniform. I stole new clothes. I already spoke French. That was very helpful.' He removes his arm from her shoulders and plays a chord, then another. He watches his hands critically, mouth pulled down so his chin disappears into his neck. Time passes. He seems to have forgotten about her. She sits very still.

Finally, quietly, he says, 'My mother spoke French to me.'

She doesn't know what to ask. She is nothing. Joan's letters are nothing. His life seems immeasurably large.

He stops playing. 'Elaine,' he says, abruptly cheerful, twisting to look at her. 'Child. You must help me. Clarissa has gone home, and I have no one to make a dance on.'

She is afraid. This is not how she thought it would happen. 'I'm wearing jeans,' she says.

'Well,' he says, 'go find something else.'

She hurries through the dark hallways to her locker, terrified and elated. This is a test. It must be. He must know how far he has thrown her off balance. She struggles into tights and a leotard, neither exactly clean, pulls her hair up. In the back of her locker, tucked in a slipper, is a baggie of cocaine. She sets a pinch on the back of her hand and inhales it, welcoming the burn. Carrying her shoes, she runs back to Mr K, making little leaps as she goes, invincibility accumulating in her body. She passes a framed poster of Clarissa in an arabesque as Giselle and gives it the finger. While she sits by the mirror and puts her shoes on, trying to stretch as she does, Mr K moves around the center floor, humming to himself, making tiny motions, shifting his weight this way and that.

'Come, child,' he says. 'Stand here.'

She goes to stand in the middle of the room and looks at herself in the mirror. She is as she always is, except that Mr K, dapper in his suit, is studying her, only her, with one finger pressed to his lips. He swivels around, looking at their reflections, side by side. 'Yes,' he says. 'She is very nice, that girl, very pretty, but now you must forget she is there.' He steps in front of her, obstructing her view, taking her face in both his hands. 'If we make a dance, we make it in this room, not in the mirror.'

She can smell him. Cologne and tobacco, something sour on his breath, some kind of pomade in his hair. His eyes are pale blue with dark rings around the irises. She has never noticed the rings before. He is going grey at his temples and in his eyebrows. She sees his nostrils expanding and contracting. She wants him to kiss her, to breathe into her, to descend upon her like an angel, but he says, 'And you must not be so nosy. You will make more of yourself if you are not the conniving kind. Promise. No more. You will put Joan's letter back and forget about it.'

She promises.

He stares at her, then nods and releases her face. He says, 'Okay. Begin like this.' He lifts barely onto his toes, suggests a tendu. 'Then this.' He turns, sweeps a hand toward the floor. 'And prepare and quick sissonne changée one, fouetté two, piqué, arabesque, chassé, big assemblé, then like this, then hold, sissonne ouverte, then something light, maybe turn, turn, turn, then assemblé, attitude, and so on, yes, yes, like so. Yes? Do you see?'

She hesitates, finds she understands. 'Yes, I see,' she says. He moves away, leans against the barre, gestures for her to begin. She dances into the silence, beginning their conversation.

'Good,' he says. 'And next this.'

JANUARY 1975 – TORONTO

Joan waits in a car behind the theater, watching the green metal stage door. A bald man in a boxy suit smokes in the yellow light of a sodium lamp set into the cinder blocks of the theater's back wall. Soon – she hopes it will be soon – that lamp will go out, will be turned out by a stagehand who is in on the plan, and she will flash her headlights so Arslan knows where to run. The KGB minder looks neither fast nor particularly vigilant; he looks cold. Joan has been watching him for an hour, wondering why he has no overcoat and no hat for his bald head. Maybe he underestimated the Toronto winter and left his warm things behind out of Soviet machismo, or maybe some official regulation compels him to be miserable. What does he think of Canada? Of the polite, busy streets, the neat rectangles of neon affixed to the buildings, the construction cranes everywhere? What will he think when Arslan makes his run? Joan hopes that the man will sympathize, even unconsciously, and allow Arslan to slip away. She knows the hope is naïve, but still she hopes. She hopes for any advantage.

The man claps his hands against his biceps and paces back and forth, seven steps away from the door, seven steps back, sending up a plume of smoke as constant as a steamship's. Joan is smoking, too. She cranks down the window an inch to let out some of the haze. Frigid air flows in. Butts and grit fill the ashtray of the Chrysler 160 that was given to her, along with detailed instructions, by the Canadian woman who met her at the airport that morning, one of Arslan's many international female friends.

Joan fingers the headlights lever with one hand and touches the key, already in the ignition, with the other. The Chrysler is a cream-colored, eager-looking car, long in front and stubby in back. Earlier, elsewhere, she had practiced starting it while simultaneously flashing the lights. Three times, with the Canadian woman in the passenger seat, she practiced driving the two miles from the theater to the parking garage where she will trade this car for one with New York plates. She knows the way, with a few extra turns thrown in for safety, and she knows an alternate way. From the parking garage, she knows how to get to the highway that will take them to the border and then to New York.

The Canadian woman, Felicia, had expressed skepticism that Joan was the right accomplice for Arslan's escape. 'I thought you would be a race car driver or a secret agent or something,' she said as Joan navigated through the city, feeling like she was taking a driving test. 'More of an aggressive person. To be completely honest, I can't make out why he was so set on you.'

'I don't know either,' Joan said, 'but I couldn't say no.'

'He doesn't want a fuss, or people, or a celebration. There's going to be so much fuss and so many people eventually. I think he wants to stave it off so he's not overwhelmed right away. He said he doesn't want chatter, so don't chatter. You know he doesn't speak English anyway.'

'We spoke French.'

'Oh. You've met him?'

'Yes, of course. Haven't you?'

'No, but it feels like I have. I got involved in his case through friends. I saw him perform two years ago. In Paris. It changed my life. He's extraordinary.'

'Funny, that's where I met him. In Paris. I was with the Opéra Ballet. It could have been the same day as when you saw him.'

Felicia says nothing. The air is spiky with competition. She is older than Joan, in her mid-thirties, and her clothes are conservative but high quality. She wears a sizeable diamond engagement ring and a wedding band.

Joan wants to tell her about the dressing room floor but only says, 'I would do anything to help him.'

'So would I,' Felicia snapped. 'Of course. Communication has been difficult, to say the least.

139

We never knew what got through to him. It was simplest to do exactly what he wanted. Arguing would have taken too long, and the more messages we passed back and forth, the more likely he was to get caught, and that'd be it. We've had a terrible time planning. This should work, though.' She paused and then said, 'As long as no one fucks up.'

At the moment, Joan's sole wish in life is not to fuck up. The mechanism of how she has become Arslan's getaway driver, his escort to the New World, is not entirely clear. From what she can gather, he informed his network of friends, to their universal puzzlement, that he wanted to be met by Joan and conveyed to New York by Joan. That he has chosen her fills her with an ever-shifting combination of amazement, confusion, joy, a desperate feeling she suspects is love, and a fear of failure that pursues her through the days and nights. She has scarcely slept since she learned of the plan.

Months earlier, his first letter had materialized like a hoax or an omen. In Paris she had given him the address of her mother's house in Virginia, but this mysterious, portentous cream-colored envelope with a French stamp had somehow found her New York apartment. She had not known what to expect – a friendly note? a sexy one? – but could not have guessed that inside would be a stiff card bearing an admonition from an unknown Frenchwoman not to tell anyone that Arslan had written to her and then, from Arslan, three sheets of thin, grey paper, densely scrawled over on both sides. It was an oddly impersonal treatise on dance, in French, detailing what he perceived as its limitations, its glories, its future. *Please tell me,* he wrote at the end, *about dance in the USA.*

So she had written back as best she could, describing the company's repertoire and the choreographers who cycled in and out depending on how territorial Mr K was feeling. She told him what they were rehearsing: short ballets of Greek myths, a long ballet about Wyatt Earp. She tried to explain how Mr K made dances, how he was always asking his dancers to be faster and sharper and more controlled and more turned out and how he was expanding their vocabulary of steps. Then she answered questions Arslan had not asked. She told him about her mother and how she had thought ballet was cute when Joan was little but now understood almost nothing about her life. She told him about her bed behind the sheet in Elaine's apartment, about how all she had ever wanted was to perform with the company and how strange it was that a dream, once realized, could quickly turn mundane. She skimmed over her doubts about her own talent, her fears about what she would do when she was inevitably shouldered out of the company. The Frenchwoman's note had instructed Joan to mail any response to her address in Paris, and she would try to get it to Arslan.

A few weeks later, sooner than Joan had expected, an envelope arrived that contained a stern note in English from a West German informing her that secrecy was imperative and then another discourse on *la danse* roaming over more sheets of the thin, grey paper. She replied again, this time sending her letter to Berlin, telling Arslan more about herself, asking him questions about where he lived, what his days were like. *I think about you all the time,* she wrote. *I worry about you.* Another letter arrived before her reply could possibly have reached him, accompanied by another warning to keep her mouth shut, this time from a woman in Milan. More letters followed. They were never personal, but they were increasingly passionate. He seemed to be working himself up, churning out long screeds about artistic paranoia in the USSR and the way the system built magnificent dancers and then smothered them. He listed ideas for new ballets. He wanted to make a ballet about nuclear war, another about a rock band, another set to the dull peals of Russian Orthodox church bells, another set to the sound of crickets and performed in near darkness. Each letter was chaperoned by a haughty European admonishment to keep the correspondence secret. Joan told no one. She was only being obedient, but she inadvertently passed a test of trustworthiness. When word got out that Arslan was coming to Toronto with a small touring company, a letter arrived from an Englishwoman, a soloist with the

Royal Danish Ballet, the first of many sets of instructions.

Arslan insists that you should be the one to help him in his hour of need. I wish with all my heart it could be me – Arslan feels the same – but we don't know when another opportunity like this will arise. As you probably aren't aware, he hasn't been allowed to perform in the West since '73. They think because he is a Tatar and because he is interested in choreographers other than Petipa (or, more accurately, regurgitated 'Petipa') and doesn't like idiotic dogmatic ballets, he can't be trusted. They are right, of course, but another dancer was injured, and so they are allowing him to go to Canada with this little circus troupe (everyone else in it is a thousand years old or completely terrible or both, by the way, but that means for once he gets to dance the lead, their way of bribing him). For reasons unknown to me, he has chosen you to help him. He is too stubborn to be dissuaded, and so you must do it. Don't make the mistake of believing he is in love with you.

Waiting behind the theater, watching the bald man smoke, nervously tapping her fingers on the hard plastic steering wheel, Joan thinks that Arslan must be in love with her. You could only trust someone you love with a task this important, this

143

dreadful. She remembers his eyes on her in Paris. Two years have not diluted the memory. Something was sprung open by what they had done – she had felt the new space, the possibility – but then he was gone, and impossibility swung shut behind him, and she thought she had been foolish to imagine there was anything more than a fuck on a floor. She thinks she confuses the articulation of dance with the incoherence of sex. Within sex, bodies tell you nothing. They are incidental objects, assemblages of moving parts in a pleasure generating mechanism. For him, she was probably nothing, barely a blip in his faraway life. She had accepted this. But then the letters, then the summons to Toronto.

The stage door light goes out. There is a shout, a slam. She fumbles to turn the key in the ignition, almost forgets to flash the lights, then jerks the lever back and forth, gasping out loud with fear. The asphalt appears in white light, disappears, appears again. The brake lights of parked cars flash like the eyes of surprised animals. Arslan runs toward her, an apparition becoming solid, his white tights glowing, and then he is at the car, struggling with the door behind her. She hears him flipping the handle – a metallic clapping accompanied by a slight shaking of the car as he begins to tug frantically – but she does not make sense of what is happening until his face, wild, is at her window, yelling something. The bald man is almost to them, charging flat-footedly across the parking lot. As Joan twists around to unlock the door, she catches a peripheral glimpse of the minder's face. He looks terrified, as though he were not the pursuer but the pursued. His eyes plead against what is happening, his own failure. Then Arslan is in the car. All the bald man can do is scrabble at the Chrysler's stubby rear end as Joan throws it into gear and jolts away, not roaring and squealing like in a movie, just driving, but still moving faster than the bald man, the back door hanging open until Arslan, splayed across the seat, pulls it shut.

Arslan is still ranting in Russian. She glances at him in the rearview mirror. His face is tight with fury at her, the idiot who forgot to unlock the car door, who might have let him be seized by the bald man, dragged away to a different car, an airplane, back to Moscow. 'Je suis désolée,' she says, then says it again, grateful she has to concentrate on driving and can't turn around and assess the devastating discrepancy between the look in his eyes now and the one she has been polishing in her memory. After her third apology, he falls silent.

The drive to the parking garage is short, quiet, and uneventful. She stops at yellow lights, signals when she turns. In the mirror, he watches the city. Sometimes he cranes around to look out the back, maybe checking to be sure they are not being followed or maybe getting a longer look at something that has interested him. The plan had been

145

for him to crouch down, but she lets him sit and look out the window. She doesn't want to speak to him for fear of rekindling his anger, and she sees no reason for him to hide. No one is chasing them. Who would, really? It has already worked. He is already free. She half hopes the bald minder decided to run away, too, that he will become a Canadian.

In the garage, as planned, another car is waiting, this one a Buick with New York plates. Not as planned, Felicia is standing beside it, smiling, shimmying with anticipation like an overexcited dog. The key was supposed to be in a magnetic box under the front bumper, a change of clothes for Arslan in the trunk.

'Qui est-ce?' Arslan says.

Joan pulls into a parking space. 'Felicia. Ton amie.'

'*Zdravstvujtye!*' Felicia calls, bending down to wave at Arslan through the window. He stares coolly at her through the glass. 'Welcome!' Felicia says, opening the door for him. 'Welcome to Canada!'

Slowly, he emerges. Joan gets out and hovers between them. She is more anxious and embarrassed for this woman than she thinks she should be, given how unfriendly and rivalrous Felicia was during the day, but she has intuited that Arslan, already on edge because of the locked door and the weeks of tension that must have led up to this moment and the dawning reality of his defection,

146

will not welcome an improvisation on his request for no fuss, no people, no chatter. Felicia is already chattering. 'You have done a very brave thing,' she tells Arslan, staring at him with an intensity that excludes Joan. 'The free world welcomes you. We are so very, very happy to have you, really, I can't express how honored I am to witness this moment. And I want to assure you that I understand your sacrifice. I do. Really, I do. I hope we might have the chance to get to know each other better.'

Arslan is looking away, across the mostly empty garage to where a narrow window lets in cold air and frames ashy city darkness perforated by a smattering of lit windows in a tall building. He stands in his white tights and slippers, mouth pursed in annoyance, arms folded in the blousy white sleeves of his prince's shirt across his cream-and-gold waistcoat. He has the appearance of an impatient time traveler. Felicia steps toward him, perhaps to embrace him, and he stiffens, fending her off without even acknowledging her.

'Would you translate?' Felicia says to Joan. 'Please?'

'Elle dit –' Joan begins.

Arslan looks at her. 'Vêtements?' he says sharply.

'What did he say?' asks Felicia.

Joan hesitates, not wanting to be rude but also wanting to leave, to be rid of this woman. 'He's wondering where his clothes are.'

'Oh. Yes. I have them here.' Felicia, crestfallen, opens the trunk of the Buick and takes out a brown shopping bag. Arslan is already unbuttoning the waistcoat and stripping off the loose shirt. His torso is narrow, pale, armored with compact muscle. Hooking his thumbs in the waistband of his tights, he looks at Joan as he pulls them down, revealing his thighs and the flesh-colored, neutering triangle of his dance belt. The corner of his mouth curls, and he winks. She is forgiven. Felicia, reproached by his nakedness, turns away to study the streaks of salt and dirty water on the cement. She holds the bag out to Joan. Inside is a grey sweat suit, socks, and a pair of black high-top Chuck Taylors. Without quite looking at him, Joan hands Arslan the pants first, then the hooded sweatshirt, the socks, the too big shoes. Dressed, his fine head dwarfed by the hood, he looks small and painfully young and tired, like a high school athlete after a lost game. His ballet clothes are a pale puddle on the cement.

'Allons-y,' he says to Joan.

For ten days after they reach New York, Arslan refuses to leave the apartment Joan had hastily rented in Chelsea before going to Toronto, explaining to a mildly bewildered Elaine that she needed her own space. A dwindling platoon of reporters camp out on the sidewalk, tipped off by someone in the company. SOVIET BALLET STAR DEFECTS IN CANADA, announce the headlines. *American ballerina drives getaway car all the way to New York love nest.* The newspapermen bribe people who live across the alley to let them spy from the fire escape. Joan and Arslan smoke and smoke but don't open the windows for fear of eavesdroppers, and the tiny rooms are hazy and stale. In Leningrad Arslan had been given an apartment in a former palace with large windows and fine things that were chosen for him. He tells her this slowly, painfully slowly, with the aid of the Russian-English dictionary they keep on the nightstand. He expresses some disappointment with the neighborhood, which he seems to have expected to be glamorous, not gritty, with piles of garbage and men loitering on stoops, and she shows him the words for *cheap* and *available* and *hurry*. They communicate best in French, but he has ordained that they must speak only English. Conversation drips slowly, as though from a leaky faucet, with suspenseful gaps between words.

Lawyers come and go. Mr K brings a samovar and smoked fish and Chinese food and pastrami sandwiches and piles of new clothes – Levi's, underwear, baseball tees, a sport coat, checked shirts like the ones Mr K favors, a necktie, dancewear – but even in the presence of visitors, Arslan will only put on a pair of running shorts, yellow with white trim. He sits bare chested and cross-legged on the unmade bed, enthroned, smoking and nodding at what the lawyers and their translator have to say. When the visitors are gone, he tosses the shorts aside and retreats under the covers. Sometimes he is playful, making funny faces at Joan and reciting English phrases passed among the male members of the Kirov: 'Cool chick, please be meeting you, very sexy.' Sometimes he stares moodily at the ceiling and smokes in silence, extinguishing his butts in an ashtray shaped like Mount Rushmore.

'Who is?' he had asked on their first night together, pointing at the enamel faces.

'Presidents,' she said. 'Their faces are carved in a mountain.'

His black eyes are set in a narrow, expressive, high-cheekboned face, and he screwed the whole thing up in exaggerated confusion. She had gotten up, naked, and gone to her stack of books on the floor – a bookshelf had not been among the bits and pieces of furniture she'd bought in one rushed sweep through a consignment store – and found her eleventh grade history textbook, which she had kept out of a vague concern that someday she might need to look up something historical. There was no picture of Mount Rushmore, but she found a painting of George Washington and pointed to it and then the ashtray. By the time she got to Roosevelt, Arslan's interest had waned, and when she went for the dictionary, he grabbed her arm and rolled her onto her back. While he kissed her, she thought it was just as well. The whole thing would look like a Communist monument to him anyway, and he would either think too much or too little of it.

'Marvelous girl,' Mr K says every time he comes

to the apartment. Clasping her face in his hands, he kisses her cheeks. 'Beautiful, marvelous girl. I knew I saw something in you in Paris. You have a brave soul.' He takes her by the arm and shakes her at Arslan. 'Très belle, non? Très courageuse.'

'Oui, oui. Très belle,' Arslan agrees, and then they speak to each other in Russian while Joan wrangles the samovar and empties ashtrays. They drink gallons of dark tea from glass tumblers Mr K brought, sweetening it with sugar cubes. Mr K shakes his head with a show of great reluctance at something Arslan asks, and Joan wonders if they are talking about her. Arslan has told her he wants to dance with her. She is not good enough. She knows this. Mr K knows this, too, but Arslan has never seen her dance and he is, as the Englishwoman said in her letter, stubborn. She sits on the floor and stretches. The subway rumbles under her building, and her few dishes rattle on their shelf. Mr K has told her not to worry about missing a week of class. He says she is right to stay by Arslan's side, guarding him. She is a good girl.

As the days pass, she is becoming restless, tired of flipping through the dictionary, of weathering Arslan's periods of bleak silence, of breathing old smoke, even of sex. The urgency of their first coupling in Paris and the rough, clutching grief of their second – conducted in the Toronto parking garage in the backseat of the Buick after Felicia had finally slunk off – has evaporated, leaving behind something residual and perfunctory, if also frequent.

151

He is not what she would call an attentive lover. But she foresees no satisfying resolution to her restlessness. As soon as they leave the apartment, she will lose him: to Mr K, to the company, to the reporters, to the whole country. His defection has been taken as a national compliment. In all likelihood, he is the best dancer in the world, or he will be as soon as he makes use of his new freedom. He is, by his very greatness, a vindication of the Soviet system, proof that the brutal heat with which they forge artists and athletes does, in fact, yield new, better human forms, and yet he has risked everything to escape (to liberty!), and she (Joan!) is the angel who bore him safely into the bosom of his new homeland. Our vindication tops their vindication – so imply the breathless magazines, the politicians quoted in the newspapers. Everyone wants what we have, they say.

Joan is tired of the apartment, but at least while she is in it, she has Arslan. She watches him with a hoarder's eye, fearful of the moment when he will go outside. Her old life seems dull and unappealing now; it is like a shabby, outgrown dress she doesn't want him to see her wearing. Out there, he will see her in the corps, no longer his rescuer but one of many identical girls, a bit of background, a swan or a peasant or a wili or a shade, and she will see him not as the man who smokes in her bed and wallows in her bathtub and splays naked in her armchair, flipping through the English-Russian dictionary, but as she had first seen him: onstage, removed, at the spinning center of everything. She is having her own momentary flare of fame (her mother called to say an unfamiliar woman claiming to be her fourth grade teacher had gone on the local news and called her 'lion-hearted' and 'a patriot'), but when the political drama settles and there is only dancing, she will not be able to keep up. All her life she has wished for more talent, for better feet, longer arms, and the fact that her wish has gone unfulfilled now seems like vindictive cosmic spite. She has asked him why he chose her, but he does not answer beyond rolling his eyes if he's gloomy or telling her because she's so pretty if he's flirtatious. In low moments, she returns to the question, asking herself why he did this to her, why he had come from Russia to torment her with her own limitations.

They had stopped short of the border and, to be on the safe side, put Arslan in the trunk of the Buick. The bored customs official gave Joan's driver's license a cursory inspection and waved her through. She exited the highway at Niagara Falls and wound her way to a lookout spot with a dark parking area. 'Les États-Unis,' she said, letting Arslan out of the trunk. They stood together at a railing above Horseshoe Falls, side by side, the metal bar vibrating under their hands from the force of so much water. The river, black and flat and gleaming, vanished at the brink as though lopped off by a sword, the dark, slick water turning white and pulverized as it poured into space.

Colored lights played over the descending scrim. A plume of rising spray turned from a ghostly amber twist to a blue one to a white one.

'Qu'est-ce que c'est?' he shouted over the roar of water.

'C'est une . . .' Joan didn't know the French word for *waterfall,* and surely he could see for himself it was a waterfall, surely they had waterfalls in Russia. He was asking something else, something for which she had no answer in any language.

On the eleventh day, without fanfare, while Joan is in the bath, he gets dressed in flares and a checked shirt and goes outside. She hears the front door close, calls for him, hears nothing, splashes out of the bathroom, dresses in a panic, and rushes down the stairs while buttoning her dress, her hair still clipped up messily on top of her head. Outside, Arslan is posing for the one photographer who has won the war of attrition. He leans jauntily against the brick building. 'Joan!' Arslan says, apparently delighted to see her. He beckons her over, and she comes to lean beside him. The photographer steps forward, releases her hair from its clip and fluffs it over her shoulders.

In the photo, which runs in all the newspapers, her panic is invisible. She looks happy, tucked under Arslan's arm, her hair messy in a way that suggests they have been too busy in bed to emerge until now. The next day he goes to class, and then in the spring there is his grand debut with the company, as Albrecht in *Giselle.* The ovation goes on and on. Joan stands in the rear, in a row of girls all wearing long white tutus and wreaths in their hair. They are wilis, the spirits of jilted maidens who died of heartbreak. They have danced the gamekeeper Hilarion to death, but Albrecht is saved by Giselle. The principal who danced Giselle runs offstage, returns with an armful of red and white roses bound with a huge blue ribbon. She curtsys low, offering them to Arslan. He accepts, plucking out one red rose to give back to her. Joan watches him bow and bow to the roaring maw of the theater, and she remembers the waterfall. Here is the answer to his question.

FEBRUARY 1976 – PARIS

Joan's left hand is tucked under Arslan's elbow, in the warm crook. Beneath the wooden slats of the Pont des Arts, the Seine slides between its stone embankments, crusted with patches of gold from streetlamps. A shallow lid of clouds has closed over the city like an oyster shell. Snowflakes fall but do not stick, and the iron railings gleam with half-frozen damp. At the center of the bridge, Arslan gathers Joan under his arm and faces downstream toward where the sharp prow of the Île de la Cité cleaves the arches of the Pont Neuf. The island's narrow buildings huddle shoulder to shoulder, facing out at the encroaching metropolis, the towers of Notre Dame peeping over their roofs as though from within a circle of protective bodyguards. To the right, the bridge leads to the dignified gold-ribbed dome of the Institut de France. To the left, the Louvre.

'This city is exquisite,' Joan says. 'It's trite to say so, but I never get used to it. It makes me greedy. I want to stuff it into my pockets.'

'What is this word?' he asks, his cheek against her temple.

'Which word?'

'With "x."'

'Exquisite. It means beautiful. But more than that. Like . . . so delicate and perfect it's almost painful.'

'Painful . . . it is not help.'

'Perfect down to the smallest part. Like the most lovely ballerina possible. Delicate, fragile, almost too beautiful to look at. She is exquisite.'

'Exquisite,' he repeats, and a slight shift in his body betrays that his mind has left her, is following that ghostly ballerina off the bridge and away into the Parisian night. She should have thought of a different example. To remind him of her presence, she leans against his side. Grasping her shoulders, he turns her to him, bends to nuzzle her neck.

Her happiness is also exquisite, excruciating, barbed with fear. At any moment, it will be taken from her. The company, which will go to Amsterdam next and then London, did a matinee that day but no evening performance, and afterward Arslan sought her out and told her to put on a dress and meet him later in the hotel lobby. When she did, he took her hand in full view of the dancers hanging around the front desk and led her out into the city. They had a glass of wine in an art nouveau café, squeezed side by side behind a tiny round table, and he talked to her about dance. Lately he has been going off, away from the company, to work with other choreographers, other companies. Mr K is annoyed with him, possessive. 'People come

157

because of me,' Arslan told Joan. 'They buy tickets because of me. He knows this. Everyone knows this. But I can't dance only here, only his dances. I stay in one place, I lose inspiration. I lose inspiration, I lose my soul. I can't come here and do same thing again, again, again. What is point, you know?'

Yes, Joan said, of course.

'Is difficult, these new things, jazzy things, swing things, American things. I don't know these things. They are not in me. Like eating too fast. Sometimes they –' He closed his hands over his throat, bugged out his eyes.

'Choke you. Get stuck.'

'Yes. Stuck. But I want to know. Is important to know.'

Yes, Joan said, it is.

They took a taxi to the Left Bank to hear a piano recital in a tiny church with fluted columns and real candles that dripped wax from iron candelabras onto the stone floor, making a slow patter. The pianist, an old White Russian who played in a tailcoat, kissed Joan three times after Arslan introduced her, his long mustache tickling her cheeks. They went with him to dinner in a restaurant with red and gold walls, white tablecloths, red leather booths, a low ceiling of dark wood. Waiters who resembled the pianist in both mustache and tailcoat brought them caviar and vodka and borscht and chicken in cream sauce and more foods that Joan couldn't identify but that seemed, like everything else on this night, romantic and profoundly Russian, part of a lost, maybe imaginary world of snow and sleighbells and gold onion domes. Drunk, she had reclined amid all the red and let their unintelligible conversation drift past. The pleasures of his native language transformed Arslan. In Russian, he was quick and lively and ebullient, a man who laughed, who made the old pianist and the waiters laugh. Here in Europe, without the comforting barrier of an ocean, Joan would have expected him to feel his exile more keenly, to fall into one of his glooms. She would have expected the vast, brooding bulk of his homeland to exert some dark magnetism on his soul. Instead: gregarious good cheer, an affectionate hand on her knee.

His moods are mysterious, but she has a sad certainty that this one will cool and fade soon enough. Maybe tonight when they are still in bed he will tell her he is tired and send her back to the room she's sharing with Elaine, recently promoted to soloist, or maybe tomorrow he will flirt with another girl in the wings when she is watching. He will vanish after a performance without telling her where he is going. She might catch a glimpse of him leaving the theater with a sparkling flock of strangers in evening clothes, his arm around some woman's waist. She is always losing him, but he is never quite lost. A year has passed since she drove him across the border, and they remain inextricably, inconclusively enmeshed.

He goes away. He comes back. More and more slowly, but he comes back. When they are alone, lying quietly, he holds her the way a child holds a stuffed animal: for comfort, for security, out of a primate's urge to cling, to close one's arms around a warm, soft object. Eventually, she knows, he will decide not to come back, but something – a force she wishes she could identify – binds him to her.

Almost as soon as they emerged from the apartment in New York, even before his debut, the first cascade of applause, he had begun to wander. For two months, maybe three, she was the main woman, the lead – the one on his arm at parties and events, famous as his accomplice, the brave girl in the news story – but she slipped bit by bit down into an ensemble cast. The gossip columns lavish question marks and exclamation points on items linking him to socialites and actresses. He always says the women are friends, but they are never friends. His sexual interest is a visible, obvious thing, easily tracked and monitored. He can't be bothered to conceal his affairs, his flirtations, his wanderings. Why should he? Even as he tortures her, she sees he is simply living the life he prefers, a life of variety, and she sees there is no reason, really, why he should give anything up for her, why he should love her. The recriminations of women can be shrugged off, walked away from. A mass of recriminating women will not deter other women from taking their turns with him.

After cheese, after dessert, after cigars and

aperitifs and black tea sweetened with jam, Arslan led her to the river, and they had walked to the Pont des Arts.

She tastes vodka and cigars on his mouth. His tongue lazily invades and then retreats. He leans away, studies her face, and smacks a peck on her lips. She presses her face to his neck, knowing they will go to his room soon but preferring this. They are more alone here than they will be in his room, where the shadows of other women dance around the bed. In his room, she fights his waning interest. Her sense that he is sliding away even when he is right there, as much of him touching her as possible, makes her worry she is losing her mind. She has tried to be sexier, more daring in bed, but her attempts only seem to bore him. They will go to his room – his room is where this night must end – but even with the elaborate lingerie she is wearing and the erotic stratagems she has stored up, she will disappoint him. Going to his room will only hasten the end, but here, above the river, at the center of this exquisite city, they are caught in a romantic force as powerful as a solar flare. Even he must feel it.

'Thank you for this night,' she ventures.

He nods, his chin moving against her head. 'Yes, was good to see Iosif. He still plays beautiful. If he was dancer, he would have stop thirty years now.'

'That's true.'

'I will like to be old man.'

'No, you won't.'

'Yes. Why not? Less trouble with women, no class every day, no worrying about being great dancer, no worrying about being old man because – hey – you are old man.'

'You bring the trouble with women on yourself, Arslan.'

He tsks, but affectionately, squeezing her. 'Joan, you only hear not important part.'

After his defection he had tried to dance with her. He'd been generous, really, staying late in the studio with her, lifting her again and again. But every time he would say, 'Is no good.' Then he would demonstrate, and the difference between what he wanted and what she could do caused her, horribly, to cry. Sometimes he stormed off in disgust, leaving her alone with her weeping reflection, and sometimes he gathered her into his arms, kissing her cheeks and nose, saying, 'Always she cry. She is like baby.'

Why had he even bothered? She could never be his partner; Mr K had told him so when they were still holed up in the apartment. Why had he written those letters? Why had he chosen her to drive the car, to escort him from one life into another? Had he considered how her life would be changed, too? There were so many others: better dancers, better drivers, more beautiful women. But when she asked, even begged, for the answer while sitting in a heap on the studio floor, Arslan rolled his eyes or slammed the door or worked alone in the center as though she weren't there. She couldn't gauge how much of the impasse came from their language barrier and how much was willfulness and how much was just the way he was.

'My little American,' he says on the Pont des Arts, murmuring into her ear. 'My silly little thing.' She moves closer, angling her hips against him, standing up in demi-pointe, wanting to shinny up him like a monkey. 'Thank you for dining with couple old Russians. You were' – he pauses as he does before trying out a new word – 'trouper.'

'I loved it,' she says. 'You don't have to thank me.'

Gently, he extricates himself from her arms. 'But unfortunately tonight is not for us. I have to leave you now. I'm sorry, baby.'

She steps back, confused, vibrating with the low hum of incoming pain. 'What do you mean?'

'I'm sorry. I have to go. I promise a friend to make a visit.'

'You're just going to leave me here? I have to walk back to the hotel alone in the middle of the night?'

His face has begun to close. His eyes wander out over the river. He wants to be away from her. 'I will give you money for taxi. Come on, Joan, don't ruin things.'

'*I* shouldn't ruin things? What was all this for?'

'All was what for?' He shakes his head, knowing he has garbled the sentence.

She opens her arms to encompass the river, the

bridge, the streetlamps and snowflakes, the Louvre's solemn procession of windows, the elegant Haussmann apartments, the black needle of Sainte-Chapelle's spire. '*This*. This perfect night. Why did you put me through any of it?'

'Why? Why? Why?' He tips his head back and forth, mocking. 'You always ask why. I don't know why. I don't *want* know why. I don't *care* why.'

'Is it the language? Could you say why in Russian?'

He half turns away in exasperation, his torso twisting, arms swinging loose, head rolling up and away, then he rotates back. Like all his movements, it is eloquent.

'Never mind,' she says. 'Clearly I'm not worth the trouble of an explanation.'

He shakes his head. 'I don't understand.'

'Yes, you do, Arslan. You just pretend you don't so you seem oblivious instead of like a selfish, spoiled child. No, you don't care if you're selfish and spoiled. You ignore this whole inconvenient world where other people matter, and that makes you smaller, it makes you less of an artist, even if you don't know it. People aren't just bodies. *You're* not just a body.'

He is shaking his head at the river, impatience radiating from him. She is breathing hard, as though she has been dancing. She feels her rib cage flexing. 'I keep letting you throw me away. It makes me sick. I wish to God you had asked someone else to help you defect. From now on, you can leave me alone. Consider our debt settled.'

Her last words make him look at her. 'You drived a car. That's all. You do nothing. You are little girl in corps. You get attention, get notice. I give up *everything*.'

'Not everything. Not everything, Arslan. You didn't give up fame. Or wealth. Or people falling all over themselves to please you.'

He lunges and grasps her by the arms. She stands straight and still as a soldier, not flinching, even though his face, close to hers, has never looked so angry, so helpless. He left his brother and mother behind, but he has never mentioned them to her. She read about them in the newspaper. She also read that his teacher with whom he had lived when he was at school in Leningrad was fired and rumored to have been imprisoned. 'You don't understand,' he cries. 'You know nothing.'

Joan is frightened but lifts her chin. 'You're the one who doesn't understand.'

'Okay,' he says, stony. 'So. Then, good-bye.' He turns and strides away toward the Left Bank, his footsteps hollow on the bridge, off to see whoever is expecting him at two o'clock in the morning. When he is gone, Joan finds herself sitting on the wooden planks, looking through the iron railing. The lights are not for her, not the river, not the immense loveliness. The bridge itself, she has heard, is slated to be demolished and rebuilt. The Germans bombarded it; too many barges have crashed into it; it is not sound. The new bridge will look the same except with wider arches to let the boats through, and it will be steel, not iron, stronger. She doesn't want to go back to the hotel. Elaine might be in their room, and Joan wants no witnesses to the end of this night. Or Elaine might be with Mr K or with someone else, and the empty room will be another kind of awfulness. She will cry here, where no one is watching, in the company of so much beauty.

Elaine had not bothered to find a new roommate after Joan left, and so it is easy to let her move back in. She helps Joan return her bits and pieces of furniture to the consignment store to be sold at a loss; her double bed is traded back for a twin; the sheet of printed Indian cotton is tacked up again. When Joan is out, Elaine checks for the box of letters from Jacob and Arslan and finds it under the bed again, as though it had never left, Arslan's letters still tied with the pink ribbon, Jacob's now in several neat bundles tied with ribbons of their own. She draws a hammer and sickle in lipstick on the bathroom mirror, making the hammer look like a penis. 'Welcome back, *putain*,' she writes underneath.

In the mornings they split a banana, go to class, go to rehearsal. At night, Elaine goes out or to Mr K's, and Joan stays in, sleeps, watches the TV Elaine bought in her absence. A dullness settles over her. She wonders out loud to Elaine how much of her life she wants to spend sliding one foot out from the other and back again, lifting one arm over her head and lowering it. She says, 'I feel like I'm working on an assembly line, but I'm not even making anything. I'm just *doing* something that disappears as soon as it happens. I used to feel like I had to dance, and now I feel like I'm doing it just to keep the option open, so I don't get out of shape.'

'But what else would you do?' Elaine asks, genuinely curious.

'Nothing,' Joan says. 'I don't know. I'm just depressed.'

Arslan is always at the front barre in class with the three hotshot male dancers he pals around with and shows off for. He manages to look both complacent and intent as he goes through the battements, determined to do the movements better than anyone else, to do them as well as they possibly can be done but without sacrificing his air of ease. Elaine watches Joan watch him, forlorn and puzzled as an abandoned dog. She is torn between sympathy for her friend's pain and scorn for her vulnerability. It was ridiculous for Joan to expect that a man as brilliant and hungry and capricious and sought after as Arslan would make a rewarding object for her love. But of course he encouraged her. Elaine's theory is that he chose Joan almost arbitrarily: he needed to fixate on one person, like isolating a star to navigate by, even if the star is not the destination. She has not told Joan yet that a dance is to be made on her and Arslan by Phoenix Raiman, a choreographer whom

Elaine knows slightly from the club scene. Mr K approached Phoenix about working with the company because Arslan asked him to, and then Phoenix suggested Elaine as Arslan's partner because she wants a dancer who is *modern* and *American* and not *stiff*.

Elaine means to tell Joan, but she is too slow; somebody else does. In the apartment, at the kitchen table, Joan is composed, furious, fearful. 'Couldn't you have said no?' she asks.

'No,' Elaine says. 'Of course not.'

'Because of your *career*.'

'And because I want to. And because if I didn't do this dance, someone else would.'

'Not me, though.'

Elaine sits down across from her, feeling like a placating parent. 'If it would be you instead, I would have thought about saying no.'

'Too bad I'm such a bad dancer that no one would *think* of pairing me with Arslan. He might as well dance with an anvil hanging around his neck.' Joan slides her thumbs and forefingers out along the table's edge and then back in.

Elaine waits. She wants to tell Joan she won't sleep with Arslan, but it would sound presumptuous, condescending. She knows Joan will ask. It is what matters. The dancing is a betrayal, but there is no such thing as monogamy in dance.

'Promise you won't sleep with him,' Joan says. 'He'll probably try, but please, Elaine, please don't. This is pathetic, but I have to ask. I know you wouldn't take it as tacit approval if I didn't say anything, but I need to put it out there that this is the line of my friendship. Maybe you'd rather sleep with Arslan than be friends with me, lots of girls would, but in that case I should just move out again. I can't live with you if you sleep with him. Maybe I sound crazy. I wanted to be clear.'

'I won't sleep with him,' Elaine says.

When rehearsals start, she sees quickly that the promise will be less easily kept than she thought. Phoenix, a tall, elegant, low-jawed black woman who always dresses in pristine white layers, has an idea for a dance that is slinky, jazzy, loose, juicy. Arslan struggles. He has difficulty unlocking his hips to allow for the Latin figure-eight movement Phoenix wants; he has difficulty letting his body curve forward, like a sail filling with wind, until he falls off balance and must catch himself; he has difficulty being light and sexy, not intense and passionate. She asks him to turn on one leg while the other and his torso are extended parallel to the floor, counterbalancing each other. Elaine, who has more training in contemporary dance, finds herself in the unexpected position of offering re-assurance and advice. Arslan learns quickly, even when frustrated. Elaine is impressed by how he persists in the struggle. He could so easily demand that the dance be shaped around what he already knows, but he is fired by curiosity.

'Go out tonight,' Phoenix commands after their

third rehearsal, 'just the two of you. Go find that thing you're going to bump back and forth.'

Arslan is no stranger to the city's shinier, flashier clubs, places where he is likely to have his picture taken, and so Elaine takes him to SoHo, to a brick building with black-painted windows on an empty-looking block.

'It's not open yet,' she tells Arslan in the taxi. 'They've been having these "construction parties." No frills, no booze or anything. Just good music. Amazing music. You'll like it. The sound system is in already. It's great. No one will pay attention to us. It's mostly gay kids.'

'No booze?'

'There's a bar down the street if you get desperate. And . . .' She takes a baggie of coke from her clutch. 'I don't know. Do you . . . ?'

'Sometimes. A little.'

'Me too. Exactly.' She drops it away, snaps her purse shut. 'You haven't asked what it's called.'

'Coke. I know, of course.'

'No, the club.'

'Why? What is it called?'

'The Kremlin.'

He snorts.

A burly blond guy at the door recognizes Elaine, waves them in. The entrance, which Elaine's friend assures her will be extremely cool when it is finished, is, for now, a dark ramp with a red star glowing at the top, a narrowing space that, as they ascend, thuds louder and louder with a 4/4 beat.

Arslan takes her hand, and it seems natural because, rehearsing, they have already spent most of the day touching. She has wrapped her legs around him and been dipped backward, the crotch of her leotard a fulcrum against his waist. Before they go through the black double doors to the dance floor, they pause to do a line off a black marble pedestal that might eventually hold some bit of décor for the extremely cool entrance or might exist for exactly this purpose. Shimmering, popping, they push through the doors and into a room that is black, loud, cavernous, struck through with red spotlights, and jammed with moving flesh. The crowd is mostly black and Puerto Rican boys in cutoffs and bare chests, jeans with suspenders, tank tops, white T-shirts, denim vests, berets, nothing too crazy or flashy, some girls thrown in, white guys here and there, just people dancing. Mirrored balls hang overhead but do not turn – probably a kink to be worked out – and the room is splattered with unmoving specks of light as though by paint. Above it all, in a blue-lit glass box, the DJ leans over his turntables, the captain of their submarine.

And it feels like they are in a submarine, or something like that, a dark space apart from the world, a pressurized bubble of survival. Elaine draws Arslan into the crowd. He catches the beat, of course, and can imitate how everyone is dancing, but he still looks like an impostor. He reminds Elaine of Joan's way of dancing at clubs: too controlled, too smooth, without the little hitches and catches that make an attitude. The boys in the cutoffs have both wildness and precision; their long, bare legs slide and prance and groove, seeming to twist together like two strands of rope when they turn.

'I am terrible,' he shouts in Elaine's ear, clowning a wry shrug.

'No,' she says, 'You're –' but a man cuts in then, spins her away. He is tall and dark, a terrific dancer. Elaine tosses her hair from side to side for him, trots and turns, bops her ass up and down. When Arslan cuts back in, he is clearly annoyed, and that makes him better, looser. He pulls her hip against his, glares at her, holds her close enough that she can't quite move freely. This is what they will bump back and forth in Phoenix's piece, she understands after a while, this restriction, this assertion and yielding, his attempt to dance her way while at the same time forcing her to dance his way. Songs come and go, bleed together. They keep dancing, settling into the precarious balance they've found, solidifying it.

'Let's get air,' he says finally, pulling his shirt up to wipe his face, exposing the stomach she has seen countless times before but that now makes her avert her eyes.

They go up to the roof, where people are standing around, cooling off, making out, doing drugs, admiring the washes of skyline that show through the thin fog. The evening is warm for late

March but still chilly, and their coats are down in a heap of other coats at the base of the ramp.

'More?' Elaine asks, digging in her purse for the baggie.

'Please.'

The line warms them up some, and Arslan steps close, rubs her arms, tilts his head to the side, gives her an oddly paternal, oddly apologetic smile, and kisses her. She had expected him to, had decided not to avoid it. She thinks their dance will be about intentions, power, and unfinished things.

'Sorry,' she says, leaning back. He leans in, trying to follow her mouth, but she evades him. 'I can't. Because of Joan.'

'Joan.'

'She's not thrilled we're dancing.'

'I don't talk about girls with girls.'

'Good policy. But . . .' She hold up her hands, palms up.

'But Joan and I are finished. You don't want some fun? Maybe the dance will be better.'

'No.'

'And Mstislav? It is because of him too? You know he is probably here, dancing with boys, wearing little shorts.'

'I don't talk about men with men.'

He pouts, sees her indifference, gives it up with the ease of a man who knows he has unlimited options. 'Suit yourself,' he says.

They go downstairs again. As they dance, they balance their tension between them, rolling and compacting it like a snowball, into something Phoenix can use. Elaine is curious about Arslan but does not want him, not really. He is, offstage, just a guy. Joan would hate the way they are dancing, would be livid at the kiss, but if Arslan were not dancing with Elaine, he would be dancing with someone else. After her, he will dance with someone else, and then someone else and someone else but never Joan.

Through the small window in the studio's closed door, Joan watches Arslan rehearse with Ludmilla Yedemskaya. It is May. The season is about to begin, and they are working on the balcony scene from a new version of *Romeo and Juliet*. Behind them, two understudies mark the roles: lesser shadows, ghostly mimics. Ludmilla has a blue Hermès scarf tied around her head and is wearing a black unitard, a black shrug, and red lipstick. She is perfect for Juliet, ethereal and custard blond with precise footwork, supernatural Russian extension, and a fragile, childlike stage presence. Arslan kneels on the floor in front of her, wraps his arms around her thighs, clings to her until she breaks away and flees to the far side of the studio. Then, as if tossed by a slingshot, she wheels around and does a fluttering run back to him, balancing for an instant in an elongated, windswept arabesque before his hands catch her hips and she is airborne, back arched and legs lifted, her pelvis resting on his shoulder. He sinks down so his ass is against his heels and then rises up again as though he loves her so much he has no choice but to offer her to the sky. Joan wants the lift to be silly, like the airplane game people play with children, but it's erotic and thrilling, a human sculpture of the feeling of falling in love. Ludmilla's face is luminous, ecstatic, but her expression curdles when she catches sight of Joan through the window. From above Arslan's straining back and clenched buttocks, she sneers.

Ludmilla's defection was the kind of dramatic escape newspapermen and artistic directors dream of. Traveling with the Kirov, she'd feigned illness and disappeared into a bathroom at Heathrow where an old family friend who'd gotten out to England during the Stalin years was waiting to zip her into a suitcase and wheel her briskly into the land of tea and biscuits, innocuously presided over by distant relatives of the czars. Three days later Ludmilla had boarded a flight with a fake passport and requested asylum in New York. Arslan had known she was coming. He was waiting at the airport with a huge bouquet of red and white roses tied with a blue ribbon. The press had gone wild.

In *Romeo and Juliet,* Joan is an anonymous Capulet in act 1, and in act 2 she is one of the ladies-in-waiting who come to wake Juliet and find her apparently dead. The difficult part is pretending to be sad when she presses her cheek against Ludmilla's limp hand.

Mr K's checked shirt moves into Joan's frame

of vision. Arslan sets Ludmilla down, and she moves toward the piano, reaching for her cigarettes. Underneath, watchfully ensconced in their basket, the black dachshunds lift their sleek heads. Arslan stretches his back and turns around. Joan darts away.

She walks purposefully down the hall, ignoring the dancers stretching on the floor, and hangs a left into the company office. The receptionist, Martha, a huge grey sandbag of a woman, is on the phone as usual, and Joan slips past with a little wave, ignoring the woman's snapping fingers. She has a flirtation going with the company manager, Campbell Hodges, who is recently divorced and manages to be breezy and harried at the same time and acts more like a distracted academic than a ballet bureaucrat. He claims to hate ballet, in fact, and is always griping about his pittance of a salary, the high cost and short life span of pointe shoes, and the agony of being trapped in that cash-strapped ghetto of an office all day discussing fairy tales and tulle wholesalers and other people's feet. Really, though, he loves ballet, and Joan suspects he nursed an array of fantasies about ballerinas through his decade of sterile marriage to a prim socialite whose inheritance included a vast apartment on Park Avenue. She likes him for the tartness of his personality and also because he is not a dancer but not quite a civilian, either. Tonight they have a half-facetious plan to go out to dinner. Half-facetious because he has stated repeatedly that he believes she never eats, and she has promised, without any intention of following through, to eat a bacon cheeseburger in front of him.

Campbell's door is cracked, and a roar of his laughter blasts out through the gap. Joan sidles in without knocking. Campbell is sitting in his chair, and two of the volunteer office gophers lean over his shoulders. They are all looking at something on his desk, a book that lies open on top of a mess of paperwork, and are all grinning with a sharp, impure merriment. Campbell has one hand over his mouth, clamping down the thick black beard he has allowed to run wild since his divorce, like living in a studio in Midtown makes him a woodsman. When they see Joan, there is a general blaze of guilt and a scramble on the part of the volunteers to conceal the book. She says, 'What is that?'

Campbell says, after a pause, 'Game over, girls. Let her see it.'

The volunteers appear to be in their late teens and have the groomed, minimalist look of future society ladies. Their plain, long faces are made regal, even beautiful, by their certainty of their status. Reluctantly, one hands Joan the book. It is a scrapbook, spiral-bound, with a black cover. Like the scrapbook she kept of herself and Arslan after the defection (now relegated to the back of a closet), it has thick black pages onto which photos and folded letters have been pasted haphazardly, ringed with dried swoops of excess glue. Joan opens it in the middle. Next to a photo of a woman reclining on a pool chaise in a bikini is a note giving a phone number and commanding, *If a man answers, DO NOT HANG UP!!! Say you're calling for Mrs Palmadessa. If I'm not home, leave a message with your number and the name Dwight Davis. Say it's about work. My husband is VERY JEALOUS, but I know our meeting will be worth your while. I am 34-25-34 and a GREAT ADMIRER.*

Some of the other women had not bothered with bikinis, and Mrs Palmadessa's letter proved to be among the most decorous. Jean from Philly: *What I would really like to do is wait in your dressing room after a performance in nothing but a smile – better than a bouquet, right? And I pull off your tights and* – Joan flipped the page. *In my dream,* wrote Cynthia from Oregon, *we hide out from the KGB in a cabin in the woods and you screw me silly.*

'We just think they're funny,' one of the volunteers says. 'He never sees them. He said he doesn't want them.'

Campbell stirs. 'Would you excuse us?'

Joan closes the book but doesn't offer to return it to the girls as they leave. She's always known Arslan's world is crowded with eager women, but these words and photos, thrown at him like the volleys of roses that sail from the audience after every performance, mock her. She settles in one of the sagging chairs across from Campbell and tries to smile. He is wearing a charcoal waistcoat

178

over a maroon-and-white-striped shirt with the cuffs rolled back and the collar open. Leaning forward, he rests his elbows on the desk and cups his chin in his hands, gazing at her and making a soft putt-putting sound with his lips, which are pink and shiny in their thatch of beard. 'You flinched,' he remarks.

'What?'

'Just now. At the book. You shouldn't take it personally. They're just bored kooks indulging their fantasies, taking a shot in the dark.'

'It doesn't have anything to do with me.' But she isn't sure their wanting is so different from hers. Why do they want Arslan? His fame, his talent, his body? Why does she want him? Without realizing, she has become part of a corps with these women, unseen and scattered across the country but all alike, all in the background, unified in their hopeless, persistent desires. 'Even if he made house calls to every single one of them, it still wouldn't have anything to do with me.'

'Exactly.'

'He's with Ludmilla now.'

'Exactly.'

'I wouldn't take him back. He's a narcissist with no soul.'

'Exactly.'

'Even onstage. He's always using up too much music. He ruins whole ballets by showing off. I don't know why no one complains about it.'

'Because of the applause, darling. The applause.

Do you know every performance is selling out this season? Even the ones he's not in. People care about ballet all of a sudden. Don't ask me why. Ballet is awful.'

'You're not fooling anyone, Campbell.'

'Really? I'd hoped to fool you.'

His small blue eyes turn searching, and Joan slides from her chair to the floor, pretending a sudden need to stretch, taking the scrapbook with her. 'I'm going to quit,' she calls up to him. 'I mean it.'

'No, darling, you can't. You mustn't. Why would you say such a thing?' His chair squeaks, and suddenly he has beached himself across his desk, his piratical beard hanging over her like a storm cloud.

'I'll never be satisfied.'

'Who wants to be satisfied?'

'Who wants to be tormented by their own inadequacy?'

'Touché.'

'I think if I had just been allowed to toil in obscurity like I'd planned, everything would be better. I would admire Arslan from afar and idolize Ludmilla even though she's a bitch, but now it all seems so disappointing. So drab. Now I have to think about how if I'd only happened to be more talented, my life would be a thousand times more exciting and I'd get to really dance with him, and he would take me more seriously. It's like there's an empty space in the world that was meant for me, but I can't get inside. I can just bang on the outside.'

Campbell's face disappears. He comes around the desk and sits on the floor, leaning against a precarious stack of cardboard boxes full of binders and papers, crossing his legs. The bottoms of his shoes are scuffed and gummed from the city.

'What do you really want to say, darling?'

'I hate Ludmilla.'

'Tell me.'

'She has everything. She has the right feet, the right hips, the right arms, the right pinkie fingers, the right eyebrows, the right nostrils. It's tough enough living with Elaine, but she still can't hold a candle to Ludmilla. Ludmilla probably has the ideal lower intestine for a ballet dancer.'

'Genetic luck. Out of our hands.'

'She's disciplined. Plus, she has musicality and vivacity, and I don't know how she does it but onstage she gives off this *sweetness*. You'd never guess she was made of steel and nicotine. And – this is what burns me – no one would care about her except she *defected*. She's a traitor, when you think about it.'

'And Arslan,' Campbell said.

'He's a traitor, too?'

'Yes, technically, although I think we can agree they both had good reasons. But I meant she has *him*. For now.'

'You don't think it'll last?'

'Do you?'

'I don't know. Probably it'll last because I hate them together, and clearly I was someone terrible in a past life.'

'So it's all about you then.'

'Oh, I know. Shoot me. I'm just tired of being unhappy. It's exhausting.'

'Everyone finds someone to be jealous of. Arslan's probably jealous of Nijinsky.'

'Arslan's jealous of Paul Newman.'

Campbell smiles. In the silence, they hear Martha the receptionist grumbling on the phone, someone clipping past in high heels, a muffled run of notes from a distant piano. Campbell is not unattractive, but talking about Arslan with him has been a mistake; it has forced the comparison. As if he senses her thought and subsequent rejection, he says, coolly, 'Enough. You can't be weak in the ballet or it'll crush you.'

'Too late.'

Campbell stands and offers her a hand. She takes it and he pulls her up so forcefully that she stumbles against his chest. 'Sorry,' he says, stepping back. 'You're so light.' He smiles, warm again but sad around the edges, knowing their moment has passed. 'Nothing a cheeseburger won't fix.'

'Campbell, I haven't eaten a cheeseburger since I was a little kid.'

He holds out his hand for the scrapbook. 'Give me that rotten thing.'

Joan presses it against her chest. 'No. I have other plans for it.'

'Such as?'

'I'm going to put it in Ludmilla's dance bag.'

'Ah. Then, bonne chance.'

In the doorway, she pauses, taps her fingers on the jamb, turns back. 'I know I should be over it. I want to acknowledge that I know that.'

'Forgive and forget.'

'There isn't even much to forgive. He was always clear about who he was. I was in denial.'

Campbell tsks. 'He didn't love you, darling. What could be more necessary to forgive?'

PART III

APRIL 1986 – SOUTHERN CALIFORNIA

Some days while Joan teaches, Harry goes to his friend Dale's house after school, and other days he comes to the studio and does his homework behind the reception desk or on the lobby floor by the big window into the studio. Joan has asked him if he wouldn't like to try dancing, but he politely declined, just as he turned down soccer, baseball, tennis, and karate. At a loss, she and Dale's mother signed them both up for swim team. Harry goes and swims with little complaint, but he is fundamentally an indoor child, dreamy and thoughtful and given to abrupt, consuming interests (astronauts, trains, submarines) that require semiweekly trips to the library for books he races through, shoveling information into himself like coal into a furnace.

The little girls in Joan's classes wear black leotards and pink tights and have their hair done up in buns decorated with bright scrunchies or little pink crocheted cozies. Their limbs are too thin or too plump; their bodies are incapable of grace but full of will and infantile pomposity.

'Stand like a turkey,' she tells them, gesturing to her own lifted chest, the way her weight is slightly forward. 'Be over the balls of your feet, but not too far.' With the addition of a gauzy black skirt, she wears what they do.

She likes to teach the girls who are just starting to go en pointe. As a warning, she shows them her own feet, pointing out the knobby protrusions, the toenail that has simply given up and stopped growing, the thick yellow calluses. 'Still want to do it?' she asks them. They do. She tells them how she went through a pair of shoes every day when she was performing with the company. All the dancers got custom-made shoes. Hers came from London. Once she went to the factory and met the man who made them, and he had asked to see her feet because he wanted to find out if they were as he imagined. Joan shows the girls how to sew on the satin ribbons and rough up the pointe. She demonstrates how to tape their toes and pad them with lamb's wool. She leads them over to the rosin box, and one by one they step experimentally into the sticky dust. One day, she tells them, each of you will have your own method for getting your shoes just right. Then she leads them to the barre, and up they all go like seven baby giraffes: spindly, ankles trembling. First position, face the barre, plié, here we go, ladies, and relevé, and roll through your foot, whole foot, all the way up. Back down, and cambré back. Remember to push down to go up, and pull up to go down.

Now again in second position. Only a few minutes for the first time, but they almost look like dancers.

Chloe Wheelock is taking a beginning jazz class. Joan hadn't recognized her when she first caught sight of her through the big window, only noticed her pleasing lines and proportions. But then Chloe did an airy leap across the diagonal and came running toward the window, not seeing Joan but looking past her, her face foxy and triangular like her father's but without the smugness, her eyes hard with focus. Chloe paused, breathing hard, and saw Joan. She waved.

'I hope you aren't offended she's not taking ballet,' Sandy says when Joan runs into her at pickup time a week or two later. 'We decided jazz would be better.'

'That's fine,' Joan says. Chloe has been watching her classes, sitting very straight in a folding chair out with the mothers behind the big window, her knees together and small, pointed chin held high, her posture meant to tell anyone who might wonder that, yes, she is a dancer. Now Joan spots her in the jazz studio, sashaying in a circle with the other girls while Whitney Houston blasts through the stereo. She is mildly ridiculous looking in her shiny red unitard and cropped T-shirt. Her ponytail is decorated with curly ribbons. The song ends as the girls crowd together in the center of the floor and drop to their knees, raising their arms over their heads and wiggling their fingers. Their teacher applauds and the girls disperse, chugging from water bottles and draping towels over their shoulders with affected nonchalance, mimicking the high school girls. To Sandy, Joan adds, 'But you shouldn't wait too long if she wants to do ballet. The Russians start them at four.'

'This isn't Russia. She wants to do jazz. She's having fun. She's only seven, anyway.'

'Jazz is fine, but I'd hate for her to waste her talent.'

'So now she's talented.'

'You never asked me if I thought she was talented,' Joan says.

'Well, she wants to do jazz.'

'That's good, then. She should do what she wants.'

Sandy falls silent. Joan wonders why she doesn't just leave, then follows her gaze. In the studio, a girl is letting Chloe try on her pointe shoes. Though the ribbons are tied clumsily and the satin foot is loose around her small heel, she gets up easily, looking around from her new height. She experiments with her arms, takes a few tentative steps.

'Look,' says Sandy, 'she can do it.'

'She shouldn't. Her bones are too soft. She's not strong enough.'

'She's just playing.'

'No,' says Joan. 'She isn't.'

Harry is watching, too, from his seat on the lobby carpet. He still says Chloe is his best friend even though they have been seeing less and less of each other. Joan gathers that Chloe ignores Harry at recess, but, on afternoons when he doesn't have swimming and she doesn't have dance or gymnastics, she still appears on their doorstep or calls him on the phone to come over and keep her company or act out roles in her games.

Harry stands up and taps on the glass to get the girls' attention. Chloe drops off pointe and glances at the other girl, the shoes' owner. Sticking out his butt and going up on his tiptoes, Harry turns in a circle with his arms in a hoop over his head and then does a silly, wobbly arabesque followed by some sideways leaps, mimicking Chloe's timidity, her pride in the shoes. Usually he is so shy and serious.

As he has become his own person, Joan has stopped, for the most part, wondering if he will dance. Sometimes in idle moments, watching him running and jumping in the backyard with Chloe or standing straight and small on a diving block and then snapping out to pierce the pool like a javelin, she still dwells on the possibility, but mostly she has accepted that he will do other things, be something else. She is glad he was not a girl. Through the window, Chloe's friend waves to Harry to come in, and soon the shoes are on his feet. He teeters but stays up, sticking out his tongue and undulating his arms like wings. Sometimes late at night Joan watches a tape of *Swan Lake,* and sometimes Harry gets out of bed and watches with her until he falls asleep on the couch.

'Oh, look,' says Sandy. 'He's a ballerina.'

Joan wants to say that they are just playing, but she doesn't.

DECEMBER 1987 – SOUTHERN CALIFORNIA

Drosselmeyer makes the Christmas tree grow until its star vanishes up into the light grid, and then the Nutcracker turns from a doll to a human, and the other toys come alive, and the rats creep out into the dark house to do battle with the tin soldiers, and Chloe is the smallest rat. It is Christmas Eve, the last performance. For three weeks, on Tuesdays, Thursdays, twice on Saturdays, and on Sunday afternoons she has waited in the wings until the last big rat slinks onstage, rubbing his paws together under his chin, and then she goes scurrying out after him, lifting her knees high to show she is nervous. When the rats leap menacingly at the soldiers, raking the air with their claws, she covers her eyes with her tail, and the audience always laughs.

She has grey tights and grey slippers and a leotard of hot, itchy grey fake fur and a heavy rat's head she can barely see out of. The rats, some men but mostly women who do modern dance and wouldn't have made good snowflakes, wear grey unitards with funny ovals of fur that cover

193

their chests and stomachs like long bibs. The soldiers rush forward, swords above their heads. Their jumps are low, and their footwork is sloppy. Now is Chloe's big moment, her answering attack, running out from behind the other rats into a heroic grand jeté all alone at center stage, throwing her head back like she will when she is a famous ballerina and in a *good* company, one where the dancers don't also teach school or work in stores. She lands and does a few nimble pas de chats, first toward the soldiers, then toward the rats, then back again, her feet landing exactly where she wants them to, and she does chaînés turns closer and closer to the soldiers, driving them back until she stops and shakes her fist at them.

To her left is the darkness that contains her mom and dad and her maternal grandparents and her uncle Rodney and aunt Sarah. Joan is out there, too, as she is most nights, and tonight Jacob is with her, come to see Harry, who is dancing Fritz, Clara's bratty little brother. The high school girl who dances Clara is skinny and pimply and always smoking outside while wearing her taffeta party dress or white nightgown. Fritz breaks the Nutcracker when it's still a doll, just to be mean. If the whole auditorium were empty except for Joan, Chloe would still dance her hardest, but when Joan isn't there, the whole performance seems almost pointless. Joan had been the one to suggest she join in with a ballet class after jazz, beckoning when she hesitated in the door, telling her to find a bit of empty barre or to stand in the back when they did center work and try her best. Chloe had disliked the sight of herself in the mirror. At first her reflection shamed her for not knowing the ballet words or what to do with her arms. Her jazz clothes, silly and garish next to all those neat black leotards, marked her as an impostor.

Joan lets her come over to her house whenever she wants and applauds the dances she and Harry make up in the backyard. Joan slices vegetables for a snack and puts on ballet movies for them after they get tired and tells them stories about when she was a professional. Joan found hand-me-down leotards and tights when Chloe's mom complained about the money wasted on jazz outfits, and Joan took her to a store and bought her a pair of slippers and told her to tell her mom they'd been a free sample. But somehow, eventually, Chloe's mom had decided ballet was a good thing, and now she cares too much and breathes down Chloe's neck, watching all her classes and giving loud opinions about the other girls in the car on the way home, criticizing their technique and bodies.

The tin soldiers cower; Chloe turns to the rats, arms lifted in triumph. Applause, and then a soldier stomps once, hard, on her tail.

The director has told her to pretend to be *very angry* when her tail gets stepped on, but she does not need to pretend. The indignity of her ruined moment is a fresh pain every night. She leaps in the air, whirls around and rushes at the soldiers, full of fury, but they are not afraid of her small claws, and they catch her and spin her down their battle line, grabbing and turning her, one to the next to the next. When they finally let go, she falls to the stage in a tantrum of humiliation, beating her fists and feet against the cool, smooth surface until a big rat picks her up and carries her into the wings, still kicking and thrashing. 'Take it easy, Chloe,' he whispers, and she lets up and dangles limply from his arms.

They are to wait in the wings until the Rat King enters from the other side, wearing his crown, brandishing his scimitar, and because they need to enter as soon as he does, the rat holds her while they wait. She has complained to Joan that he holds her *forever*, but Joan timed it and amazed her with the news that they are offstage for only twenty seconds. The rat, a man named Brett who works in a lamp store, smells like BO and cologne. His rat head, which never really dries out, smells like mildew, and his breathing is loud inside it. The head reminds her of the animals at Disneyland, how they hugged her, and also of the man on the Matterhorn. The memory can't be trusted. It is too vague, too blurred by motion and sound – the descent of the toboggan, the rattle of the tracks, the roar of the snow monster – but at its center is the alien, disturbing image of her mother being embraced by a strange man, leaning back against him with her eyes closed, her mouth dropping open. Who is that man? He has no face, not really, but he kisses her mother's neck. The memory can't be trusted, but it lingers and rubs like a bit of grit between Chloe and her mother, taking on layers of nacre, growing larger but turning more opaque.

Brett groans and shifts his weight, trying to support her with his hip, but then he gives up and leans back so she is draped down the front of his body. The fur on the back of her leotard mingles with the fur on his chest, and she can feel the hot dampness of his unitard through her tights. She can even feel his heart beating. During rehearsals, she liked him. He was nice and asked her about school and showed her a special way to jump after her tail got stepped on so the audience would know how much it hurt. He wore cut-off red sweatpants over his tights and a bandanna over his curly blond hair, which she liked, but he also wore tank tops, which she didn't like because of the dingy clumps of hair in his armpits. When she informed him she was afraid of being touched by his armpit hair, he laughed and wore T-shirts instead.

But Brett's nice face and curly hair is hidden under that big, whiskery rat head with two shiny white teeth and protruding black eyes. There is also the problem of the amorphous bumps in the front of his tights, where her bottom is resting. She likes the embroidered vests and velvet jackets and shirts with long, blousy sleeves that male dancers wear, but their lower bodies, exposed and monochromatic in tights, all muscles and butt cheeks and those troubling bumps, disconcert her. She knows what boys have, has seen illustrations in books and has made Harry show her his, but those purple and pink drawings and Harry's embarrassed snail-without-a-shell seem to have little to do with the contours of Brett's tights.

Once when an Arslan Rusakov special was on TV, her father had come in with a plastic cup full of red wine, stood and watched for a minute, then said, 'So much brouhaha about one fruity little grape smuggler.'

'What's a grape smuggler?'

'A guy in tights,' he said, picking up the remote and changing the channel.

So now she can't see grapes without thinking of men stuffing them down their tights, and when she finds grapes in her lunch, warm from sitting in her backpack all morning, the sides of the baggie misted with condensation, she throws them away. She asked Joan if she could be a famous ballerina without doing all the pas de deux stuff, and Joan said no but also that she didn't have to worry about partnering for a few more years. The Sugar Plum Fairy's variation is just the kind of thing Chloe wants to do – light and dainty and self-sufficient – but when the Fairy's cavalier is around he is always holding her hand and touching her waist while she turns and lifting her by her thighs.

Her mother has come to every performance, but this is the only night her father would agree to come. At home, the stack of presents is small and wrapped in paper left over from last year. Chloe's class had done a wrapping paper sale, and while most kids' parents bought at least a few rolls, Chloe had to peddle her paper swatches door-to-door in the neighborhood because her mother wouldn't buy any, not even the silver paper dotted with tiny penguins, which was the best. At the school Christmas fair, Chloe picked out a small framed photograph of a racing cyclist for her father with an inspirational saying about perseverance printed underneath. He lost his job at the mall and is having trouble finding another one. She is under strict orders not to tell anyone even though everyone already seems to know. At night, after she goes to bed, her parents either watch TV or fight. Sometimes they fight about her.

'You were so obsessed with her being gifted – she *is* gifted. This is what she's good at.'

'*I* was obsessed? You're the obsessed one. You care about this ballet stuff more than she does.'

'I care about her having opportunities. You were always talking about her having every opportunity. You said it a million times. Like really you were so oppressed growing up. Like really it was so tragic being from Grand Rapids and having a dentist for a father. Bull*shit*.'

'I'll tell you what's bullshit. This ballet crap is bullshit. It's a fantasy for little girls. Little girls and you and Joan Bintz and her faggoty kid. The best thing I can say about it is that at least girls who do it don't get fat. Do you ever stop to think about how much it costs?'

'Of course I do.'

'Why don't we just give the whole house to the Bintzes, would you be happy then?'

A silence, and then her mother's voice, calm like a teacher's: 'Do you want me to find her a different studio? It'll mean a longer drive, which means more gas money, more of my time.'

'Because you're so busy.'

'I could get a job. It would be so much better if we just had a little money coming in. I could bartend again.'

'I'm not going to be supported by my wife. I'm not going to have a wife who's a bartender.'

'Great. Let's wait for the repo man to come. Let's move in with my parents. No, let's starve to death.'

Chloe's father, quietly: 'Shut up. You're being stupid. Just shut up.'

She thinks her father is right not to want to be supported by her mother. She imagines them doing a pas de deux, her mother lifting and spinning her father, and it is all wrong. She cries when they fight and worries they will make her stop dancing, but she is impatient with them, too. Her dancing is none of their business. She has begun to divide the world into dancers and non-dancers, and her parents are non-dancers. What they think is not important. Harry doesn't even seem to know how lucky he is to live with Joan. At school, a non-dance place, Harry is in the class for smart kids, but on the playground he embarrasses Chloe with his overtures of friendship and gestures of familiarity, and she wishes he would just leave her alone there so she wouldn't have to hurt his feelings. He is a part of a better world, the hard one, the one you have to work to get inside.

The Rat King makes his entrance, and Chloe locks into an arabesque, raising her fist over her head as Brett swings her sideways, lifts her high, and rushes onstage.

MARCH 1990 – SOUTHERN CALIFORNIA

At the end of *The Hunt for Red October,* Jack Ryan (Alec Baldwin) and the defector Captain Ramius (Sean Connery) survey the moonlit Penobscot River from the sail of a hulking black submarine. 'Welcome to the New World, sir,' Jack Ryan says.

The credits roll while a Russian choir sings. Harry and Jacob sidle out of their row and walk up the aisle. 'That's what Mom did for Arslan Rusakov,' Harry says when they are in the popcorn-and-carpet-cleaner air of the lobby. 'Mom's like Jack Ryan.'

'Mom didn't shoot anyone,' says Jacob. 'That I know of.'

Harry strides ahead, buoyant. His stride lengthens until he is half galloping toward the glass doors, his arms lifting away from his sides as though he might leap into the air. But he stops short, pivoting to face his father, radiating energy, and it is a miracle he only folds his arms across his chest and shifts from foot to foot. He always seems to be on the verge of some ostentatious movement, some theatrical gesture. Jacob has never manifested enthusiasm the way Harry does, through his body, and he tries not to let on that his son's tendency to cavort in public embarrasses him. 'Take it easy,' he says.

'I am,' says Harry. 'It was just such a great movie. But I wish that guy had gotten to see Montana.'

Jacob squeezes Harry's shoulder and is startled by the muscle. Harry is almost twelve and always doing push-ups in preparation for the fast-approaching day when he will need to lift Chloe Wheelock. 'Yeah,' he says, as they pass out through the doors and into a cool, cloudy night, the mildness of March in California still novel after seven years. 'That part was sad.'

'Do you think there's a chance someone might really have defected in a submarine? And we just never knew about it? I mean, the newspapers found out about Zuyev and Belenko, but they went through other countries first.'

'I think lots of things happen that we don't know about, but this was probably just a good story.'

'I wish it were true.'

'I think things can be true even if they didn't really happen.'

Harry doesn't seem to be listening. He is doing a kind of Russian soldier march, arms rigid, head erect. But then he says, 'I don't get what you mean.'

'I mean if a story really resonates with you, it can be true for you, even if it never actually happened. Like ancient myths. Those stories probably mattered more to people than some things that really happened.'

Harry spins around and moonwalks alongside Jacob. 'I guess. But I still wish it had really happened. I wish a submarine captain would defect.'

Defectors are an object of fascination for Harry. He keeps a scrapbook of clippings about Russian dancers, particularly Rusakov, and after Alexander Zuyev flew his MiG-29 to Turkey, he expanded his reach, adding long ribbons of newsprint about the pilot. Later, he branched out still further and pasted in photos snipped from *Time* magazine of the crowds at the Brandenburg Gate. His bulletin board is dense with thumbtacked ballet programs and pictures of Rusakov, but in a bottom corner he made room for a photocopy of the famous shot from the sixties of the East German border guard jumping over barbed wire, the nascent Berlin Wall. When he was ten, Harry had insisted Jacob take him to *Die Hard* because he wanted to see Alexander Godunov, the Bolshoi defector, play a German terrorist.

But a crumbling is happening. The Wall has fallen, and Jacob expects Harry will be disappointed if soon there is no more Eastern Bloc, no more ballerinas curling themselves inside suitcases to be rolled through Heathrow to freedom. Harry has always been prone to obsession, but the longevity of these particular fixations – ballet and defectors – has been a disquieting surprise.

'I wonder if Arslan will see that movie,' Harry says as Jacob starts the car.

'Who knows.'

'I wish Mom still knew him. Do you think she'll ever stop being mad at him for dumping her?'

Harry knows the basic outline of Joan's history with Rusakov, but he seems to sense there is more, something adult and tangled and uncomfortable, a mesh of fungal filaments that his parents have done their best to conceal. He is always poking around, asking questions, trying to turn up the loose end that will make everything clear. He does not understand that he cannot understand, that the loves of others are unfathomable. 'She's mad for more complicated reasons than that,' Jacob says. 'He wasn't very nice to her. I don't think she thinks he's worth knowing.'

'I can't believe he dated *Mom*. He's such an amazing dancer.'

'It's more important to be a good person.'

'I would kill for his *ballon*.'

Ballon is Harry's new favorite word, and he has already explained to Jacob that it describes the way good dancers seem to hang in the air longer than possible. The trick, Harry says, isn't just height but what you do with your arms. Jacob turns out of the parking lot and onto the main road. While they were in the movie, it must have rained. The streets are wet, and the stoplights fall on them in long red and green ribbons.

All boys have their heroes, Jacob has told himself

again and again, but there is a needy quality to Harry's worship that reminds him ominously of how Joan had given herself over to Rusakov as though to a doomsday cult. Jacob had doggedly churned out letter after letter during that time and cast them into the postbox's dark mouth like pennies into a well. He sent her banal accounts of his daily life mingled with philosophical musings meant to impress and saccharine paragraphs of supportive mush meant to hasten her realization that Jacob, not Rusakov, truly loved her. Her responses, when they came, maybe one to every ten of his letters, were cruelly unfiltered tracts detailing her feelings of being paralyzed by her love for the other man, frozen around it. Stupidly hopeful that her misery might translate into corrective action, he would send stern yet loving replies, urging her to abandon what was clearly an unhappy and unhealthy situation, a man who did not love or appreciate her, because she deserved more, he would declare, she deserved *everything*. After a period of silence, her next letter would arrive, exactly like the last.

After a minute, Harry says, 'I just can't believe he was Mom's boyfriend. It's so crazy. Why do you think he liked her?'

'Because your mother is a wonderful person. Anyway, I don't know if he was really her *boyfriend*.'

'He was. There are all those pictures of them together.'

'Which pictures?'

'In Mom's scrapbook. The newspaper ones, and then all the other ones – normal camera pictures.'

'She has a scrapbook?' Jacob's voice rises. 'She showed you this?'

'I found it by accident. It was in the garage.' Harry opens the glove compartment and roots through a jumble of cassette tapes as though demonstrating how he might stumble upon something in the course of his normal rummaging.

'You shouldn't go through other people's things.'

'I wasn't! I was just exploring.' He closes the glove compartment without choosing a tape. 'Mom wasn't mad. We went through it, and she told me where the pictures were taken and stuff and about when the company went to Europe, which was the first time Arslan left America after he defected. I guess everyone was worried he was going to be kidnapped or something and taken back to Russia. Anyway,' Harry says, looking sideways at Jacob, clearly skeptical of his objectivity, 'it really seemed like he was her boyfriend.'

'Usually if you're someone's boyfriend you're nice to them and supportive of what they do. I don't think Arslan ever took Mom all that seriously, which was hard for her because she tried really hard to please him.'

Jacob worries he's taking the discussion too far, getting into too much nuance, but Harry only makes a noncommittal noise and says, 'Did you know in Europe ballet audiences applaud all together? What's the word for it? Mom told me.

Like, *clap clap clap clap* all at the same time, on the same beat.'

'In cadence,' Jacob says.

A year before, Jacob had decided he was weary of gifted children. They had become monotonous in their specialness, and he was tired of dealing with their overbearing nightmare parents. Fortunately, he is well liked in the district and was offered a job as the principal of a new middle school in a new town, out on the edge of civilization, where the new houses stand shoulder to shoulder, an advance guard against the empty hills. The students chose the coyote as their mascot, after the clever creatures that steal their neighbors' cats and yip and howl in the night. Jacob suggested to Joan that they might move, get a nicer house closer to school, even one with a pool, and she has begun to warm to the idea. Truthfully, he wouldn't mind trading in the Wheelocks for some new neighbors. Gary has become a sad sack, shuffling between his car and house, never going out on his bike anymore. Jacob would never have expected to be nostalgic for Gary's dandyish outfits, but he would be grateful to see the old suspenders and cuff links instead of the new baggy khakis and rumpled shirts. Late at night, the blue flicker of a television spills into their backyard.

The painted trim on the Wheelocks' windows and eaves is peeling and their stucco is mildewed. A row of cypress trees grows tall and shaggy beside their driveway and casts a serrated shadow onto the Bintzes' front lawn, stunting the grass. The lightbulbs in the fixture over their front door have all gone out and not been replaced; only their doorbell, a button of peach-colored light, interrupts the darkness. Jacob allows himself to be dragged to the ballet twice a year or so, and the Wheelock house reminds him a little of the vine-covered, narcoleptic kingdom in *The Sleeping Beauty*. Joan, too, presiding over Chloe's and Harry's training with alarming intensity, has started to seem like something out of a ballet, a dark sorceress.

Jacob has come to accept that there will be no second child, but he keeps waiting for Harry to turn out more as he had expected. There is nothing wrong with being considered a little weird by other kids, but he had been certain Harry would be nerd weird, that his would be a life of the mind. Instead, Jacob finds himself in the company of a son who sings scores by Tchaikovsky and Prokofiev in the shower and has a favorite brand of tights and possesses troubling thonglike undergarments and can do endless pull-ups and spends all his time with girls and idolizes Arslan Rusakov. Not a single day passes when Jacob is not treated to the name of his wife's former lover coming from the lips of his son. Arslan this, Arslan that. And Joan, despite her stated antipathy for Rusakov, does nothing to discourage Harry. She buys the videotapes he circles in ballet catalogs, obligingly records every PBS special that features

209

Rusakov. They have an entire cabinet devoted to their ballet video library, rows of tapes marked carefully in Harry's evolving handwriting: *The Best of Rusakov, Swan Lake, Rusakov Dances Jerome Robbins, Coppélia, Phoenix Raiman Tribute.* Joan and Harry sit on the couch together, pausing, rewinding, and discussing like football coaches watching game films. Harry knows all the other dancers, too, gets excited when Elaine Costas appears. There is a recording of *Romeo and Juliet* from when Joan was in the corps. She covers her eyes when she is onstage, even as Harry shouts, 'There you are! There you are!'

Jacob had taken down the photo of Joan and Rusakov from their hallway, claiming a need to redecorate, but Harry rescued it and spirited it away to his bedroom.

'Dad,' says Harry from the shadows of the passenger seat. 'Will it make you uncomfortable if I ask you something?'

Jacob hesitates. When his mother, Harry's grandmother, voices her usual lines – 'Isn't ballet something girls do?' or 'Couldn't Joan have left well enough alone?' – he defends his son and wife fiercely, and when she once asked Harry why he couldn't have a hobby that wasn't for queers, Jacob had taken her outside and told her she had a choice between being banned from seeing her grandson or shutting up. Still, he has wondered – wonders every day – if Harry is gay. All he knows for sure is that his son envies another man's *ballon*. 'Maybe,' he says, 'but I can live with a little discomfort.'

'Okay. This is it. How do you know if you're in love?'

They are only two blocks from the house, so Jacob pulls over and switches off the engine. He thinks for a minute before speaking. 'I think it's different for different people, but the conventional wisdom is that when you're around the person you're in love with, you feel happy, more than happy – euphoric. And you want to be around that person all the time. You don't notice that person's faults. Some people say their hearts beat faster. They feel jittery. I think you know it when you feel it.'

He and Harry are both staring forward out the windshield as if they are still driving. All those years ago, when Jacob drove Joan out to the beach with plans to kiss her, the tension of loving her had been so electric, so torturous, that he had worried about cardiac arrest, about being killed by his own desire. Now that he is finally – finally, after more than twenty years – sure of her love, the longing has vanished. He still loves her, but no passion, especially not one germinated in a hothouse of adolescent despair, could survive so much familiarity and certainty. She has changed, too. She is not so wary anymore, not always in retreat, not unknowable. They are two animals inhabiting the same den, each accepting the presence of the other, going about the business of living.

'Is that helpful?' he says to Harry, who is quiet. 'I don't know how to describe the feeling except in clichés. And being "in love" is different from loving someone. The really intense feelings don't last. Does that help? It's a big question.'

'Yeah, it's just, in ballets, people just kind of put it out there, you know? But in real life, you're supposed to be cool.'

'Maybe sometimes.' Tiny droplets have collected on the windshield, shutting them in. Jacob is much more nervous than he would like to be. 'Are you in love with anyone in particular?'

'Of course he's in love with Chloe,' Joan says that night in the bathroom while she plucks her eyebrows at one sink and Jacob, in T-shirt and boxers, flosses at the other. 'Anyone can see that.'

Jacob attends to his incisors, making a rabbit face. 'I didn't. Why didn't you tell me?'

'He hasn't told me directly. I didn't want to gossip about him.'

'All we ever do is gossip about Harry. It's half the reason people have kids.'

Joan puts witch hazel on a cotton ball and wipes her brows. 'Yes, we definitely talked over the gossip possibilities before Harry was conceived.'

Opening wide to access his molars, Jacob grunts, conceding.

'Anyway,' Joan says, 'he's in class with Chloe four days a week. She's always over here. They're the age for crushes now. It's the natural progression. I think it's unrequited, so what difference does it make?'

He rinses out his mouth and spits into the sink, then he straightens up and looks at Joan, his lips wet. 'Unrequited? She thinks she can do better?'

'She's just a kid. She thinks she's cool. But now you can stop worrying he's gay.'

'I wasn't. Now I'm worried about Chloe Wheelock breaking Harry's poor vulnerable heart. Let's drop it. I feel uncomfortable intruding into our kid's hormones.'

'You're the one who brought it up. I'm right about the gossip – see?'

'I still hope he falls out of love with her soon. He will, won't he?'

'I don't know. I don't know her very well.'

'What? What do you mean? You spend all your time with her.'

She is tired and doesn't want to explain that she and Chloe communicate mostly through touch, gesture, French words. Joan knows Chloe's knees well and her ankles and wrists; she is always touching them, shaking them loose, adjusting their angle. In fact, her deepest knowledge of the girl is of her joints. When Joan is giving Chloe a combination, she demonstrates what she wants, skimming across the floor, sketching the movements, murmuring their names, saying, 'Like this, en arrière, and then –' and then, with her body, she suggests a glissade or a pas de bourrée and says, 'See?' And Chloe sees. But the girl's character is not yet fully formed, and the parts of it that most concern Joan – grit, discipline, expressiveness, sensitivity, control – are unproven. She is not far enough into her novitiate for Joan to know if she will see it through, if dance is an infatuation or a calling.

'Let the puppies have their love,' she says to Jacob.

'The puppy,' he says. 'His love. Anyway, are we really sure he's not gay? Maybe he wants to *be* Chloe.'

'That's something your mother would say.'

'I thought he was in love with Arslan Rusakov.'

Joan rubs lotion vigorously onto her arms, concentrating on turning the white swoops of cream into a sheen on her skin, examining her elbows, interweaving her slick fingers and pulling them apart with enough force to make her knuckles sting. Harry's fascination with Arslan is her fault, of course. He thinks his obsession is his own, but he has caught it from her. If she had known from the beginning how serious Harry would become about ballet, she might have been more careful not to let her voice or her face betray how important this man had been, but it has been such a relief to have someone around who wants to talk about dance. It has been such a pleasure to let her son begin to know her, not just as she is but as she was.

'He is a little bit,' she tells Jacob. 'But it's not sexual. It's a dance crush. I don't know what I would do if it were sexual.'

'So you worried about him being gay, too?'

'I wouldn't care if he were gay.'

'What then? Too weird to have your son be in love with your ex?'

Joan meets his eyes in the mirror. Sometimes she thinks he is giving her more opportunities for sarcasm as they get older, and sometimes she thinks she's just been spending too much time with teenagers. She says, 'What would be weird about that?'

'Whatever it is, it's already weird. And what's this scrapbook you apparently have of you and Arslan?'

Facing him, she loops her arms around his waist, leaning back, making him brace to support her weight. It's been so long since he's seemed jealous or possessive that the peeved look on his face makes her pleasantly nostalgic. She'd had so much power over him once. Power was her prize for not loving him fully, her compensation for not having been loved by Arslan. She wishes she could tell him that he, the boy who helped her find her classroom on the first day of high school, is the great miracle of her life. He has always pushed her to seek contentment, and he had waited patiently for her to realize that he would be the source of it. But, to express her gratitude, she would have to acknowledge how she had entered their marriage stupidly believing she was making some kind of compromise. 'Oh, that.'

'Do you send him valentines?'

'I do. Big red construction paper hearts with glitter. I don't know . . . the scrapbook . . . it's a thing I made when I was young and crazy. I was trying to prove that what was happening was real.'

'I think Harry wants to trade me in for him.'

'No, he doesn't. Not really. Because then Arslan would just be his boring dad. Besides, he likes you.'

'He *does*? Oh, good. Sometimes it seems like I'm the only dad in town who has to feel inadequate because he's not a famous ballet dancer.'

'I think all men probably struggle with that from time to time.'

'Is it too late to challenge this Arslan guy to a dance-off?'

'It's never too late for a dance-off.'

Gently, he disengages her arms, sets her upright. 'All I'm saying is that sometimes this whole thing with Harry and Arslan gets weird.'

'I know. You've said. And I've said that Arslan is the obvious choice of idols for Harry. But I really think it'll fade. Harry will get better. Arslan will get older. Harry will want to be the one who's a god. This is how it works. I've seen it before.'

'Why couldn't he have stayed in Russia where he belongs? Why couldn't you have left him at a Canadian gas station?'

She puts her palm on his stomach, and he sucks in, stretches up on tiptoes, and lifts his arms over his head in a ballet pose, looking down at her with mock hauteur. She says, 'I've asked myself the same thing.'

Jacob lies awake. When he is sure Joan is asleep, he slides out of bed and, turning the doorknob slowly so the latch doesn't click, goes out into the hall. Pumpkin-colored light from the streetlamp washes down the stairs, and Jacob descends quietly through it, barefoot. Without turning on any lights, he navigates the darker, cooler downstairs, his toes curled under to avoid catching on corners or table legs. Only when he is in the garage, on the chilly, dusty concrete, does he feel for a switch. The fluorescent bars flicker and pop on, humming. He looks around at his parked car, the pile of bikes, the washer and dryer and sacks of plant food. Two boogie boards lean against the wall, still crusted with sand from the summer. Cardboard boxes are stacked in one corner, never unpacked after the move, full of stuff that did not fit easily into this new Californian house and life: winter clothes, relics of childhood, relics of grandparents, things saved because to throw them away now would be to admit the foolishness of having saved them in the first place. The top box has JOAN written on it in black marker and creased flaps that are already partly open, scraps of tape curling back from their edges.

Now that Jacob has come all this way, committed to this self-indulgent and possibly upsetting fact-finding mission, it occurs to him that Harry has probably hoarded the scrapbook away in his room with all his other Rusakovian treasures, and he is preemptively annoyed with Joan for letting that happen. But when he pulls the flaps back and peers into the box, there is a large rectangular album bound in light-blue vinyl textured to resemble leather. Jacob takes the book and boosts himself up onto the washing machine, his bare heels bumping against the cold white enamel. He wishes he had thought to put on a sweatshirt. He opens the book.

The first pages are full of postcards of Paris. He has never been to Paris, but he knows its landmarks well: the Eiffel Tower, the blocky Arc de Triomphe, the blockier, sootier façade of Notre Dame. He studies the opera house, its arches and columns and squashed green dome. Statues stand up on the roof, but he can't quite make them out, even when he bends close to the page. In an oversaturated postcard of its interior, the gold plasterwork is banana yellow, the seats and curtains a lurid red. There is a program from a performance by the Kirov. Jacob finds Rusakov's name. There is a program from a performance by the Paris Opéra Ballet. He finds Joan's name. He thinks of Europeans all clapping together, like Harry said. *Clap clap clap clap.*

Next she has pasted in envelopes with exotic postmarks – Madrid, Berlin, Rome – their top edges carefully slit open. Inside are letters from Rusakov, all in French. Jacob takes them out and looks at them but does not understand. Languages have always been his bugaboo; he has no aptitude for them. He reads the letter from the English dancer. *Don't make the mistake of believing he is in love with you.* Pages of pasted-in clippings from the time of the defection follow: fragile rectangles of newsprint with long tails folded to fit in the book, some with yellowed photographs of Joan and Rusakov together on the street outside her apartment and then, later, in evening wear at dinners and balls, Joan smiling, skinny in chiffon. He remembers standing at the newsstand in Chicago and staring at these same pictures. *Library's down the street, buddy,* the guy said every time.

The snapshots stun him: the youth of the people, their pervasive beauty, their ease in their bodies. His jealousy, which he had thought was gone, eroded to nothing by the passage of time, rears up. There is Joan, her bare legs curled under her, nestled against Rusakov on a green couch at a party, stuck to him like a limpet. Rusakov, holding a drink, looks up at a man in a tweed blazer who sits, legs crossed, on the couch's arm. There is Rusakov, smirking, shirtless and barefoot in running shorts, sprawled in a chair. Rusakov on the Brooklyn Bridge, in Central Park, on the steps of the Metropolitan Museum of Art, his head cocked sardonically to the side, hands in his pockets. Rusakov again and again. Mugging, clowning, glowering, pondering, dancing, preening.

Eerily, Rusakov sleeping, his young forehead slightly furrowed in dream concentration. Jacob can't let himself think about Joan taking that photograph, crouching beside the bed, framing the defenseless face and greedily making a memento out of it. Joan in a party dress, Joan in bell-bottoms and platform sandals and too much makeup. He can tell by her shy, intense expression that Rusakov is the photographer. Joan in leg warmers sitting on the floor of a dance studio, Rusakov's head in her lap. She looks tender, her fingers buried in his hair, but he is amused, hoisting an eyebrow at whoever took the picture. Programs from ballets. Clippings about Rusakov that no longer mention Joan. More snapshots, but they are less intimate. Group shots. Joan still smiles but is not happy. A plane ticket, a postcard of a bridge made of delicate iron fans on stone legs, and then blank pages.

APRIL 1991 – SOUTHERN CALIFORNIA

For his thirteenth birthday, Harry has requested that Joan and Jacob take him and Chloe to see *The Phantom of the Opera* in LA Though Harry is pretending to be enthusiastic, Joan knows he has engineered the trip more for Chloe's benefit than his own. Gary has changed jobs again, and money is too tight for the Wheelocks to be buying theater tickets. Worse, Gary is in a religious phase and has begun to disapprove of a growing list of things that might include musical theater, especially when it concerns lust, opera, and French people. He isn't so sure about Chloe dancing around in a leotard. 'He's a big Jesus freak now,' Harry said. 'He's always getting together with a bunch of dads to pray.'

'What does Chloe think?'

'I don't know. She goes to church with him, but I don't think she's getting into Jesus, really, except to be nice to Gary. I don't think she likes to say bad things about Gary because everyone else does. He's such a dick.'

'Harry.'

'You and dad call him that.'

'Maybe he is kind of a dick,' Joan allows, 'but, please, Harry, don't pass that on to Chloe.'

'Mom, I'm not stupid. I want Chloe to like us.'

Last month, Chloe told Joan she was hoping to be taken to see *Phantom* for her birthday, but instead she had come to class with CDs, a gift from her mother. 'It's the original cast recording,' she said brightly and requested they listen to it during barre. The other girls were excited by the prospect of dancing to music with singing, so Joan had indulged her, watching Chloe mouth the lyrics in the mirror, refraining from reminding her that her battements didn't need to be quite so emotive.

The Bintzes have moved to a new house, and so they drive back to their old neighborhood in Valle de los Toros to pick up Chloe. They study their former house the way someone might scrutinize an ex-lover from across a restaurant, taking in the little sprucings the new owners have done, agreeing that it looks smaller and older now that they don't live there. The previous summer they moved to a new tract of pink-stucco, tile-roofed houses near Jacob's school. They have a rectangular swimming pool and a wheeled aquatic robot that scoots around the bottom vacuuming up leaves. They have a guava tree in the backyard that yields hard, grey-green fruit nobody will eat and an orange tree that periodically explodes with more citrus than they can use. Joan has bought an electric juicer, but overripe oranges still fall and split open on the patio, enticing the bees. The new house is bigger than the old house and lighter and more modern, and these advantages bring her a straightforward domestic pleasure. She had thought she would miss the old house, the place where their family had taken shape, but her loyalty has shifted, along with their furniture and boxes of stuff, into this comelier shell they have found for their lives. Jacob takes a lordly pride in sitting on a chaise and surveying the blue water of the swimming pool. They believe they are owed sunlight, newness, and abundance. They have become Californians.

The new house is only six miles from the old one, still in the same school district. Harry and Chloe go to the same middle school, although Joan wishes they didn't. Harry says that Chloe at school isn't really Chloe, but he won't give details. He seems to think the real Chloe is the one in the studio, the one who is mostly movement. Joan has begun to work on partnering with them. Harry's crush on Chloe is an advantage; he is focused on her, determined not to drop her, not squeamish, not selfish, not annoyed with how much effort he must put into being scaffolding for another dancer. He dances with the other students, too, because he is the only boy, and he is a conscientious partner to them all because he doesn't know how to be otherwise.

Chloe flies from the Wheelocks' front door, smiling broadly with a mouth full of braces, running down the front walkway in a clingy calf-length dress printed with pink and yellow roses. Her turned-out feet are quick in blocky white heels. Her hair, which has darkened over the years from a baby blond to the dirty color of tarnished brass, is loose on her bare, bony shoulders. Joan is startled. She has not seen Chloe outside of the studio for a while, and, as girls this age do, she seems to have changed overnight. She still has a child's skinny shape, but something is different. Perhaps the body is collecting itself in preparation to change, getting ready for the exertion of growth. Despite all the hours Joan spends staring at Chloe in the studio, molding her, this gawky adolescent who jumps into the backseat, radiating excitement and smelling strongly of cheap body spray, seems unfamiliar, and the whole expedition to LA is suddenly embarrassing, as though they were four strangers going on a double date.

Joan wonders what Chloe's fragrance is supposed to be. Freesia? Rose? Middle school girls have an insatiable enthusiasm for making themselves reek of imitation melon or gardenia or strawberry. Joan has prohibited her students from wearing anything scented to class – no sprays, no lotions – but still she catches them sneaking plastic bottles of purple and pink liquids out of their dance bags during breaks for a restorative spritz. They have strange ideas, these girls, of what it means to be a woman. Mr K, she sees now, was clever with his courtly little gifts of perfume. *This is the kind of woman you are,* he tells the dancers he chooses to elevate. *This is how you should smell.* According to Elaine, he has fewer muses these days. He no longer sleeps with them but still picks out their perfume. His health is irregular, Elaine says, but apparently nothing can deter him from going out and spending an hour at Bloomingdale's, smelling and wafting and pondering until some stray puff of fragrance finally captures the essence of a certain teenager in pointe shoes. If Joan has a muse it is certainly Chloe (not Harry, whose instruction she approaches with both maternal pride and pedagogical terror – she is too close to him; like a sculptor, she needs distance to take in the whole), but she has no impulse to mold any part of the girl besides her dancing. She believes that the less she knows about Chloe, the better she can see her.

As they drive north, Harry passes one of Chloe's CDs forward between the seats, nudging Joan in the shoulder. 'We're going to hear all this again in a couple hours,' Joan says, but she pushes the disc into the slot.

There is a bit of dialogue about a chandelier, and then the car is flooded with churning organ music. 'Yow,' says Jacob, taking a hand off the wheel to turn down the volume.

'Thank you so much for inviting me,' Chloe says sweetly to Joan and Jacob.

Jacob glances in the rearview mirror. 'Of course, kiddo.'

'We're glad you could come,' Joan says, 'but Harry invited you. He's the one with the birthday.'

'Thanks, Harry.'

Joan turns her head so she can see Harry out of the corner of her eye. He leans against the window, pleased and blushing. 'Yeah,' he says. 'It's cool. Just don't tell anyone at school. They already think I'm weird. I don't need anyone thinking I'm into musicals.'

'Weird is good,' Jacob says. 'Weird means you're interesting.'

'No,' says Harry. 'Weird means you're weird.'

'I won't tell,' Chloe says magnanimously. She leans forward, grasping the back of Joan's seat. 'Joan, when you used to dance in Paris, were there ghost stories about the opera house?'

'Oh, some. There are ghost stories about most old theaters, I think.'

'Did anyone ever die there?'

'I'm sure. In fires and accidents. Probably of natural causes, too – audience members having heart attacks and things. And, way back, the whole opera company used to live in the building.'

'Do you think it's haunted? Did anything spooky ever happen?'

'Spooky?' She remembers the red velvet box on the third loge, her first glimpse of Arslan, her reflection in his dressing room mirror. 'No, not really. The basement is a little spooky. It's stone with archways and things, kind of like a crypt. There are lots of different levels. There used to be

226

stables. But now it's mostly just stuff in storage, like sound equipment and old props and things.'

'Is there really a lake underneath?'

'There's water but not really a lake. When they were building, water kept seeping through and ruining the foundations, so they gave up and made a cement tank for it. There's a grate in the basement you can look through and see the water down below. Someone told me the water was for if there was a fire. I don't know if that's true. Performers aren't really supposed to go down there. You have to make friends with the stagehands.' Joan wishes she were the kind of person who could make a good story out of that old murky cistern.

But Chloe seems delighted. 'Wow,' she says. 'That's so cool. So maybe the *Phantom* story is partly true.'

Harry stirs. 'Made-up things can be true,' he says. 'Dad says it better, but it's like, if a story matters to you, it's true for you, even if it never happened. Like myths. Right, Dad?'

'Right,' says Jacob, pleased. 'Or Bible stories.' After the words are out, Jacob glances at Chloe in the rearview mirror, remembering that Gary is now a Jesus freak.

'I feel that way about *Swan Lake*,' Joan offers quickly. 'Some other ballets, too. *Romeo and Juliet*.'

'Shakespeare was so lucky to have that ballet to base his play on,' Jacob says.

'Ha, ha. The problem is I've only seen the play once. I've seen the ballet a million times.'

227

Chloe still says nothing, and Joan worries that Jacob offended her or she thinks they are being ridiculous, but then she says quietly, 'I feel that way about pretty much everything.'

Joan reaches back with one arm. She finds Chloe's familiar hard knot of a knee in the space behind her seat and pats it.

Harry is glad the theater is dark for several reasons. The first is that he is mortified. He can barely bring himself to look at the effusion that's happening onstage, all the singing and acting, the mist and the candelabras, the organ and the electric guitar, the decadent opera house set with gold, bare-breasted sculptures, red drapes, and a huge chandelier. For people to walk around onstage *singing* seems unnatural, a desecration of a space intended for the rigors of dance. Of course some ballets are all about drama and passion and swelling music, and of course dancers emote, but all that ardor is kept in check by their silence. Onstage, the girl Christine and her young suitor Raoul are singing a duet, and it all seems too obvious, too easy, too literal. They just sing the lyrics someone else wrote. Anyone could play these parts and get the point across. These performers are just people: people who can sing, which Harry cannot, but still just people. Dancers are not just people.

The second reason he appreciates the darkness is that, since he doesn't want to look at the stage, he can look at Chloe, at least some of the time. His mother, without making a big deal about it, bought seats for herself and his dad on the other side of the theater from him and Chloe. He sees Chloe five days a week at dance, but they are always in motion, always observed. Since his family moved away, they are never quiet and still together anymore, the way they used to be when they watched TV or read books or hung out in the backyard. She had come to swim in his pool once right after they moved in, dropped off by Gary, who did not even turn his head to look at the house before speeding away, but their old friend-ship, which had worn deep, inviting grooves through the old house and yard, could not seem to find purchase in this shiny new place. Harry had been excited about showing her the pool and by the prospect of her two-piece bathing suit, but they had become awkward and hostile with each other, brought up short by the smooth rectangle of water as though by an ancient riddle. If they were younger, they would have dived for rings or invented events for pool Olympics or done water ballet. If they were older, they would have known to float peacefully on the rafts or lie roasting on the chaises. But they didn't know how to play anymore. They treaded water, chins at the surface. Chloe's head looked small, sleek, and mean. 'I thought it would be a bigger pool,' she said. 'I guess it's nice, though.'

She ducked beneath the surface and pushed off

the bottom, turning into a long streak against the sun dapples, the pink halves of her bathing suit powered by her churning feet to the far end of the pool, where her sleek head popped up again and one thin arm emerged to clutch the edge. 'This is boring,' she called.

'Let's practice a lift,' he suggested.

'No, I'm going to go talk to Joan.'

'Fine,' he said, and then he turned a backflip and settled down on the bottom of the pool, leaden as a crocodile, holding his breath until her legs climbed the steps and he was alone.

Chloe sniffles more or less continuously through the first act and dabs her eyes with a tissue she takes from her little beaded purse. She cries when Christine sings with the Phantom; she cries when Christine sings with Raoul. Her indiscriminate rapture in the face of so much excess – material and emotional – troubles Harry. More and more he has noticed girls reacting to movies and songs and pictures in magazines in ways that don't make any sense. Girls always seem to be straining and crying for some invisible thing they recognize and want but that seems completely obscure to him. They seem to want to have something to want, as though wanting was an end in itself.

In the lobby, before they sat down, Harry had seen a clump of middle-aged women all wearing white ceramic Phantom masks pinned to their sparkly theatergoing outfits, and he had recognized the edgy excitement in their eyes, the elevated pitch of their voices, the way they clumped together. They were grown-ups, but they were also like the girls in his class. Girls, he is beginning to conclude, love to feel. They're hooked on it. He doesn't love to feel. He wishes he felt less. Life would be less confusing if he felt less, especially for Chloe, and would be more pleasant if he wanted less from her. He wants her to be nice to him at school, to dance with him and only him at dances. (Why won't she dance with him, a boy who actually knows how to dance? Why does she prefer to dance in a group with her smug-but-awkward girlfriends and then with boys who just shuffle back and forth like crippled, sweating bears?) But Chloe's face, flickering in the light from the stage, wet with tears, is so pretty. He is pleased to be the one to have brought her here, given her what she wants.

Love for Chloe lodged in him before he can remember, administered like a baby vaccination, and he isn't prone to changing his mind, even though the project of loving her has become steadily more complicated. Even when they were very small, she excluded him at school, always turning away, choosing someone else, making it clear that the hours spent playing in each other's houses and backyards had no bearing on the way things would be in public. After he started dancing, they had become both closer and more estranged. No one else understands the harsh regime they've chosen to live under, the time and

231

pain lavished on every tiny rotation of wrist or ankle, the relentless need they feel to get better, to work harder, but at school she is worse than a stranger. When people laugh at him for doing ballet, she sometimes almost seems to agree with them that it is normal for her to dance but freakish or stupid for him to do the same. The fineness of his body, its small neatness and the precision with which he moves draw mockery, but the same qualities make her desirable. At dances, the shuffling bears line up for her.

The third reason Harry is glad for the darkness is that, at the end of Raoul and Christine's song, when the Phantom has taken over and howled his echo of it, Chloe finds his hand and holds it. She doesn't look at him, and he is startled by the creeping fingers that tug his left hand out from where he has tucked it under his thigh and interweave with his own. The sensation in itself is nothing new. They hold hands all the time when they do partnering work, and so he thinks maybe she has taken his hand purely out of habit. Or maybe out of gratitude for bringing her here. Maybe his reward for ceding his birthday to her is this slightly sweaty pressure in the darkness. Or maybe she thinks he is as swept up in the ludicrous love triangle happening onstage as she is, wanting Christine somehow to give herself to the masked genius living under the opera house but also to marry the handsome aristocrat and go to parties and have a mansion. The story would be better as a ballet, he thinks. Closing his eyes, still holding Chloe's hand, he clears the stage of sets and people and mist and candelabras and puts himself at its center, alone, and imagines how one day he will be the best dancer and Chloe will want to dance only with him.

JULY 1992 – UPSTATE NEW YORK

Elaine sits at Mr K's bedside and watches him sleep. His sleep is no longer simple rest. Dutifully, regularly, he subsides into unconsciousness, sometimes because of the drugs, sometimes because something in his ravaged, over-grown interior reaches up and pulls him down into oblivion. Several blankets are piled on him even though the evening is warm. When his raspy breathing grows deep and regular, she crosses to open a window. His hospital bed is in the dacha's living room because the bedroom is upstairs, and stairs are no longer on the agenda. Elaine sleeps alone up there, under the steeply sloped ceiling, oppressed by the dark wood and lace that he loves, the paintings of troikas and peasants and birch trees. There are icons on the walls, too, heavy with gold leaf, but he is not religious, only sentimental. Arslan once sent him a balalaika as a joke, but he received it in seriousness and keeps it propped beside the fireplace. The house is decorated to remind him of a house on the Black Sea where he spent summers as a child.

Only the top half of his face shows above the

blankets. The contours of his skull protrude through his wispy hair and thin yellow skin. His nose is marked by a dark lesion, one of the few remaining now that his body is too exhausted even to disfigure itself. Out the window, in the fading light, fireflies dawdle over the long meadow. The far line of fir trees atop the steep slope down to the river has turned to a pronged shadow. Not tonight, but often when he is asleep, she goes out to the barre on the porch and stretches and goes through the battements. She has stopped performing – she is Mr K's associate artistic director – but the closer he comes to death, the harder she has been working at the barre. She hears his voice in her head issuing polite, rhythmic orders: *one, and up, and three, and plié, and just the upper body, good, and out, and fifth, and out, and fifth, yes, and turn.* When she runs company class, she feels like a medium speaking with his voice. *And up and out and pa pa pa pa. No, like this.* 'You think you can stave off mortality,' he said once when she came inside drenched in sweat. 'You think you can be too strong for it. You think, child, that you're working a spell out there.'

'I'm just staying out of trouble,' she told him.

The New York Times has his obituary all ready to go. The fact-checker has called to confirm that Mstislav Ilyich Kocheryozhkin, known as Mr K for obvious reasons, was born in Moscow in January 1924, days after Lenin's death, to a

Bolshevik mother who disavowed her aristocratic family and a father who was one of the architects of the Second Five Year Plan. He attended ballet school in Leningrad until his father was sent to the Gulag, at which point he was conscripted. At the end of the war, he deserted from the Red Army in Berlin and made his way to Paris and eventually New York, where he found a wealthy patron and began to choreograph for fledgling ballet companies. He was believed to have contracted the virus sometime in the early eighties, and he kept his diagnosis a secret for more than seven years.

Yes, Elaine said, as far as she knows, that's true. The other things the newspaper will print are true, also: that he is perhaps the most famous choreographer in the twentieth century, that he was among the first to make ballets that didn't rely on stories or romance, that he trained his dancers according to a system of his own devising, emphasizing speed and clarity of technique over emotional expression, that he nurtured many great American dancers along with famous defectors like Arslan Rusakov and Ludmilla Yedemskaya. The fact-checker is businesslike, offers brisk condolences for her vigil. As his replacement artistic director, he asks, how will she handle the burden of his mixed legacy? There are more questions – a black, tarry pit of curiosity bubbling under his *mmhmms* – but the boundaries of politeness exclude them.

She is not infected. Every day, as she and the

nurse watch his wasted body convulse around the tasks of discharging sputum and diarrhea, she gives silent, ashamed thanks. She could have contracted it, certainly. She had many opportunities, but she was lucky, beyond lucky. Over the years, she had usually supplied him with a condom, and even when she hadn't, he was as likely to give up in the middle as to finish, which, the doctor said, had probably diminished her odds of infection, not that withdrawal (a charitable way to put it) was a viable method of protection. For the past five years, since well before she knew he was positive, they have not had sex. When she was younger his indifference had hurt, but now she is grateful for it. She would have liked more passion over the past eighteen years, to have been loved more fully, but now she will keep on living when she easily might not have. There is even an element of revenge to her health, something – at last! one thing! – she has not because of him but in spite of him, though she knows she will suffer when he is gone.

He stirs and coughs. Yellow eyes open beneath the bony overhang of his brow. She takes a cup of water from the nightstand and holds it for him so he can sip from the straw.

'What do you want to open the window for?' he asks in an abraded whisper. 'You'll catch your death.'

'Wishful thinking. I'm not coming with you.'

'You see, I have made you Russian after all. Gallows humor about someone else's gallows.'

She straightens his blankets, folding them neatly under his chin. He watches her face. She sits; there is a silence. She asks, 'What do you think today?' Lately, they have started talking more about death, almost gossiping about it, speculating as if it were as changeable as the weather. Together they wait for his death as though for a bus.

'Today I think it is like inside a theater with all the lights out, after everyone has gone. Black, with a damp smell, but large. What do you think?'

Night has fallen, and, outside, the crickets are droning. 'I don't know,' she says. 'I don't know if there can be blackness. There definitely won't be smells.'

'Who are you to say there won't be smells? Then no sights, no sounds either?'

'Do you think you'll have a body?'

He coughs, and she holds a tissue under his mouth for him to spit. 'Today, I hope not,' he says. 'It's too much trouble. But then there will be no ballet.'

'No, I suppose not.' Elaine tries and fails to make sense of the idea that there could be ballet after death. The absurdity of it casts a shadow over ballet in life. Why, she wonders, would you spend your life doing something that will be useless to you when you're dead and have no body? But everything will be useless when you're dead, she thinks.

A whole, bare arm emerges from under the covers, a hinged broomstick, and reaches for her. She takes the assemblage of bones that is his hand. 'You know,' he says, 'I would like to do one thing before I go.'

'Skydive?'

'Serious now, Elaine.'

'I'm sorry. I'm listening.'

'I said I would marry you. Years ago. Maybe you don't remember.'

'I remember.'

'I should have done it long ago, but now . . . maybe it is wrong to ask you to marry a corpse, but I will ask anyway. I think it will be nice to die married. My mother wanted me to marry.'

Shocked, she lets go of his hand because she is afraid she will squeeze too hard and hurt him. He watches, mildly interested in her surprise but no longer able to get worked up over anything. She has been stunned by how little anger he directs at death, this man who could fly into a rage if the temperature in a dance studio was one degree too warm or if some poor girl had a hair out of place. Finally, she finds her voice. 'I'll have to call your obituarist and give him the news.'

'I like a little surprise at the end. Like in my ballets.'

'You probably didn't have a chance to run out and buy a ring.'

'On the contrary.' He straightens one finger. 'In the little Palekh box on the bookshelf.'

The box is a two-inch cube, varnished black with a tiny firebird picked out in glowing reds and golds on its lid, a swirl of burning plumage flying over the bare branches of a silver tree. Inside is an enormous emerald held with fragile teeth to a tiny gold band.

'From my mother,' comes the whisper from the bed. 'One of the few things she kept from her family. A little insurance, maybe. She gave it to me before I went to the front. I don't know why. Most likely I would have died, been buried or burned with it in my pocket. I think she wanted to lose everything all at once. No one has worn it in fifty years. More.'

An idea of the emerald's provenance crackles through Elaine. A cave in India; merchants; traders; a journey overland; St Petersburg; a soldier fleeing through the rubble of Berlin. 'I can't.'

'No, girl. You must.'

In August, Joan looks out her kitchen window at Elaine lying beside her pool, flat on her back on a towel, eyes closed, offering her body, still taut in a black bikini, to the sun. She is maybe too thin now, all greyhound contours of muscle and bone. Nearby, on a chaise, Harry is equally flat and still. The two of them look like anesthetized patients waiting for some cosmic surgeon to open them up.

In the preceding months, Elaine had called a handful of times, usually while Mr K slept. She

240

was taking the train back and forth between the dacha and the city a few times a week, trying to care for both the company and Mr K and always feeling guilty about one when she was with the other.

'It would be more convenient if he wanted to die in the city,' Elaine said, 'but there's no changing his mind.'

'Don't worry about the company,' Joan told her. 'It can take care of itself.'

'The thing is,' Elaine said, lowering her voice, 'if I never left here, if I stayed with him all the time, I would lose my mind. All I can do is watch him and wait and give him water or drugs. At least in the city I get to yell at people, tell them what to do. There's nothing for me to tell him to do. It's a little late for the whole Lucy and Ricky routine. Oh. I haven't told you. We got married.'

Joan was sitting outside on her patio with the cordless phone. The pool reflected purple evening and a crescent moon. 'What?' she said. 'Really?'

'Really.' There was a whistling kind of inhale, a pause, and then a shallow cough. 'Sorry, I've taken up smoking weed. I used to think it would make me fat, but now I'll try anything just to chill out a little bit. You know? I used to do all that coke. I wouldn't know what to do with that kind of high now. I would have to sit here and wait for it to go away.'

'You married Mr K?'

'Yes, in holy matrimony. For the brief period till

241

death do us part. He popped the question. A justice of the peace made a house call. It was sweet, in a macabre way. The hospice nurse witnessed and our neighbor from down the road. I think they would have been more suspicious except Mstislav told them I was already his sole beneficiary. And then he said, "She's always dreamed of being a widow."'

Joan couldn't bring herself to say congratulations. 'I'm sorry, Elaine. This sounds really hard.'

'Don't be. You should see the ring.' A long pause. Joan could hear the roar of the Hudson crickets. Finally, Elaine said, 'It is hard.'

Every time they talked, before hanging up, Joan told her she was always welcome to visit, that she should consider a change of scene when she had the time, which was, of course, code for after Mr K was dead. Elaine had never seemed particularly interested, but after the funeral and the end of the company's summer run, she had called and announced she would be arriving the next day and would Joan pick her up at the airport?

On the curb outside the baggage claim she told Joan she would be staying for a month. It has been three weeks. Joan doesn't mind – she and Elaine have not lost the knack of being roommates – but Jacob shows signs of feeling crowded and marginalized. Most nights after dinner he retreats upstairs with restrained grumpiness to read or watch TV in the bedroom, ceding the family room to the other three so they can continue working their way through Harry's collection of ballet videos. Harry absorbs Elaine's new commentary hungrily, like she is a guru on top of a mountain and he has walked for days to meet her. He has questions. What does she think of the guy dancing Mercutio? Who is that girl dancing the Lilac Fairy?

Elaine says the guy is pretty good, that he dances in Holland now. The girl was subbed in at the last minute, impressed everyone, and then tore up her knee two weeks later and had to retire. No, she doesn't know what became of her.

Elaine is modestly helpful around the house. She does the dishes, buys groceries, offers to chauffeur Harry wherever he wants to go – he is thrilled to have a principal dancer, a flesh-and-blood *artistic director* driving him around – but mostly she behaves as though she has checked in to a sanatorium, sleeping for ten hours at a time, picking through the refrigerator, surreptitiously smoking joints out by the back fence, spending hours standing in the pool under a broad-brimmed hat and reading a book. She doesn't seem sad, exactly, though Joan knows she is. She hides it well. She says she did most of her mourning while Mr K was still alive. When she thinks no one is looking, she worries at the huge emerald on her finger, turning it toward her palm and rubbing it with her thumb as though it were a blister. She seems distracted, the way Joan feels when Harry is away on a school trip and part of her tries to follow him clairvoyantly through his day, probing the ether for any sign of distress. 'I catch myself wondering how he's doing,' Elaine has said. 'Like how he's doing with being dead. What he's up to. If he needs me. Where he wants to go on our honeymoon.'

Joan thinks she should be doing more to draw Elaine out, pry back her layers of careful control, but she doesn't know how. Her attempts are, for the most part, met with jokes and deflections. 'You can freak out, if you want,' she tried once.

'I don't,' Elaine said, not quite snapping, but firmly. 'Don't worry. I'm not going to suddenly explode and rend my garments and then be catatonic in your guest room for a week. I'm comfortable this way. There's always a little motor going somewhere, processing, but it's private.'

'Fine,' Joan said. 'That's fine.'

Sometimes Elaine comes to the studio and sits in a folding chair by the mirror. She watches Joan teach, mans the stereo, drinks from an enormous thermos of black tea. Twice she has taught the advanced class, five girls including Chloe plus Harry. She sounds uncannily like Mr K as she walks up and down the barre correcting them. The students are dazzled by her and frightened of her demanding brusqueness, the way she might seize an underperforming arm or leg and shake it at its owner as though confronting a dog with a chewed-up shoe.

Out on the pool deck, Elaine rolls onto her stomach and fiddles with something she pulls from under Harry's chaise – a small box that must be metal from the way it catches the sunlight. She sticks a joint in her mouth – Joan supposes for one foolish moment that it could be a hand-rolled cigarette – and lights it. Holding it at the end of one outstretched arm, she maneuvers onto her back again, then expels a cloud of smoke. The arm comes down to her mouth in a graceful curve, a swan's neck bending to feed.

'Elaine,' Joan calls, going out and crossing the patio to stand over her, 'are you smoking marijuana in front of my son?' She should be angry, but Elaine's brazenness has disarmed her. She's like a tourist from Balletland who doesn't know the most basic local customs.

Elaine looks up at Joan. The sun is a star against the black space of her sunglasses. She cracks her lips and smoke sidles out. 'Well, he wouldn't have noticed except you said so.'

'I know what pot smells like,' Harry interjects, propped up on his elbows. The position emphasizes how narrow his waist is compared to his shoulders. His shoulders seem to have passed into manhood, while the rest of him is still boyish and gangly. 'It's fine, Mom. Elaine is grieving.'

Elaine holds the joint up, proffering it to Joan, who shakes her head. She twists onto her side to stub it out in the lid of her little box, which holds a half dozen more skinny paper twists. Carefully, she tucks the remnant in with its brethren, shuts the lid. 'Sorry,' she says. 'That was presumptuous.

But it's so delicious here in the sun. I couldn't resist.'

Suddenly it is deeply annoying to Joan that Elaine has chosen to rest on her life as though it were a lily pad. 'Try,' she says. 'I know it's not very bohemian of me, but I don't actually encourage Harry to do drugs.'

'I wasn't *encouraging* him. I didn't offer him any. I wouldn't.'

'Mom,' Harry says again, soothingly, 'it's fine.'

'You don't get to decide,' she tells him.

Elaine swivels up so she is sitting Indian style. The tendons in her groin stand out like guy wires holding her bikini in place. There is nothing to fold or pooch out on her stomach; the skin stretches taut around the shallow knothole of her belly button. With an air of giving Joan the straight scoop, she says, 'Harry will have to make up his own mind, anyway, Joan, since he's going to be a dancer. You remember how it was. If you're going to just say no, you'll have to say it a lot.'

Harry perks up. 'You think I'm going to be a dancer?'

Elaine aims her sunglasses at him. 'Don't you want to be?'

'Yeah, obviously. But you think I'll make it?'

'You're special,' Elaine says. 'There are no guarantees, but you have the talent. Some people think you just need to work, but they're wrong. You need talent, too, and the right body, obviously. You've got those, so now you have to work harder than everyone else. The second you think you're good enough, it's over. Then you're a complacent sack of shit, and you're wrong. There's no such thing as good enough.'

'Don't promise things,' Joan says to Elaine. 'Especially not while you're high.' Harry is slipping away from her. She has thought for some time that he is gifted enough to be a professional, even a star, but she has only vaguely considered the intrusive mechanisms that will start to take over. People with more power will move in and shoulder her aside, claim jumping on her son, her student. He is already becoming a commodity. She experiences a tickle of anticipatory jealousy. This is the beginning of people wanting him to dance what they choreograph, wanting him to make money for them, wanting him simply to be present on their stage or at their gala or party. Soon girls and women will want him to bestow attention and love and sex. Even as she wants him to succeed, Joan wants to keep him for herself. She envies the talent that will propel him away from her.

'I didn't promise anything,' Elaine says. 'Best-case scenario, I promised a lifetime of feeling inadequate.'

'I don't think it's helpful to tell him he's special. I don't want him to be disappointed.'

'Of course he's going to be disappointed,' Elaine says. 'Harry, you're going to be disappointed sometimes. Is that okay?'

'Yes!'

Elaine pats his foot. 'You don't know what you're talking about. You'll have to come to New York next summer for the intensive.'

Harry hesitates. 'What about Chloe? Can she come?'

'She can audition. You'll have to audition, too. I can't just ordain that you're coming. Maybe I could. No, I won't. Chloe needs to finish growing. I can't tell what she'll look like in a few years.'

'She's having an awkward time with puberty,' Joan says. 'She's very good. She'll work it out.'

'Can you tell what I'll look like?' Harry asks Elaine.

'You – yes. Partly because I know your parents and partly because I can just see it. I get more excited about boys in general. There are fewer boys. Harry, you can't tie your career to any other dancers. You can't only do what Chloe does.'

'I know.' He nods gravely but looks unconvinced.

'You're bossy for a pothead,' Joan observes.

'You should hear me without it. I'm Mussolini.'

Joan goes inside and gets her cigarettes out of their hiding place above the fridge. She returns to the pool, steps out of her sandals, sits down next to Elaine's towel, and puts her feet in the water. Below, the wheeled cleaner robot glides in long arcs over the curvature of the bottom, vigilantly patrols its tranquil beat, sometimes running so high up the walls that part of it breaks the surface, dipping up into the air like a dolphin's back. Elaine and Harry are talking to each other, uninterested in her, but they stop when she clicks her lighter, unites the tiny flame with the paper. 'I guess we're all adults now,' she says.

'I knew you smoked,' Harry says. 'I have a *nose*.'

'Okay, then. Don't start, though. You'll never be able to stop.'

'I don't do things just because you do them.'

The sound of bees comes from the orange tree. A mourning dove sings its four notes. Joan is the architect of this moment, but all along she has been building herself out of it, cheerfully walling off her son's future. It is too late to undo anything. She has made Harry a dancer and can't unmake him. She wouldn't want to, but she is sorry to be left behind again.

MAY 1993 – SOUTHERN CALIFORNIA

In the early mornings, before her parents wake, Chloe makes herself coffee and does her exercises. She stretches. She lies on her back and spins a bicycle tire around one ankle and then the other. She does handstands and yoga poses in the living room and pull-ups on the spring-loaded bar she ordered from a catalog and wedged in the doorway of the downstairs bathroom. She does these things, but each day she does them more slowly, with fewer repetitions, spending more and more time lying on her back and contemplating the ceiling, wondering if she should quit ballet.

Several reasons present themselves for quitting. For starters, dance takes up all her time and makes her tired and is hard and not fun. Second, her mother, who is a fat cow and doesn't know anything about ballet, is always riding her about staying focused in class. And it doesn't help that puberty, slow to arrive, finally overtook her like a plague and has spent the past year, her fourteenth, widening her hips, throwing off her center of gravity, robbing her of turnout. No matter how little she eats, the hips will not be fought back – the wideness is in the bone. Her pelvis has spread like a stain, pulling her femurs and knees out of alignment, changing everything forever. The hips are her mother's fault, genetically speaking, and are resented as such, as though she had conceived Chloe as part of an elaborate plan to cultivate her dancing and then, via anatomical time bomb, sabotage it. Chloe used to be good; ballet used to feel natural, not easy but not like an impossible struggle against her own limbs.

Harry, too, is undergoing the grand transition they've heard so much about in health class, but he seems to be having an unfairly easy time, simply growing taller and stronger. *His* arms and legs aren't clumsy saboteurs but have assumed pleasant masculine proportions and continue to cooperate with his wishes. Pure physical luck – along with the political advantage of being Joan's kid and Elaine Costas's honorary kid or whatever and the numerical advantage of being one of the relatively few boys who do ballet – is why he got into a better summer intensive than she did (moral outrage: another reason to quit), the one in New York. The worst thing that puberty (such a gross word) has inflicted on him is a change in the way he smells, and she should know because they have been spending more and more time on partnering work and her face is always in his armpit or chest or, if something goes wrong, crotch. He doesn't smell bad, but sometimes she tells him he does, whispering spitefully as they practice a promenade, him walking a slow circle around her, rotating her on her pointe. Joan says this difficult time will pass, that Chloe will learn how to dance in her new body, but she isn't giving Chloe any breaks. 'Push *down* with your leg, don't pull up!' she shouted a few days ago as Harry lifted Chloe. 'He can't support you unless you support yourself. You need to *engage*.' Harry, trembling, lowered her back to the floor.

'*He* needs to get stronger,' Chloe said. 'I can feel him shaking.'

'He does. Harry, you do. But he's working on it. You have to help. It's meant to *look* effortless, not *be* effortless.'

For her fifteenth birthday, Harry gave her a book on famous ballerinas, including Emma Livry, who died in 1863 at the age of twenty after her tutu caught fire from a gas lamp onstage at the Paris Opéra, and now Chloe has nightmares about dancing while engulfed in flames. This morning, after plunging into a bottomless orchestra pit, trailing sparks through the blackness as she fell, unable to scream, burning and flailing in silence, waiting to splash into the water Joan said was under the Opéra but never getting that relief, she woke with scratches on her torso and blood under her fingernails, the sheets tangled around her ankles. If she quits, maybe the dreams will stop.

When her father comes downstairs in his bathrobe, Chloe tells him she was finishing homework and that she has eaten breakfast. There are no dishes in the sink and her clothes are soaked with sweat, but her father pours himself a bowl of Lucky Charms and says nothing. He has stopped going to church. He has been working in a store that sells mailing supplies. He doesn't care that her mother has started bartending and is gone most nights. As Chloe passes by his chair, he reaches out and grabs her, pulling her into a sideways hug. He so rarely embraces her that her first impulse is to pull away, but he holds fast, his shoulder digging into her ribs. Not knowing what else to do, she pats him on his head and gently pries his arms off her. 'It's okay, Dad. It's just breakfast,' she says.

She showers and walks to school. Halfway there, Bryce pulls up next to her in his truck and rolls down the window. 'Hey,' he calls.

'Hey.'

'What are you doing?'

'Knitting a sweater. What are you doing?'

'Nothing.' His truck crawls along in the bike lane. He says again, 'Hey.'

'Hey what?'

'Maybe I'll see you after school.'

'No. I have dance.'

'Maybe I'll see you at lunch.'

'Maybe.'

At lunch she goes out to the parking lot, to the far corner where Bryce has parked his truck under a pepper tree. Small green leaves and hard pink peppercorns sprinkle the hood and flatbed. The cab is cool in the shade, and she finds herself almost dozing off even while Bryce kisses her and grasps her wrist to press her hand against the front of his jeans. 'You're so hot,' he whispers. 'You're like crazy hot.' Other students pass by, talking and laughing, but their voices seem as irrelevant as birdcalls and only add to Chloe's lull.

When the bell rings, she says, 'Is it okay if I stay here and take a nap?'

'Don't you have class?'

She has biology. 'Free period.'

He doesn't like the idea, but she has let him feel around inside her underwear and knows he will want to keep her happy. She is already folding her sweatshirt into a pillow. 'Just don't get me in trouble,' he says.

When she wakes sometime later, the parking lot is quiet and Harry is staring at her through the driver's window.

'Hey,' she says. 'How long have you been standing there, creeper?'

'They were calling you to come to the office. Mrs Ferguson asked me to look for you.'

'Am I in trouble?'

His face is strange, reluctant. 'I don't think so.'

'But I ditched.'

'I'll walk with you.'

'I should probably get used to taking care of myself, since you'll be so far away this summer. Off with the *good* dancers.'

He doesn't say anything but doesn't leave, either. She knows he feels bad about the intensive but not bad enough not to go. Taking her time, she sits up and straightens her clothes, pulls down the mirror and checks her makeup, wiping crumbs of mascara from the inside corners of her eyes, licking her index finger and smoothing her eyebrows. It bothers her how he doesn't tell her to hurry up but just stands there waiting. Only eight boys were at the auditions in LA and almost a hundred girls. She had made it through several rounds, and then she had waited, breathless after a combination, the number four pinned to the front of her leotard, while the people from the company conferred. A lady with a bun of white hair said, 'Will numbers three, nine, seventy, fifty-two, and twenty-one please stay? The rest of you, thank you very much.'

True, Chloe had been skipping class in the weeks before audition to hang out with Dylan, who had been more of a real boyfriend than Bryce because he took her to the movies and they had gone all the way, and, true, she had fallen off pointe during an easy set of turns in the audition and been sluggish with her footwork, but the rejection had still come as a shock. Joan *knew* these people, had told them to look out for her. Maybe if she'd been Joan's daughter they would have taken her along with Harry. Maybe Elaine didn't like her and had told them not to take her. The next day she had told Joan the whole thing seemed really unfair, and Joan had been surprisingly bitchy and unsympathetic and said, 'You can't expect to slack off and still be good enough. Ballet isn't about you. Art isn't about you, what you want.'

'I know that!'

'Maybe I pushed you too hard. Maybe I misunderstood – I thought you were serious.'

'I am.'

'You're not, and if you don't see that, I don't know what the point is.'

'I *am*,' Chloe had protested, and for a few weeks, she was determined again. She started the morning exercises, trying to get stronger and sleeker, but her commitment is already dwindling.

'Don't you have class?' she asks Harry.

'Yeah, but, like I said, Mrs Ferguson asked me to find you.'

For the first time it occurs to her that something is wrong, and she slides out of Bryce's truck and walks with Harry across the parking lot. 'What's going on?' she asks.

'I don't know,' he says.

She knows he is lying. When Joan started coaching them in pas de deux, the promenade was the first thing they learned. Chloe stood on one pointe with her other leg back and bent in attitude, and she and Harry grasped hands, their index and middle fingers extended along the inside of each other's wrists, their arms making an S shape, and he walked in a circle, turning her. The step looks simple but is difficult. She can feel his pulse in his wrist. He becomes a part of her balance; they are one system of weights and counterweights. They might as well be standing on a tightrope together. *He's a glorified butler,* her mother likes to say. *No, he's doing a lot,* she replies, even though, when they moved on to lifts, Joan had told him not to grab but to support. *You're like a waiter lifting a tray,* she said.

As they come into the principal's office, two things happen at once: she sees her mother sitting in a chair, and Harry puts one arm around her waist and grasps her under the elbow with the other hand, holding her up.

Carefully, Harry closes his bedroom door and pads downstairs. He doesn't think Chloe is asleep, not really, but he feels he should honor her charade. She is under the covers in his bed, curled on her side, breathing through her mouth, her eyes closed. Outside, the streetlights have come on, but the kid next door is still dribbling a basketball on his driveway. The sound, echoing around the neighborhood, is crisp and sharp. The kid is bad at putting the ball in the basket, but he's good at dribbling and turning and faking and jumping, graceful and smooth. Harry has watched him before. Sometimes minutes pass without him even taking a shot at the basket while he and the orange ball orbit each other.

In the kitchen, Harry's father sits at the round yellow breakfast table they brought from the old house. A plate of cold spaghetti and three empty beer bottles are in front of him. His mother is outside smoking. A glass of something sits at her place but no food. When she sees Harry, she steps on her cigarette and comes in.

Harry takes his usual chair. 'She's pretending to be asleep.'

His mother turns her face away, staring out into the backyard. 'Poor thing,' she says for the thousandth time.

'I got hold of Sandy finally,' Harry's father tells him in a man-to-man tone. 'She knows Chloe's going to spend the night here.'

'Is she mad?'

'It was her sister I actually talked to. They're at a hotel. She said Sandy's pretty sedated.'

'Oh. Like with drugs?'

'I assume.'

At school, when Mrs Ferguson asked him to go find Chloe, she had told him her father had died and her mother had come to get her. He asked how Gary died, and Mrs Ferguson hesitated before saying he'd killed himself. *How?* Harry asked, knowing the question was impolite but wanting to know. *It's not very nice,* Mrs Ferguson said after another hesitation, *but you'll find out eventually. He used the exhaust from his car. He died in their garage.* Harry knows the Wheelocks' garage well, its oil-spotted cement floor and naked lightbulbs, the big oily, dusty springs that groan when the door lifts open. Gary has a workbench with a pegboard full of tools, and there is an old red leather barber's chair you can swivel around fast enough to make someone dizzy. Chloe's whole body had flowed out of his grasp like water after Sandy said, 'Daddy's dead. He killed himself.' She sat on the rough office carpet, gasping for air, and when Sandy crouched down beside her, she lunged forward and knocked her over, clawing at her face, not making a sound except shallow gasps. It had taken Harry and the principal and Mrs Ferguson to pull her off. Sandy had looked so amazed, so sad, lying there with three long scratches down her face, her skirt pushed up to show her plump knees.

'Sandy's sister didn't sound too happy with Chloe for reacting the way she did,' Harry's father goes on. 'I tried to tell her that Chloe doesn't really blame Sandy. This is a coping mechanism. It's cruel, but it might help her get through the next few days.'

'Days?' says his mother, still staring out the window.

'I don't know.'

She turns back. 'Why would she blame Sandy? Gary was so obviously depressed. He has been for years.'

Now they both look at Harry. Chloe, curled in his bed, had raged against her mother in an incantatory whisper, muttering and hissing that Sandy was *a crazy bitch who was never happy, and he knew she would never be happy, and so he was never happy,*

259

and it should have been her *instead*. 'I think she thinks Sandy was really hard on him,' Harry suggests.

His mother's high forehead creases. 'It's odd what children think about their parents.'

'How so?'

'I mean, I think Gary was pretty hard on everyone. I think he felt like he'd gotten a bum deal in life. But I still don't know how he could have done this to them. Harry, make sure *you* understand this wasn't Sandy's fault.'

Harry points to his mother's glass. 'What is that?'

'Vodka.'

'Just vodka?'

'Just vodka.'

'Can I taste it?'

'Okay.'

'Joan,' his father says, startled.

She pushes the glass toward Harry. 'It doesn't matter.' She watches as he sips the terrible liquid, and then she tells him, 'She can stay in your room, but you get your sleeping bag and sleep on the floor.'

'What, you think I think this is my big chance?'

'If things get out of control,' his father says, 'like if she seems like she's getting too sad, you come wake us up.'

'What's too sad?'

'Just if you feel out of your depth.'

After a while, Harry goes back upstairs. He pulls his sleeping bag from the hall closet and eases his bedroom door open. Chloe has not moved. The sleeping bag is green and pilled from use, and when he spreads it on the carpet, it looks drab and uninviting. He stands uncertainly, feeling like an intruder in his own room. It's much too early to sleep, but he doesn't want to turn on a light. He has homework, but probably he won't have to go to school tomorrow. He sits on the edge of the bed. 'Chloe,' he says, 'do you want something to eat?'

'No.'

'Can I do anything?'

'No.'

'Your mom's in a hotel with your aunt.'

'I don't care where she is.'

Carefully, slowly, not wanting to alarm her, he lifts the covers and slides in beside her, leaving space between their bodies but resting his hand on the saddle of her narrow side. He knows he should be ashamed, but he can't help hoping that eventually she might turn and let him embrace her, her flat chest and belly against his, closer than they are when they dance, or at least closer in a different way – still and quiet, not always moving. He is sure he knows her body better than anyone else, much better than the boys who get to touch it everywhere, probably better than she knows it. When she walks toward him in the halls at school, he prepares, without thinking, to lift her. He knows the exact weight of her body, the limits of its strength, the smell of its sweat. His fingers have left bruises on her inner thighs, her hips, her arms.

He is in high school. He is supposed to love no one, everyone. He is supposed to ferret out willing girls and take what he can get. For everyone else, Chloe seems to be one of those girls. He has heard she rides around in cars with older kids playing a game where you shed an article of clothing if you were the last one to touch the ceiling after spotting an out-of-state license plate. She doesn't even try. She just sits there and strips in silence until the boy driving the car kicks everyone else out. Other kids do these things – drink and party and hook up – for fun, but Chloe never seems to be having fun. Her rebellion is considered, serious. Rumor was she'd gone all the way with that guy Dylan, who girls said looked like Kurt Cobain even though he was always so buried under base-ball hats and hooded sweatshirts and tangled, bleached hair that he didn't really look like anything.

'Did you read the book you gave me for my birthday?' she asks. 'The ballet book?'

'No.'

'Do you know who Emma Livry is?'

'No.'

'She burned up.'

He rubs her back the way his mother rubs his when he is sick or sad, feeling the sharp edges of her shoulder blades through her tank top, the bumps of her spine, the flat wings of muscle. Her

262

grief makes her distant despite the nearness of her body; her vertebrae slide under his fingers like worry beads. He wants to wipe away some of her sadness. 'Chloe?' he whispers. 'You know I love you.'

She is very still. He wishes he could take the words back: they were worse than trying to cop a feel under the guise of offering comfort, even more selfish. Finally, her voice muffled by the blankets, she says, 'Do you remember when we rode the Matterhorn at Disneyland? That first time we went? When we stayed in the hotel?'

'Yeah, I think so.'

'Do you remember a guy coming on it with us?'

'A guy?'

'Yeah, a guy with a ponytail.'

'No. I thought it was just us and your mom. Why?'

'I have this memory of being on that ride and seeing a guy with his arms around my mom, and I don't even know if it's real. I've never been able to shake it. I think it's real because it always comes back.'

'You could ask her.'

'I couldn't.'

'I don't remember a guy.' He does, actually, vaguely remember a guy, a ponytail, a little girl, but he sees no good in saying so.

'That doesn't mean he wasn't there. We were so little.' She is quiet. Under his hand, her side rises and falls. It strikes him as strange that her skin should be so warm in the midst of her pain. She rolls onto her back, the streetlight touching her pointed chin, her small, sharp nose. With the movement, her tank top rides up and his hand slides thrillingly onto her bare, narrow stomach. He thinks she might shake him off, but she hardly seems to notice he's touching her. 'On one level,' she says suddenly, 'I know I love you too, because you're my oldest friend and because I just do, but on another, I basically can't imagine what you're talking about right now. I don't believe he's dead. But he doesn't seem alive either.' She draws a ragged breath. 'We love each other – so what? What difference does it make?'

The mixture of elation and humiliation her words cause is familiar. He settles into it, feeling at home.

JULY 1994 – NEW YORK CITY

The dancers doing the pas de deux are married Russians, not defectors, just dancers looking for opportunity. They danced in the Bolshoi until the collapse of the Soviet Union brought new freedom and also a collapse in their funding. The company was pleased to have them in New York, and so here they are. They own a chic apartment in SoHo, paid for by the advertisements she does for luxury watches and by the clinics he holds for young students and small companies, bringing some old-school Russian refinement to the more aggressive American style.

Their white costumes are lovely and simple against a plain backdrop lit pale blue, and their dance is one of Mr K's most famous short works, a storyless, virtuosic duet set to an otherwise forgotten scrap of Tchaikovsky. The performance is in honor of the second anniversary of Mr K's death, and the summer intensive students sit together at the back of the third balcony. Chloe would have liked to be next to Harry, but another girl, Cassandra-with-the-Turnout, snaked through at the last second and stole her seat.

Waiting at the airport for their flight to New York, Harry had turned to Chloe and said, 'Just so you know, things might be a little different at the intensive than at school.'

Paging through *Cosmopolitan*, Chloe said, 'What do you mean?'

'Socially.'

Affecting indifference, she'd let it go at that, although she already suspected something of the sort. After the previous summer, when Harry had gone to New York and she had gone to San Francisco, he'd come back with more confidence. His dancing was markedly better, so much better she'd begun to feel self-conscious being partnered by him, especially after he started offering tips he'd picked up from his *many* female friends in New York. *My friend Natasha says this. My friend Kirstin says that. This girl Jennifer I know switched to a shoe with a firmer shank, and she says it made a big difference.* His confidence provided armor at school, too. He wasn't popular by any means, but he didn't get picked on anymore, either. Not that she is up on such a high social perch. Since her father died, she has given up hooking up with boys; she has given up schoolwork; she has given up on her mother, who tends bar six nights a week and doesn't even seem sad; she has given up crying; she has given up pretty much everything except dancing, and she can't even seem to do that right.

'Chloe,' Joan has said more than once, 'not every

266

dance should seem angry.' But anger has made her turns blisteringly quick, her jumps unusually propulsive for a woman. She dances so hard and so long that blood seeps through the satin of her shoes. In San Francisco, she danced herself into a knee injury and had to sit out the end of the session, seething as she watched the others do their showcase performance. The Sugar Plum Fairy is no longer the role she dreams of but Manon, the fallen courtesan who dies in a swamp.

And it turns out that, indeed, Harry in New York is someone very different from Harry in California, although Chloe can't tell if he's actually changed or if it's all context. She is just another girl, but he is one of the boys, one of the straight boys, even one of the cutest straight boys, and a star. An aura of promise surrounds him. He is called on to demonstrate in class. He knows all the teachers and most of the students from last year, and he knows how the subway works and which bars don't card. He has been invited to take company class twice already, and the session is only half over. There are whispers about him, rumors he might be invited to apprentice with the company after the summer. The girls trample one another trying to get to him in partnering class.

Onstage, the pas de deux is in its last fervent coda. Chloe knows the dance well, has learned it with Harry, and she waits for her favorite moment, when the woman steps quickly toward the man and he catches her in a fish dive, one arm supporting her abdomen, the other around her extended leg so she is almost upside down, her body curved like a fish jumping out of the water. But these Russians have their own way of doing things, and instead of just stepping toward her husband, the woman leaps at him from what seems an impossible distance. He catches her inches from the stage. The audience gasps. Chloe's hands spring up from her lap in surprise. A minute later, another fish dive. The leap is headlong, reckless, full of faith.

As they leave the theater, Chloe elbows through a pack of girls until she is at Harry's side. Gripping his arm, she whispers, 'When we get back, let's sneak into a studio.'

'Why?' he says at a normal volume.

'Shh. Just for a little while.'

'I should really sleep.' Tomorrow Arslan Rusakov is coming to teach a special class for the boys, and Harry is nervous. More than nervous. Harry seems to believe that only Arslan's opinion matters, that all the other people already oohing and aahing over him don't count for anything. This man, this stranger, is the only one who can convince him he will be a dancer.

'We won't get in trouble. It'll help you sleep. I want to try something. Please.' Disliking herself for it, she puts a girly plaintiveness into her voice.

He is not as pliable to her will as he once was, but he still gives in. When they are back at the school – a short walk, just two blocks from the theater – they pass rapidly through the dorm to pick up their dance bags and descend to a small basement studio where no one has much reason to go. They turn their backs to each other and put on whatever they find in their bags. Chloe sees Harry hesitate, holding a dance belt, but he hurriedly tucks it in the bottom of his bag, staying in boxers instead. He changes his black pants and dress shirt for track pants and a T-shirt. Chloe wriggles into tights under the dress she wore to the gala and then lets the dress hang around her neck while she pulls on a leotard. In the mirror, she sees Harry peek at her bare chest.

'What do you want to do?' he asks when she is sitting on the floor, tying the ribbons of her shoes, and she sees the tension in his face and hears it in his voice. He still wants her, despite all his other options.

'The fish dive,' she says, 'like they did it.'

When Harry comes into the big studio, Arslan Rusakov is already there. He wears black drawstring pants, a black V-neck sweater, and white slippers, and he is standing and talking to Elaine, his weight on one leg, arms folded across his chest. His hair is darker than when he defected and shorter, cropped close to his head in an almost military style. The lines between his eyebrows and from his nose to the corners of his mouth have deepened with middle age, giving his face a sternness that is only slightly mitigated by the air of amusement that sits on him like a rakish hat.

Not that anything about his appearance could surprise Harry, who remains committed to his lifelong scrutiny of the man. Just two months back there was a ten-page spread in *Vanity Fair* of Arslan at his island property in Maine. He has a converted barn where he choreographs avant-garde works for his small eponymous troupe. One shot showed the dancers at the barre in summer, the barn doors open to a vista of rocks and ocean. The facing page showed him alone at the barre in winter, the windows framing falling snow. In fact, in some ways, this man, this stranger, is more familiar to Harry than people he knows well. Harry hasn't just looked at Arslan every day, the way he looks at his friends or teachers or parents: he has studied him, hungrily trying to mine some deeper under-standing from the glossy surfaces of photographs and video, to figure out what makes him the greatest ever. Yes, he's perfectly centered, as if his own private axis pins him to the earth. Yes, his positions are always precise, even when he's tran-sitioning from one step to the next. No, he never falls out of a turn or an attitude; he seems able to balance forever. Arslan has elevated an entire art form. Because of him, ballet will never be the same. Michael Jordan doesn't do it for Harry, but he understands the guys at school when they talk about him. If you can do something perfectly, you are a god.

A handful of other boys are already at the barre, stretching and warming up, all in regulation black tights, white T-shirts, and black slippers. They sneak covert glances at Arslan from between their knees or over their shoulders, trying to seem workmanlike and unconcerned. Arslan rarely teaches. They have been told they are exceptionally lucky. Harry catches Elaine's eye as he sets down his dance bag, and she gives him a cursory smile. Usually she has little to do with the summer students, but she was the one to arrange Arslan's visit.

Two weeks before, after it was announced that Arslan would teach them, Harry had gone for a walk in the evening to clear his head, working his way downtown, farther and farther, letting the people and the food cart smells and the traffic noise and the heavy, humid air wash over and around him. The sky was overcast. He was sweating. He wouldn't have been sure he would remember where Elaine's building was – he had only been there once, for dinner the previous summer, and knew it was in Tribeca but nothing more specific – but then he happened to pass a Japanese restaurant with window decorations he recognized and realized he was on the right track. Farther down the block, past a fancy shop with huge windows sparsely occupied by purses on pedestals, there was a heavy green door, and next to the brass button marked '4' was a label that said 'Kocheryozhkin/Costas.' He pushed it, and then pushed it again.

In a moment, a crackle, and then Elaine, sounding unfriendly: 'Yes?'

'It's Harry,' he yelled into the speaker. 'Can I come up?'

Another crackle, a buzz, and a loud click. Harry pushed open the door and climbed the stairs. Elaine was waiting for him on her landing. She was barefoot. An indigo cotton bathrobe printed with white horses hung open over her leggings and loose tank top. An elastic headband held back her hair. She looked young, much younger than Harry's mother, and he wondered what she did when she wasn't at the studio or the theater. What had she been doing before he rang her buzzer? It occurred to him that if he ever had that much privacy he might never stop masturbating, and the thought made Elaine's solitude titillating and mysterious.

'Harry?' she said.

He stopped just below her. 'Would you please not tell Arslan who my mom is?'

She held her door open. 'You must have been really worried to come all this way. Come in for a bit. And you don't have to scream into the intercom. You're like an old man sometimes, kid. Take your shoes off.'

Harry followed her to the kitchen, where she took two Diet Cokes from the refrigerator, and then into the cavernous living room. She pointed him to a sofa. Through an open door, he could see her bed, which had a wrought-iron headboard and pale green bedding and was unmade. He looked away, blushing. The apartment had white walls and wide, caramel-colored floorboards covered irregularly by thin rugs in geometric patterns. Sheer white curtains hung from iron rods, and potted ferns crowded the wide window-sills. A tall chrome sculpture stood in one corner, and on the walls there were a couple paintings of trees and one of a frozen river. 'I like these paintings,' Harry said.

Elaine gave a little snort of amusement. 'You said that when you came here last year. Do you remember?'

'I guess not.'

'I remember. I thought they were a funny thing for you to notice. They were Mr K's. I don't like them very much, honestly, but I got used to them. I don't know what I'd put up instead.' Elaine picked up two ferns and set them on the floor to make a perch for herself beside an open window, where she settled, one foot tucked under the other knee, and cracked her soda.

'Are they valuable?'

'Yes. And old.'

'Did Mr K miss Russia?'

'Yes, but I think he liked to play up being home-sick, too, for drama, as a reason to be melancholy. He grew up in the city, but he only bought paintings of the countryside. I think he missed the idea of all those trees and rivers more than he missed any real place. Our house upstate was his mini-Russia. I wish you could have known each other.'

'Does Arslan miss Russia?'

Elaine smiled, narrowing her green, feline eyes, and Harry felt a desire to be touched by her, though he couldn't gauge if he wanted something sexual or only a maternal caress. 'I don't know,' she said. 'Probably. He could go back now, though, to visit, and he hasn't. Harry, I haven't told him that he'll be meeting the son of an old flame. I had the same thought as you, that he should see you dance first.'

'I don't want any special treatment,' Harry said vehemently.

'Of *course* not,' Elaine agreed, matching his passion, gently mocking.

'I'm really nervous.' Something occurred to him, looking at Elaine sitting among her ferns, and he decided to be daring. 'Hey, do you have any weed?'

She laughed in a loud, startled way. 'Are you a pothead now? Is this my doing? I brought you to New York, and now you've got reefer madness?'

'No. No, I just thought it might make me less nervous.'

She looked out the window. Her hand dipped into her robe pocket but emerged empty. 'I'm not your dealer,' she said after a pause, 'but you can have a glass of wine if you want one. Do you?'

'No, that's okay. I'm not done with my Coke.' Feeling stupid, he took a long swig and sat forward on the couch, his hands wrapped around the can. A rumble came from outside. 'Was that thunder?' he asked.

'I think so.' The ferns rustled, and the sheer

curtains billowed gently. Elaine grasped the window frame and leaned back, angling her torso out so she could look up at the sky.

She tipped back upright. 'Definitely going to rain. Hey, what's wrong, kid?'

Harry said, 'What if Arslan doesn't like how I dance?'

'Kid. I know I told you not to be complacent, but don't worry so much.' Elaine stretched her arm outside, palm up to check for droplets. She studied her hand, wiped it on her robe. 'He's just a guy. He's a brilliant, brilliant dancer, but he's not God.'

'My dad calls him the Jedi master.'

'Maybe he's that.' It had begun to rain, and she dropped off the windowsill and replaced the ferns. Harry helped her close the windows. Rain tapped politely, asking to be let in, and then started hammering and hammering against the glass.

'I wish I weren't scared,' he said. 'I don't mind being *nervous*. I like that feeling when you're about to go onstage, and your stomach is full of that crazy whirring feeling, and your heart is beating really hard. I like that. I feel like a rocket about to launch, or something. But this . . . it's like it's *too* important. I just feel awful.'

'Listen,' Elaine said, coming to sit beside him on the couch and patting him on the knee. 'You have to use what you have. You have to take the fear and use it to wind yourself tighter and tighter, and then, at the right moment, you let go, and it'll drive you forward. When I'm afraid, I do extra barre work. It reminds me that everything I know is still there. Fear comes and goes. You'll learn how to deal with it. Okay? Look at me. Okay?'

'Okay,' Harry said.

Elaine took a small glass pipe from her pocket. 'One toke,' she said, 'and then I'm putting you in a taxi. This is me treating you like an adult, Harry. You're a dancer to me now, not Joan's kid. So be discreet, okay? I don't want all the intensive kids talking about how I got you high. I could get in trouble.'

'Okay,' he said.

But in the taxi back to the dorm, he wasn't sure if he felt anything, even though he had talked Elaine into a second hit, had held it as long as he could. The city, revived by the rain from its turgid afternoon, glimmered with menace. He wished, briefly, that he had never started dancing so that he wouldn't feel this way. He wished he could have stayed at Elaine's, tucked under a blanket on the couch. With a pang of guilt, he imagined her in the blue robe with nothing underneath, inviting him into the bedroom, the green bed. Then he thought of being in the green bed with Chloe, then with Natasha, the girl he'd slept with the previous summer and so was easiest to imagine. His thoughts began to accelerate. He shifted on the cracked pleather seat.

Once, in an acting class at school, the teacher had told them all to lie on the floor and push their thoughts away, breathe them out through their noses, squeeze them out through one arm and then the other, and then push what was left down through their bodies, their legs, out through their toes, until they were left with dark, empty space.

He closed his eyes. He pushed away Elaine, and Chloe, and Natasha. He pushed Arslan away, and then his mother, and he pushed away the taxi, the rain, the streets, the clouds, the sky. He became a void. For a moment, he held the entire universe at bay, and then he let go, let it all fall back into his body as though from a great height. He jolted in the seat and giggled. The cabbie looked at him in the mirror. Every cell in his body was alive. He told himself to remember this feeling, this certainty, this knowledge that his body was *his* and that it was the most important thing, all he needed. It was beautiful to be in this taxi, this city. He felt like a sparkling silver parachute had opened around him, delicate as the billow of a jellyfish.

Head down, Harry crosses to an empty spot on the barre. He has been following Elaine's advice to do extra barre work, focus on the fundamentals, and he tries to settle his mind, to open lines of communication with his body. Putting the arch of one foot on the barre, he stretches his hamstring, then bends the leg to get at his hip flexor. He is bruised and sore from where he and Chloe crashed to the floor together. They had not known how to turn their cautious schoolroom fish dive into an explosive, daredevil catch – there was a reason the audience had gasped in amazement at the Russians – and without anyone to teach them, Harry had seen little hope of figuring it out. But Chloe would not be deterred and leapt at him from across the room like a predatory cat. He needed to get his right arm wrapped around her torso and his left arm around her leg, but there wasn't enough time. She slipped through his hands like, truth be told, a fish and landed hard at his feet. 'Let's not do this right now,' he said after the first try, helping her up. 'It's too hard. We need someone to coach us.'

But she was already stalking away, back to where she started. 'Ready?' she said, and hurled herself at him again.

That time they both went down, his shoulder taking the brunt of their weight. 'Chloe!' he said, roughly pushing her off him. 'This is stupid. We're going to get injured.'

She stood up, her lip bleeding. 'Ready?'

It was on their eleventh or twelfth try that the miracle occurred, after they had stopped talking and their breathing and Chloe's footfalls were the only sounds in the studio. He knows he could not replicate the feat, not for a million dollars, but somehow that time when Chloe flew at him, eyes blazing in her tiny face, he had snatched her out of the air in a perfect fish dive, as good as the Russians', maybe better, maybe more ferocious and brilliant and dangerous. After, as it dawned on them that they had not gone down in a heap, his arms, which had locked around her of their own accord, refused to lift her up and set her back en pointe, and instead he held her, almost upside down, her arms open and relaxed, and they watched themselves in the mirror, winded and bloodied and full of disbelief. In fact, he never put her on her feet but instead lowered her to the floor of the dreary basement studio. Things had proceeded rapidly, unstoppably. He had peeled off her leotard and tights like one long snakeskin, exposing her imagined flesh, her familiar shape. The level of her surprise that he was not a virgin had offended him enough to make them both laugh, although he thought to himself that, really, she *shouldn't* have been surprised. The girls at the intensive were after him like a pack of baying hounds. He had tried to tell her before they even got on the airplane, but she was so used to him being a loser that she had been slow to grasp the new order. Even with an eleven o'clock curfew and morning class, the liberation of being in New York shocks him, like he has been woken from hypnosis.

Arslan warns them that he runs a fast barre. He hopes they are sufficiently warmed up. 'Prepare,' he says, and they begin with pliés. He walks around the room as they go through the battements, pausing occasionally to adjust someone or demonstrate a correct position, thumping his own legs with a closed fist for emphasis. Twice he stands behind Harry and watches in silence for long, unnerving seconds. When Harry does ronds de jambe en l'air, Arslan comes close and grips his thigh with both hands. 'Hold more still,' he says. 'Keep pulling up.' Harry studies himself in the mirror. He sees his arms and legs, the sweat on his face, Arslan moving toward the other side of the room, and, ghosted over all of it, he sees himself and Chloe as they had been on the floor. They were so used to watching themselves in the mirror, neither could keep from looking. In sex, as they never would in dance, they had looked perfect.

After only half an hour Arslan moves them to center floor. First tendus, then more adagio ending with diabolically slow grands battements en cloche, their legs swinging forward and up, then all the way back like bell clappers, their ankles wiggling and their feet curling to grip the floor as Arslan tells them to bring their heels forward, hold their turnout, not to sacrifice placement for extension, things they have heard a thousand times, nothing that will make *them* like *him*. 'And we're not leaning back, are we?' he says pleasantly while they tremble. 'No. Not even a little.' Then petit allégro and finally three at a time into grand allégro, which he makes tricky, giving them an enchaînement of turns and jumps so quick their legs must beat together at hummingbird speed. 'And *one*, pa pa pa,' Arslan shouts at them. 'And *up*, ba ba ba, and front, and stay. Good!' Kyle, Harry's roommate, loses control and crashes into Phillip, a catty, slinky boy who, when Harry was fresh off the plane last year, had administered his first kiss, declaring that he would be the one to decide if Harry was straight or not.

As he careers through the combination, Harry wobbles on the edge of control, struggling to roll down into his landings, to breathe, not to neglect his arms. When the music ends, he stands with Kyle and Phillip, chest heaving, waiting for what Arslan will say. He has danced better than the others – he always does – but he is never happy with his performances, and now he is crestfallen to the point of near panic. He hadn't been able to focus, to marshal all his nerves and all his cells the way he knew he could. Why had Chloe chosen last night of all nights? Why had she left him bruised and distracted? Did some part of her want him to fail?

Arslan has been leaning against the barre near the piano, and he pushes off and walks slowly toward Harry, stopping in front of him. He cocks his head, smiling with one corner of his mouth. To be looked at by someone he has spent so much time looking at is unsettling. 'Who are you?' Arslan says in his soft accent.

'Harry Bintz.'

'Not such a great name for a dancer. Do you know Fonteyn's real name?'

'No.'

'Peggy Hookham. Not the same, is it?'

Harry had not planned to tell him, but suddenly

he needs to. He can't bear to listen to what Arslan might say about his dancing, must head him off. 'You used to know my mother,' he blurts. 'Joan Bintz. Or, Joan Joyce, I guess back then.'

The amusement falls away, and the eyes sharpen, searching Harry's face. 'Joan? You are Joan's son?'

'Harry,' says Elaine from beside the piano, 'maybe this could wait until after class?'

Everyone is looking at him. He has never been so embarrassed. Of his dancing, of his lame ploy to distract the one person in the world whose opinion matters most to him by bringing up his *mother*.

'No, it's okay.' Arslan is smiling again, smirking really, but seriousness has pooled under his ironic façade. 'How is Joan Joyce? I have not seen her in many many years.'

'She's good. She teaches ballet.'

'Yes? She taught you?'

'Yes.'

'Well, Joan's son, what are you working on? What would you like to show me?'

Harry hesitates. Finally, reluctantly, he says, 'Ali the slave boy.' There are other variations he knows, but he is best at Ali. It is a role meant for a small dancer, a quick dancer, a good turner, all of which Harry is. But, really, the reason he has worked so hard on the dance (and the reason the studio is now heavy with silence) is that it was the show-piece that secured Arslan's gold medal at Varna. In the States, Arslan had sworn off Ali forever,

282

saying the Kirov had treated him like a performing monkey, he was tired of Ali, this was meant to be a free country, no?

'The slave boy,' Arslan repeats, dragging out the syllables. 'It is difficult one.'

Harry smiles. 'At least it's short.'

'That's what they say about me, too. Difficult is good. You are not an artist if you only do what is comfortable. You must always find new challenge, new pleasure. Okay, Joan's son. Let's see it.'

The other boys step back, pressing against the walls as though Harry is about to attempt a feat of dangerous sorcery. Some look envious, others smug, others nervous. Harry walks to the front corner. He wishes he were in costume, bare chested above blue and gold harem pants, gold cuffs on his biceps.

'Prepare,' says Arslan. In the moment of stillness that precedes the piano, as Harry steps into fifth position and pushes up into demi-pointe, he empties his mind, pushes it all away. He finds that he is, in fact, prepared. A buoyancy rushes in, driving away his fear.

Elaine watches Arslan watch Harry. She has tried to shield the boy from the most rhapsodic bits of the speculation surrounding him, the comparisons to Rusakov himself. And those whispers aren't out of nowhere. They have similar proportions, Harry and Arslan, similar lines, similar instincts. The biggest difference between them has to do with presence and attitude. Arslan onstage is impish and arrogant but can also be dark, even grotesque; Harry is sweet, earnest, noble, perhaps a tiny bit too effusive, but that can be ironed out. He is so young, too young to be complex. There is no telling how good he might become. As he whirls through the slave boy variation, he surprises even her. He is a gravity-defying dervish, full of bravura and brio, all the things male dancers need to be full of. He does the horribly difficult pirouettes where he pliés on his supporting leg without losing momentum. He does the turning jumps cleanly and with good height. His takeoff is naturally quick; he doesn't need a low plié to get off the ground, even in fifth position. And there is a welcome hint of interpretation beyond the technique, a hint of defiance from the slave. Even before she'd seen Harry dance, years ago, when Joan had pulled that gap-toothed school picture from her wallet, Elaine had recognized him as a potential asset for the company. Now is the time to secure him. When he is still young and his technique still pliable. She wants to protect him from injury, to choose the right moment to unveil him to the public.

The creases in Arslan's forehead deepen. Any flippancy is gone. Elaine wonders if he will be threatened. Or if he will try to take Harry for his own weird company, spirit him away to Maine and make him dance in a purple bodysuit to Arvo Pärt or Balinese gamelan music. Mostly she wonders if he will see what she wants him to see. The piano ends, and Harry is on one knee, his head back and his right arm lifted. Then he drops the arm and stands up. He makes a little bow to Arslan and another to the pianist.

Thoughtfully, Arslan drags one hand over his mouth and chin. 'This is good,' he says, 'but it can be better. How old are you, Harry Bintz?'

'Sixteen.'

'Sixteen.' Arslan paces a few steps one way and then back, hands on his hips. 'Okay. Your arms. On the last jump, organize them better. And use your breathing better. Take breath, and up, and breath, and up. Yes? In the middle . . . I don't know how to say exactly. I will show you. Here, when you come out of the turn and into lunge pose, you know, like this' – he comes into the middle of the floor and demonstrates, making a shape like the blade of a sundial: one leg bent at the knee, the other stretched behind him, an arm continuing that leg's ascending line to point at something high in the distance – 'then up into the arabesque, but not pushing with back foot. Push with other leg. The whole leg. Straight up. Pop. It must be straight. It is very exposed.'

Arslan pops into an arabesque en relevé. He is only in his early forties, but Elaine is still impressed by how undiminished he is. He could easily still dance the major roles if he wanted to. But he is interested in other things. 'And then,' Arslan says, 'you take these two steps, but you must already

285

be prepared to jump. You are preparing even before the arabesque.'

Two small steps, and he is in the air, spinning, knees bent like a genie's to lend an exotic flair, and then when he lands, he seems unable to resist the pull of the variation, of memory, and so he continues on, the piano chiming in, the room holding its breath because no one has seen this particular man do this particular dance in almost twenty years. Arslan does the final, uninhibited leap, legs flying, and then he is on one knee, and the boys are hooting and applauding. Arslan waves a hand, pleased but pretending to be abashed. His half-suppressed smile says the ongoing miracle of his artistry is nothing, only a trifle. 'Come,' he says to Harry, 'we do last bit again. Together.'

And they do the final chaînés again and the wild, flailing leap, ending side by side, each on one knee, arms upraised, looking into the mirror. Arslan is staring not at his own face but Harry's, and Elaine sees in their reflection that, as she had hoped and feared, he understands.

PART IV

JULY 1977 – NEW YORK CITY

Arslan opens his door wearing only shorts, blue with white piping. Joan asked him once if he had ever deigned to get dressed in his apartment in Leningrad, but he had not answered, not really, just said that there he wore a fur robe like Peter the Great. On this July night, which is miserably hot and offers little relief from a hotter day, his undress makes more sense than usual, doesn't seem so much like an affectation, a flaunting. He is sweating. It shines on his chest and trickles through his sideburns. 'Joan,' he says, out of breath. Wearily, he waves her inside, half fanning himself, half directing her.

'Why are you so hot?' she says. 'It's hot, but it's not that hot.'

He shrugs. A set of hand weights is out on the parquet floor beside a rubber mat. It would be such a simple thing for him to say he's been working out, but, true to form, he can't be bothered. She wants to think he gets a sadistic pleasure from frustrating her, but she doubts the impulse is that coherent. The door to his narrow strip of a balcony is open, and she goes to it, drawn as always by the black carpet of Central Park, beaded with round white streetlamps that illuminate irregular patches of green. The low skyline of grand apartment buildings to the east is blocky and yellow grey, and to the south are to the towers of Midtown, windows lit in an indecipherable code.

'I hate the city in the summer,' she says. 'It's like living inside a dog's mouth. I thought there would be a breeze up here, but there isn't. You should send a letter to your co-op board demanding breezes.'

'Did you come to talk about weather?' He flops into a black leather Eames chair and regards her. The apartment is all black and white and glass except for a couch in harlot red. The walls are mirrored. She resists looking at herself but then gives in, wondering what he's seeing, if he can tell she's drunk. She has been across the park at Campbell Hodges's new girlfriend's apartment, another sky palace, though one with more conventional décor: heavy drapes, floral rugs, chintz sofas. In the mirror she looks flushed and messy but also, she thinks, fetching, silhouetted as she is against the glowing city night. Her sundress is pretty, though not glamorous like the tight and shiny dresses Ludmilla wears with her ridiculous head scarves. The Disco Babushka, Campbell calls her.

'No,' she says. 'I came to ask you something.'

He rolls his eyes but purses his lips in a half smile. When he is languid and sardonic like this, she knows he is horny. His mood gratifies her, is contagious even though she had planned to be frosty and remote. She puts a hand on her hip and leans against the doorframe. Campbell had invited her to lunch to celebrate his girlfriend being out of town, and together they had eaten shrimp cocktail on the absent woman's roof terrace and sampled her excellent wine collection and then, into the evening, her assortment of ports and sherries. Sometime around sunset, Campbell had told Joan that, according to the all-knowing Mr K, Arslan and Ludmilla are secretly engaged.

'Always questions,' Arslan says. 'What can the question today be? Don't tell me. I will guess.'

'Don't guess.'

'You want to know whether I like your dress. Yes?'

'No. Arslan, I'm serious.'

'I am serious, too. I like this dress. I would like to see behind of it. Turn around, please.'

Joan steps away from the door and turns in a circle. His attention, thrilling and humiliating, compels her.

'Yes, I like other side, too. There. I have answered. Good-bye.' He smirks the infuriating smirk she both loves and despises. 'You're still here? There are more questions? Or maybe you have something else you want to show me?'

Joan wants to go to him. She grasps the doorframe with one hand. 'Are you going to marry Ludmilla?'

He pauses, nods. 'Yes.'

'Why?'

The smirk again. 'Why not?'

'That's not an answer. Why don't you ever answer me?' She had thought she would cry. Campbell had been sitting on the floor while she sat on a ruffle-skirted sofa, his head lolling against her knee and his fingers caressing her ankle. She had moved her foot away, and he had said, 'If I know something, do you want me to tell you?'

'It sounds like I won't like it.'

'No.'

'Okay.'

'Okay, tell you?'

'Yes.'

He had poured her more sherry, and he had told her about the engagement, and she had cried, surprising herself with the violence of her short, spluttering sobs. 'Darling,' he'd said, immediately contrite, 'I'm sorry. I always forget this thing with Arslan was real. I do that with other people's dramas. I think it's all a game and act like an ass just to stir the shit. I didn't mean to spoil our day.' Later, still guilty, he had insisted on paying for her taxi. She told him she was going straight home.

She had cried again in the taxi, but now her eyes are dry and her voice steady. This unexpected reprieve from tears steels her to her mission.

'I deserve an answer,' she tells Arslan.

He rests a bare foot on his Lucite coffee table and swivels from side to side. The chair squeaks.

'You want to know about Ludmilla or you want to know about you?'

'This isn't about me.'

'Is always about you, Joan.'

'That's rich.'

The fine head tilts, trying to catch her meaning; the black eyes belong to a hawk or eagle. 'Rich?'

His English has improved dramatically in two years, but his accent is still strong, and she likes tripping him up when she can. 'It's ironic you would call *me* the selfish one.'

Ironic he knows. *Ironic* is one of his favorite words. 'It's i-ron-ic,' he says, giving each syllable its own little moment in the sun, 'you don't understand. Ludmilla is very good dancer. I want to be with very good dancer. You want to be with me because I am very good dancer. Why else? Because we make good conversation? Because we are happy all the time? Because we are so good in bed together? Even when you wear your little stockings and say your little dirty things, we are still – it is . . . I can see is work. Like with dance. Is not natural between us.'

She ignores the pain of this, saving it for later, pressing forward. 'Do you even love her?'

He considers. 'Yes,' he says, fingers flicking the question away. 'But love and marriage are not same. Only American schoolgirls think this.'

'I feel sorry for Ludmilla. She's in for a bad time.'

He slides farther down into his chair, the leather creaking, his knees moving farther apart and his head lolling back, black eyes watching her. The posture seems almost submissive, but she knows better. Pretending to smother a yawn, he asks, 'Why did you come here?'

'I don't know. No, I know, but it already seems stupid and pointless. I wanted to understand.'

'What is to understand?'

'I wanted to know why you chose me. We didn't even know each other. What did you think I was? Why did you write me those letters? Why did you want me to come to Toronto?'

He looks at her pensively, with some annoyance, and the lights go out. They both exclaim, not complete words, just sounds of reflexive surprise, his an odd, foreign bark.

The chair creaks, and he brushes past her to the balcony that is little more than a shallow ledge with a railing. She follows. Beyond the railing: nothing, only darkness. She senses the park as a lower, softer sort of darkness, and the buildings on its far side as solid, squared-off hunks of it, barely perceptible against the sky. 'What is this?' he says.

'A blackout.'

A siren is already wailing, the sound floating away like the call of a night bird. Maybe it is only the heaviness of the heat, but the darkness feels close, stifling. Joan wants to pull away from it, but there is nowhere to go. Above and below, she hears doors opening, people stepping murmuring onto their balconies, all looking out into the same vanished city as Joan and Arslan. Her question seems irrelevant in the dark, or maybe it is that the answer has to do with irrelevance. She could have been anyone. Most theaters have a red light in the back for the dancers to spot off of as they turn. She had been that light for Arslan as he considered defecting, a fixed point to look at, to steer by, unremarkable except in its use.

When Joan reads in the newspaper how thousands of people were arrested for looting and arson and running wild in the dark streets, how people ripped the grates off storefronts with chains attached to the bumpers of cars and smashed the windows and took everything inside, how muggers mugged one another, stole what had already been stolen, she is not surprised. Darkness is permission, if you want it to be. Arslan had pressed his hand flat against her hip, not pushing her away but seeming to steady himself. They had turned together and gone inside, retreating from the night and also burrowing farther into it. There was nothing else to do.

When Harry is a newborn and Joan happens across a newspaper article about the spike in births nine months after the blackout, she is not surprised that others had felt the same recklessness, the same constricting, driving momentum. Within her body, in the deeper darkness there, she had committed a theft.

DECEMBER 1995 – SOUTHERN CALIFORNIA

Joan whips around the corner into the kitchen, surprising Jacob as he loiters against the island, flipping through a catalog of travel accessories and picking at a bowl of pistachios. 'Have you seen Harry?' she asks. She is wearing a ladylike dress, navy blue with a pleated skirt and a narrow brown belt around her narrow waist, sheer nylons, and brown high heels. She loves Christmas, loves *The Nutcracker,* which they are about to go see for the zillionth time, but refuses, as a policy, to ever wear anything holiday themed. He tried to coax her into a red blouse for his school party, but she had worn black, which had seemed unnecessarily contrary.

'Narcissus?' Jacob replies. 'I think he's out by the reflecting pool.'

'We're going to be late.'

He follows her out into the living room. 'You don't have to tell me. I'm ready. Do you think this year they'll change it up? The whole thing will end before intermission with the rats tearing down the tree and eating Drosselmeyer?'

Joan stands at the base of the stairs and shouts up them, 'Harry!'

Jacob flops into an armchair. As he often does around his son these days, Jacob feels equally amused and annoyed. He has become increasingly convinced that there is something autoerotic about ballet, with all that mirror gazing and body perfecting, and lately Harry has done nothing to dissuade him. Ballet, like other pursuits that require immense determination and reward showmanship, seems to foster hubris. But maybe all art fosters hubris. Joan's angle is that a little confidence (she will not say Harry is arrogant, even though Jacob can see she is bothered by his arrogance) will sustain a dancer through hard times. It provides a little support, a little cushion.

With Harry off in New York, ballet is mentioned less frequently in the house – the house is, in general, much quieter – but ballet has also stolen his son, replaced college with a GED (*Just for now*, Joan says), and created a thousand awkward variations on conversations with new acquaintances in which people learn Harry is a dancer and then, thinking they're being subtle, try to find out if he's gay.

You're boring, Jacob wants to tell them. His ambivalence is private, nothing compared to his pride in Harry. *Your thoughts and your sneaky little questions are boring. You could never do what my son does, and he could do so many other things, too, if he wanted.*

Joan stands with her heels together and the toes of her brown pumps sticking out to the sides. She lifts her chest toward the silent upstairs. 'HARRY!'

Harry slides down the banister in one of his dandyish new outfits: shiny, stiff-looking jeans, black Converse sneakers, a tight tweed vest over a white shirt and narrow black tie. He wears a tweed cap that Jacob thinks makes him look like a newsboy, but Harry has already informed him that he, Jacob, knows nothing (nothing!) about fashion outside of (smirk) principal chic. *Excuse me,* Harry says, *for not wearing a tie that looks like a big crayon.*

Harry lands on one foot and spins around to grab Joan, dipping her backward like Fred Astaire. Unfazed, she accepts the manhandling and bends gracefully over his arm. Jacob thinks of the photo of her with Rusakov, arched in the same way, her throat exposed. He fingers his necktie, which is red with tiny green Christmas trees and which he had chosen in defiance of the other Bintzes. They think he's uncool. They think his job is dull and that his friendly ties and collection of knock-knock jokes, which are meant to put kids at ease, are evidence of a lack of seriousness, sophistication, and discrimination. Sometimes he has an urge to remind them that he is the only one with a college degree, let alone a doctorate, that he knows things they don't, but he resists. He doesn't want to talk himself into thinking less of his family.

'All right,' Harry says, righting his mother. 'Let's go. Yippee. Bring on the technical fireworks.'

Jacob pushes himself out of the armchair. 'Looking sharp, Harry,' he says. 'Chloe will be wowed.'

'Oh,' Harry says, shifty, squaring his tie in a mirror on the wall. 'Yeah. That reminds me. Chloe and I are taking a break.'

'Harry,' Joan says, arrested in the act of opening the front door. 'You broke up? Since when?'

'This afternoon. It's not totally final yet. I just told her I thought I needed some time.'

'You broke up with her right before a performance?'

'I wasn't planning it. Things are a little unclear right now.'

'Unclear? After all these years?' Jacob says.

'One year. Nice tie, by the way.'

Jacob ignores the tie comment and presses his hands to his heart the way ballet princes do. 'But the longing! All those years of longing!'

'People change, Dad,' Harry says in the superior tone he has brought back as a souvenir from New York. 'People change.'

Except for a few stray remarks on the opening of new movie theaters next to the freeway and the closure of Long King Chinese Palace where they ate every Friday when Harry was little, they are quiet for most of the drive. Only when Jacob is hunting for a parking place at the theater does Joan twist to face Harry in the backseat. 'How do people change?'

His answer chills her, and the chill lingers as they present their tickets to the white-haired ushers, find their seats, flip through their programs until the lights go down. It stays with her through the overture and the party scene and Drosselmeyer's gift of the Nutcracker to Clara. This production, put on in a large, professional auditorium, follows a version that uses children for Clara and the Nutcracker. Chloe is the Sugar Plum Fairy and will not appear until the second act. Joan has seen her perform twice. She is doing well in the role. There are still traces of a strange fury in her (or hostility, or something – Joan has never satis-factorily been able to name the disquieting vibe Chloe's dancing took on after Gary's death), but Joan thinks only a practiced eye would notice. Indeed, the practiced eyes of Chloe's auditioners, while beguiled by her sharp, beautiful face and crisp technique, had not missed her misplaced ferocity. 'Your little Valkyrie protégée,' one of them had called Joan to ask, 'can she tone it down? Be sweet and pretty? To be totally honest, we don't have a lot of good options, and we like the idea of having someone so young and fresh and local, not to make her sound like produce. We thought we could pitch newspaper stories about her as a rising star. It's a shame your son isn't available, too.'

'Chloe will be wonderful,' Joan had promised, liking that word: protégée. She had not expected to find much in teaching besides a little extra income, something to do, a way to keep fit. She had not anticipated she might be able to re-create, even improve, her young self through the body of another. Chloe's unusual stage presence worries her – things would be simpler, careerwise, if she were just sweet and pretty – but sometimes Joan envies her strangeness. At least Chloe is different. Her imperfection makes her interesting.

But Joan was right about Chloe as the Sugar Plum Fairy – everyone is happy. Chloe is excellent in performance and terrible at auditions, no matter how many times Joan has tried to convince her that the two are not so different. Auditions bore her, and she resents the necessity of proving herself. She had only gotten into the summer intensive in New York because Joan had pitched her hard to Elaine, but then she had made a good impression and been asked back. She is very good, really – far better than what Harry had called her in the parking lot: mediocre. He used to worship Chloe, but now he thinks that, as a dancer, she's mediocre at best. And that, he told Joan, was how he'd changed.

'I'm not sure I respect her as a dancer,' Harry had gone on, 'and that's starting to get to me. You know, honestly, I'm not sure we have the best training system in place in this country. It seems unfair to get kids started down a road when they're doomed to failure. Like in Europe lots of schools take X-rays of kids' legs to see what kind of turnout they'll be able to get before they let them in. That's not the worst idea. Right? Like it's a little harsh, but it makes sense. I don't mean to be a jerk, but

Chloe's hips aren't ideal for a dancer. And the U.S. is so decentralized. I probably shouldn't have languished here for as long as I did.'

'*Da,* Comrade Bintz,' Jacob said. He mostly speaks to Harry in jokes these days. '*Da,* we take leetle children from families, X-ray legs, send to People's Ballet Factory.'

Joan had been tongue-tied. 'Chloe's not mediocre,' she finally managed to say. 'She's very good.'

'Maybe for the corps somewhere.'

'There's nothing wrong with the corps. The corps does the most work for the least glory. You'll be in the corps.'

'I don't think so.'

'You don't think what?'

'I think they're planning to bring me into the company as a soloist. Just to make more of a splash. Otherwise I'd already be in the corps.'

'Everyone has to go through the corps,' said Joan. 'It's part of the process.'

'Arslan didn't.'

'Obviously you don't have to if you're coming from another company. But, Harry, you should want to earn your place. If you're not in the corps, you'll never have the same understanding of how ballets work. And I'm sorry you had to *languish* here for so long. That must have been terrible for you.'

'I'm just saying.'

Jacob parked the car and shut off the engine. 'Also,' he said into the silence, 'you might be barking up the wrong tree as far as what makes a good relationship. What if the best dancer in the world is a big bitch?'

Joan said, 'Which she probably would be.'

'So then,' Jacob went on, 'things are great when she's dancing and miserable the rest of the time. What people can *do* isn't everything.'

'I know,' Harry says. 'You've been saying that my whole life. I know. I feel like you're trying to brainwash me with these mushy *Sesame Street* values that aren't actually helpful once things get messy. Why's everyone on my back? Dad, why are you all high on Chloe now? You used to want me to forget about her.'

'No, I didn't.' Jacob sounded wounded. 'I like Chloe.'

'I'm seventeen,' Harry said with exaggerated patience. 'I live three thousand miles away. I just think I'd like to date other people, that's all. I don't think that makes me a monster.'

Jacob opened his door. 'I see your point,' he said quietly. 'Do what you want.'

Joan has to admit she sees Harry's point, too, even though the chill will not leave her, not when the Christmas tree grows up taller and taller, or when the soldiers defeat the rats, or when the snowflakes dance their waltz, or when little Clara and the Nutcracker Prince fly in their sleigh to the Land of Sweets. She remembers how Arslan had looked at her during the brief time when he had tried to dance with her, his disappointment.

303

Usually she feels at home in the fanciful worlds of sets and costumes, music and colored lights, but tonight the familiar dances seem bawdy and farcical and accusatory. *Didn't you want this?* the snowflakes ask as they pirouette. *Didn't you make this?* Joan shivers. Jacob turns to look at her, blue light playing across his glasses, the same wire-rimmed glasses he's always had, the same face she has known since she was a child, just older. He puts an arm around her and rubs her shoulder, but she only feels colder. When the lights come up for intermission, she turns around and spots Sandy Wheelock two rows back, snuggled up next to a bald man in a golf sweater. Then she flushes with nervous heat.

'Who is that?' Tony asks.
  'Who?' says Sandy.
  'The woman who just waved at you.'
  'Chloe's ballet teacher.'
  'Should we go say hi?'
  'Not if we can avoid it.'
  'Oh-ho,' says Tony. 'Bad blood.'
  'Not really. Do you have anyone who's all tied up in the worst parts of your life? And you just wish they didn't exist?'
  'Sounds rough. Why don't you get Chloe a new teacher?'
  'Chloe does what she wants. They have this whole' – she swivels a hand in a circle – 'thing. I'm not involved. And her son has been in love

304

with Chloe forever. Darn, they're coming over. Anyway, he and Chloe are dating. He dances. Actually, he's dancing in New York now.'

As they make their way down the row in front of Sandy and Tony, the Bintzes look more uncomfortable than Sandy thinks they need to, strictly speaking. Chloe hasn't even been onstage yet, and even if she makes some horrible ballet mistake, Sandy will not be bothered. After Gary died, she stopped thinking about ballet or watching Chloe's classes or following her progress or doing anything except clapping at her performances, and for a while she had not even done that. Sandy had mourned her husband and forgiven him – for inflicting his death on them and also for the dark years that had come before – but she was not sure she would ever fully forgive Chloe for attacking her in the school office. You had to forgive your own child, especially for something she did out of panicked grief and some nonsensical, backward teenage idea of blame. But pieces of that awful day have stuck in them like shrapnel, healed over but still hard and alien and painful when you least expected. When Chloe dances, Sandy can't help but think of Gary.

And right now she would prefer not to think of Gary or death or anything but all the usual Christmas schlock: eggnog and candy canes and even the damn *Nutcracker*. Though she would never say so out loud – there are restrictions and responsibilities that come with being tragically

305

widowed – she is happier than she has been since Chloe was a baby. She took up cycling as a way to remember Gary and has gotten in pretty good shape. She tends bar at a grill near the beach, and she's in the late stages of planning to open a hole-in-the-wall strip mall pub all her own. She's good at bartending. She has fun with it. Tony was one of her regulars, and then he asked her out. It happens all the time.

Joan and Jacob arrive in front of them. Sandy introduces Tony.

'Chloe's pas de deux is a treat,' Joan says, earnest as a preschool teacher. 'She's very good.'

Sandy nods, struck by how this woman seems like more of a stranger now than when she first saw her doing ballet on her patio. It had been so suspenseful, having a little kid, wondering how she'd turn out, competing with other parents over hypothetical futures. Joan probably thinks she won, but Sandy doesn't care. Chloe is what she is.

'Yeah, she gets the best music,' Sandy says. 'The tingly-wingly fairy dust stuff.'

Jacob keeps squeezing Joan against his side like he's sheltering her from the wind. 'I remember when she was the baby rat,' he says.

Sandy smiles politely, thinking about the rat year, how she had watched every rehearsal, every goddamn, endless, mind-numbing, amateur-hour rehearsal, and how she had been such a hideous stage mom about it too, leaning forward in her seat whenever Chloe did her little solo, almost doing the steps herself. Chloe had been right when, driving home from Gary's funeral, she accused Sandy of always needing everything to be perfect, of making Gary feel inadequate. But she had the cause and effect inside out. Gary hadn't killed himself because of Sandy. He killed himself because nothing was ever perfect. 'Is Harry here?' she asks.

Jacob waves vaguely over his shoulder. 'He saw someone he knew. You try to raise a loner, and you end up with Mr Popularity.'

'Chloe's so proud of him,' Sandy says. 'She's always talking about what an amazing dancer he is and how famous he's going to be. Even though I'm sure she'd like to be in New York, too.' They stare at her like she's a space alien. Do they think she's suggesting that Chloe should have been made an apprentice, too? Probably. They're probably thinking about how to let her down easy. *You know, Sandy, Chloe just isn't as godlike as Harry. What's important is that Chloe find what she's good at, which is nothing.*

'It's been tough on the kids,' Jacob says slowly and carefully, talking down to her as usual, 'being separated. They're just kids. It's easy to forget because of the dancing, but they're kids.'

'Yeah,' Sandy says, breezy. 'They're cute. Chloe crossed off the days on her calendar until Harry got back. I couldn't even get her to open the little doors in the Advent calendar. She only cared about the advent of Harry.'

Joan puts a bony hand to her forehead. Joan is always miming things. Her theatrical flourishes drove Sandy nuts back when they were friends. 'I'm sorry,' she says. 'I'm not feeling so well.'

'Too many Christmas cookies?' posits Tony, and now he's the alien to be stared at, bless his heart. Joan's probably never had a Christmas cookie in her life.

The lights dim and come back up. 'It's about to start again, anyway,' Jacob says. 'We should go sit down.'

Chloe, waiting in the wings before her pas de deux, trembles so much that her tutu flutters. She is not exactly nervous, nor does she have the bold, predatory feeling she usually gets when she is about to attack the stage. The sensation is vague but intense – she supposes it's shock over the breakup, tension and disbelief. She has not cried yet. Since her conversation with Harry, she has felt painfully alert, both vulnerable and dangerous, as though she were wrapped in explosives. She flexes one ankle and then the other, tests her pointes against the floor. 'Are you okay?' her cavalier whispers. He is Danish, blond, poised, gay, solicitous, a soloist at the San Francisco Ballet poached for the Christmas season by the well-funded suburbanites behind this production.

'I'm fine. Why?'

'You're fidgeting.'

'Sorry.' She folds her arms across her chest.

Flowers are waltzing onstage. The music whirls. Clara and her Nutcracker sit on a throne at stage left behind a table piled with prop sweets. They are small, cute, assured. As a kid, she would have liked that: to sit onstage for the whole second act in a pretty white dress. She would not have wanted Harry to be the Nutcracker, though, because she wouldn't have wanted people to look at them sitting together and think she had anything to do with him. Funny. All she wants now is to be seen with Harry, but she can still remember exactly how it felt to always want to get rid of him.

Her cavalier is not reassured. 'Can I help?'

'No.'

The waltz accelerates, building to its finale. Chloe shakes out her legs, rolls her neck. Her cavalier extends his arm forward, and she places her hand over his. She takes a breath, pulls up, and walks smiling out onto the stage before the flowers' applause has ended. When there is quiet, a harp begins scales, up and down on top of slow pizzicato strings. Swooning cellos. Woodwinds come in from above, sailing down to join the strings; brass follows behind, taking long, stately strides, warm and wide but bittersweet. The music is like a room slowly filling with people, but not a party. Maybe a wake. Chloe dances but is barely aware of what she is doing or of her cavalier's hands gripping hers, his hands skimming her waist as she turns. She is not thinking about the Sugar Plum Fairy, about sweetness and lightness, about smiling. Harry would not even explain himself, would not do her the favor of being honest so she might hate him. He just said he needed space, time, a break, the experience of not owing anyone anything, and then sullenly, he endured her reminders that *he* was the one who had always loved *her*, her entreaties, and then her accusations of vanity and conceit, of overestimating his own talent, of setting himself up to be lonely and miserable.

'Take it easy, Chloe,' her cavalier whispers through his smile. Her wrists shake. The audience must be able to see her tremors on the balances. Her cavalier's arm vibrates as though she is sending electricity through him. Dire trombones plow downward, are caught and buoyed up by the relentlessly romantic strings. Her body is rigid, but at least that makes her easy to lift. He practically tosses her up into the air. From her new height, she glowers at the audience, at Harry in it. She is not a fairy; she is an avenging angel. The counterfeit sparkling, smiling prettiness she has worked so hard to stick to herself like sugar has been swept away. She knows what she is doing is wrong for her role, and she feels sorry for her cavalier, but she is burning. The consuming pain she felt after her father died had burrowed into her center and still smolders there like a coal fire. In New York, the teachers told her to try not to feel, to just work with the music, or to think of the movements as cold, crisp tasks her body must carry out. But she can't. Feeling is what allows her to dance at all.

A last long balance while her cavalier rotates her on one pointe and then dips her forward so her fingers almost touch the stage, her extended leg going vertical. Then she is up again and he spins her quickly between his hands. Rolling kettle-drums, bows grinding into strings. She throws herself too hard into the final fish dive, remembering Harry, the basement studio in New York, the sight of them in the mirror, and her cavalier, hissing through his teeth, almost drops her but doesn't, sets her upright. Grim faced, she gives a sharp bob of a curtsy and stalks into the wings to wait out her cavalier's variation, a tarantella. He is a very nice dancer, tall with clean lines, but her eyes won't focus on him. She stares blankly at a spot on the stage, oblivious as he passes in and out of her field of vision. Ordinarily, she would be blotting her face with tissues, wiping her chest and neck with a towel, perhaps paying a visit to the rosin box, preparing for her own variation, but now she stands, sweating, arms loose at her sides, and thinks of nothing.

Too soon, her cavalier flies offstage and, not even trying to smile, she abandons the shelter of the wings. Stage right, the back corner, her legs in croisé derrière à terre, arms low in a graceful hoop. In the instant before the music begins, she confronts the darkness, feeling Harry in it somewhere. Having to dance for him is humiliating, especially this saccharine, dainty variation that is so wrong for her. She had longed to be the Sugar Plum Fairy when she was a rat, and now she longs to be a rat. Plucked strings. She moves en pointe along the diagonal. Tiny steps, unsatisfying, nibbling at the stage. The celesta comes in, an instrument that looks like a toy piano and sounds like bells. The music is tinkling, tentative, a mouse creeping through a sleeping house. She is the rat again. A bassoon slides down a dark staircase. Piqué turns – she is getting ahead of the music. Her ankles shake. She thought she could let go of the prettiness, the carefulness, that what was left would feel instinctive, easy, but she has become unused to dancing with freedom. Her elbows and knees are sharp. It is all en pointe, mincing little steps and hops, her feet always moving, poking and prodding the stage, her arches cramping. Chaînés turns: chains indeed. She feels like she's dragging them behind her. She stumbles badly, landing flat on her feet, putting out her arms for balance. Other dancers have gathered in the wings, staring. A pulse of strings, then scrubbing cellos, then another pulse. 'What do I do?' she had asked Harry. 'What do I do now? Everything is ruined. You've ruined everything.'

'That you think that,' he'd said, 'is exactly the problem.'

She can see there were moments when she asked too much of him, but she can't be reasonable when she feels her life falling away in big, loose chunks.

She doesn't know what will be left. The chiming comes faster and faster. The rat is trapped, scurrying and spinning from one side of the stage to the other. She turns and turns. The stage tilts. The staring eyes in the wings whirl diagonally past. She is dizzy, but she does not fall. There is still the coda to do.

MAY 1998 – NEW YORK CITY

The city has changed. The absence of grit, the safety of it hits Joan like a betrayal, as though it had purposely waited until she left to undergo a course of self-improvement and is now putting on airs. She takes Jacob to see where she had lived with Elaine, and although the building doesn't look much different, the block is now quiet and leafy and prosperous: innocent in its elegance, as though it had never been perched on the edge of blight. The subway cars are mostly silver, not funky and screaming with spray paint. Times Square is full of scaffolding and construction fences, illuminated by huge video screens and billboards of beautiful people, crowded with tourists, purged of massage parlors and peep shows.

She has not been back since before Harry was born, and now she and Jacob have come to see Harry make his debut as a soloist. Joan was right: he had been in the corps, but not for long and not without fanfare and plum solos. This would be a joyful occasion, but Arslan will be at the performance. Knowing he is in the city, Joan sees him hurrying down sidewalks, passing through subway turnstiles, sitting in restaurant windows, sailing by in taxis. She had tried to think of a way she could get out of seeing him, but making too much of an effort to avoid a reunion would be undignified, would imply she was still hung up on him. He is a mentor to Harry, and she knows Harry wants her to see them together, to witness how he has forged a bond with his idol. She wonders if Arslan has guessed, when he will guess. Elaine must know. Joan has never said aloud to anyone that Arslan is Harry's biological father. She is not sure she could form the words.

Getting ready in the hotel room, she is jumpy, breaks a water glass in the sink. Jacob removes her from the bathroom so he can clean up the glass, kisses the nape of her neck. She brushes him away, and he is frosty until they get to the theater and he sees a poster with Harry on it and wants her to take his picture next to it. She does, and he insists on taking one of her.

'Sorry,' she says while he fusses with the camera. 'I'm sorry I was a jerk.'

'Hey,' he says, 'it's fine with me, but that water glass still seemed pretty broken up about it.'

Then they are in their seats, and the back of Arslan's head, his real head, the head she has held between her hands, is six rows up, tilting sometimes to catch whatever the woman beside him is saying, and then he is a precisely identified bit of darkness that never fades into the rest of the darkness as the gala begins, never stops itching at her attention, even when Harry is onstage. His performance is, objectively, extraordinary. Elaine has him doing the Bluebird pas de deux with a very good young Cuban ballerina, a real-life defector, and the two are well suited, classic, technically brilliant, romantic without sacrificing refinement. But Joan is used to seeing Harry dance. She is not used to being in the same enclosed space, however spacious and dark, as Arslan Rusakov.

Had she set out to create a dancer? If that had been her purpose, she thinks she would feel more elation at the sight of the stunning young performer now alone onstage, flying through his variation. She bore him, raised him, taught him, released him to New York. She masterminded every step of the process that made him what he is, but a part of her still pretends she has been passively swept up by something larger than herself. Harry's dancing is beautiful but frightening. The better he is, the more conspicuous he is, and the more likely someone is to do the math, ask questions, notice the resemblance, which now, as Harry becomes a man, seems glaringly obvious. When she was that silly girl in Arslan's bed, she might have thought it would be romantic for their affair to produce another dancer. She had thought then that she had so much to lose – her place in the corps, the shape of her body – but really she had possessed nothing, no one.

Afterward she must lean on Jacob's arm as they make their way out to the white tent erected in the plaza. Mercifully, he seems to have decided against having a big conversation about Arslan. He talks about how incredible Harry was. Joan's arms and chest ache from the force and speed of her blood. In the tent they are greeted by an ice sculpture of a ballerina and a phalanx of waiters with trays of champagne flutes and morsels on toothpicks and a maze of white tables and twiggy chairs. They wind their way to the bar in the back, where Joan braces herself against a table and gulps from a vodka tonic. Several hundred tuxedos and gowns filter in and settle around the bar, chattering and pawing at one another with convivial menace. Chloe should be among them somewhere, but Joan can't quite remember to look for her. 'Let's move out of the way,' Jacob says as the crowd grows dense, and he pulls her along through a tunnel of bodies that dead-ends, abruptly, inevitably, at Arslan.

'Joan,' he says, visibly ruffled. 'How nice to see you.' There is a woman on his arm, a young brunette who is unmistakably a dancer, and he turns her slightly, adjusting her trajectory, and gives her a practiced, graceful little push. Unresisting, she glides off into the party as though wearing ice skates, and Joan watches the shimmering crowd swallow up her bare, narrow back.

Jacob offers his hand. 'Jacob Bintz. Joan's husband. Nice to meet you after all these years.'

Arslan gives a Russian smile: somber eyes, lips curling in a wry wince. 'Harry was excellent tonight.'

'I'm no expert,' Jacob says, 'but he looked pretty damn fantastic to me.' Arslan stares at Joan. Jacob adds, more cheerfully than he needs to, 'He's been really pleased you've taken an interest in him.'

'He will have very good career. Who knows what will happen, but he could be . . .' He trails off, opens his hands as though releasing a bird.

Jacob puffs up with pleasure. 'As long as he's happy.'

The two men look at Joan with their four dark eyes, waiting for her to say something, but she can only look back, riveted by the strangeness. She has imagined this encounter for more than twenty years. The air inside the tent has turned thick and heavy. Their voices plow slowly through it.

'Joan,' says Arslan, 'does the cat have your tongue?'

She smiles but feels tension quivering in the corner of her lip. She presses her fingers to it. 'Your English is so good now.'

'But not perfect. It will never be perfect.'

Jacob takes her empty glass. 'Want another one?' He is asking if she would like him to leave for a minute, and she nods. Now that the first shock is over, a thrill-seeking impulse has taken hold. She wants to know what will happen when she and Arslan are alone, what he might say.

But she does not expect him to say, immediately,

forcefully, champagne flute in one hand, 'He is mine, this boy.'

'No,' she says, claustrophobic, trying to breathe, 'he's mine.'

'He must be. Once I saw, I had no doubt.'

'Jacob is Harry's father.'

'Yes. I know. Your husband raised Harry. As far as they know, they are father and son. But, Joan, don't lie. It is too late for that. I *know*. The blackout. You were full of purpose. I still remember. Like you were in Paris. Driven. I could never resist you like that.'

She doesn't know how to ask what she needs to know: if he intends to ruin her family. 'What do we do?' she says.

He sips the champagne, hand shaking. He sees her notice the tremor and says, 'I don't hide things so well now that I'm old.'

She grasps his other wrist, lets go at once. 'Hide this. Please.'

'Why would you do this to me, Joan? I have no other children.'

'That you know of. Isn't that the joke? What would you have done if I had told you? Would you have been a good dad? Would you have done all the things for Harry that Jacob has? He wouldn't be the kind of dancer he is without Jacob.' She has never quite formed this thought before, but as she speaks it, she knows it is true.

'Or without me.'

This, too, is true.

'You were never going to tell me,' he says. 'It is perfect crime. Poor Jacob, probably you have him waiting already, he has no idea, just think, oh, good, Joan loves me. I will marry her. Sure, why not?' His English is breaking apart. He gulps unsteadily at the champagne. 'I have always wanted children, Joan.'

'You could have had them. Don't try to tell me there weren't dozens of women begging to have your babies.'

'No. It's no small thing to have a baby. Maybe to you, not to me. I took women lightly sometimes but never children. Ludmilla could not have them, and there has been no other woman I would trust.'

'You've been Harry's hero since he was a little boy. Can't that be enough?'

He stares over her shoulder. 'Your husband is coming back.'

It is too soon, but the conversation will never be complete, not even if Jacob took a year to bring the drinks. 'Don't tell Harry,' she says.

'He would have better career as my son.' But he says it feebly, as a last stab.

'Arslan, if you were ever going to do one kind thing for me, let this be it.'

'I owe you, yes? For the ride from Toronto. The trip to Niagara Falls.'

'This isn't about a debt.'

Jacob is upon them, bearing drinks, resolutely cheerful, and before Arslan can excuse himself, Harry is there too, in a tuxedo, his hair still damp from the shower. His Cuban pas de deux partner is holding his hand. She is tiny, coffee skinned, all clavicle and narrow thighs in a short beaded dress. Joan greets her distractedly. Harry tells them he has just learned the company will go to Paris in the fall and dance in the opera house. 'Harry says there is a lake below?' the ballerina says in her musical accent.

Joan looks at Arslan. They think of the dressing room. 'There's sort of a cistern below the basement,' Joan says. 'With a locked grate over it.'

Arslan nods. 'There are big fish in the water, big white fish. I think they are carp. The Opéra firemen feed them. They come up to the surface like ghosts of hungry prisoners. And now there is a man who keeps bees on the roof.'

'Really?' says Joan. 'I never saw fish.'

'What is a grate?' asks the ballerina. 'What is a cistern?'

To Joan, Arslan says, 'They were there.' His eyes, crimped around their edges by middle age, are sad, not morose like when he used to descend into one of his moods or wildly tragic like when he was mourning Juliet or Giselle onstage, but soft and sad as he stands and drinks.

Later, much later, after the Bintzes are gone, Chloe sits on the edge of the fountain in the middle of the plaza. Water rains down over a jagged metal sculpture and into an illuminated turquoise pool. Through the tent's open flaps, the caterers are stripping and collapsing the tables, stacking the chairs, dismantling the bar. She should go home; she has morning class, but she feels stuck. If she had somewhere to go, she could move, but she doesn't, not really. Only back to the tiny apartment she shares with two other girls, to class in the morning, and then where? She knows she will never be asked to join the corps. Elaine made her an apprentice out of kindness, but everyone knows she is wrong for the company. Her technique is good, but her hips will always be slightly too wide. The problem isn't her weight but her skeleton, her unchangeable bones. Her stage presence, too, is an issue. She is not, as Elaine has said, a ballerina, not like Verónica, Harry's girlfriend, who is like a specially evolved bird with hollow bones and tulle plumage and unshakable calm. 'You can fake it sometimes,' Elaine said, 'cover up this thing you have with prettiness, but then you lose something. The audience can see something's missing. But if you don't cover up, they see you wrestling with the dance, and it worries them. You're gifted – uniquely gifted – but I don't know how to use you.'

Tonight at the reception, Chloe and Joan had cried when they hugged and then chitchatted to cover their tears. Watching Harry and Verónica circulate, accepting congratulations, Chloe had expected to feel jealous or at least bitter, but her jealousy seems to have finally run its course, leaving her exhausted to the point of immobility,

322

like a castaway. She had asked Elaine for the apprenticeship, begged really, in part because she didn't know what else to do – auditions for other companies had not gone well; she can't see a reason to go to college – and in part because she wanted to be close to Harry, to force him to realize he couldn't simply discard her after a lifetime of loving her. He had yielded a few times, letting her drag him drunkenly back to her apartment, but then he had closed and locked himself to her. 'What are the odds,' he had said once, 'that we would both make it? Two little kids who lived next door to each other both going pro?'

'Is that what this is?' she said. 'You're afraid I'm hurting your odds?'

'I'm saying we need separate destinies.'

A man in a tuxedo and undone bow tie emerges from the tent, glass in hand, and makes his way toward her, turning his unsteadiness into a little dance, staggering sideways until he seems about to fall over, then catching himself with a nimble hop and staggering back the other way. When he reaches the fountain, he turns a stuttering pirouette on his heels like Charlie Chaplin caught in a gust of wind and plops down beside her, nearly tipping backward into the glowing water.

'I didn't know they got a clown,' she remarks.

'Hello, Chloe,' Arslan says.

She takes the glass from his hand but doesn't bother to sniff it. True to stereotype, he always drinks vodka.

He winks. 'You want some?'

She dumps the liquor into the fountain. 'Don't flirt with me.'

'You don't like to flirt?'

'Not with drunk old men.'

'How old do you think I am?'

'Fifty?'

He cringes. 'No, not yet. A few more years. She is cruel tonight.'

'Maybe I'm cruel every night.' She has met him a dozen or so times, usually briefly, always with Harry, who never seemed overly anxious to share his mentor.

'Maybe. But always with good reason, I am sure.' His thoughts appear to wander, and she watches in the active, watery light as his face relaxes into sadness.

'No, sometimes just for fun,' she says.

'What are you doing out here? Are you waiting for someone? Harry has seen his mistake?'

'I don't know. I just didn't get any farther. What are you doing here? Where's your date?'

'You noticed my date. Then you are not indifferent.'

'But you are to her, I guess.'

'She is the indifferent one.'

'Please.'

'Yes, please. She is one of these young ones, like a balloon. I let her go, and she drifts away. Bye-bye. Not a word. Up into the sky. A nice light thing.'

'Or you pop her.'

'Only when she asks nicely.' Now she laughs, and he looks pleased. Then he is serious again. 'Are you very heartbroken by Harry?'

Two men in leather work gloves tip over what is left of the ballerina ice sculpture and drop it into a rubber bin. 'I was. But now I'm just tired.'

'I think you are too tired to go home. I think you should come in a taxi with me, to my apartment, and we will keep each other company.'

'Arslan, I'm not going to sleep with you.'

Some dark expression crosses his face, and he turns his head to hide it. 'You think I'm too old?'

It was mortality in his face, flitting quick as a bat. 'Not exactly. I wouldn't want Harry to think I was trying to get revenge on him. I wouldn't want you to think that, either.'

'I wouldn't,' he says plaintively. 'And I don't tell Harry who I sleep with.'

'That's the other thing. I don't want to be one of your girls. I feel pathetic enough as it is.'

'Oh, Chloe,' he says, putting an arm around her shoulders. His grasp is gentle, but she can feel his strength. 'You make me so sad. We are both sad tonight. Okay. Come with me anyway. We need someone to keep us company. I have a guest room. I have milk and cookies.'

She wants to be proud, to say no. At least she wants to ask why he has suddenly focused on her, but she knows if his answer is not perfect (and what would the perfect answer be?), she will have to go home to her cheap futon in her tiny bedroom partitioned from a windowless corner of her shared apartment. So instead she asks, 'Why are *you* sad?'

'I am sad because I am an old man, and nobody wants to sleep with me. And because I am Russian, and we are always sad late at night.'

AUGUST 2000 – UPSTATE NEW YORK

Elaine watches from her upstairs window as they walk slowly around the meadow, not touching but straying into each other's paths and bumping shoulders from time to time. Sometimes she thinks she should envy them, but she has no appetite for entanglement anymore. She has cleared out human mess from her life. Her boyfriends are short-lived, convenient, and never invited to the dacha. In fact, Arslan and Chloe are the first guests she has ever had here, and she is pleasantly surprised not to resent their presence, especially since they invited themselves. There is something they want to discuss.

She still calls it a dacha even though it is just a house now. She painted the paneling white and got rid of Mr K's lace curtains and most of his Russian bric-a-brac. No more troikas, no more saints frowning down at her from under their gilded halos. The samovar survived the purge because of sentiment and because her years with Mr K left her hopelessly addicted to tea, and the balalaika still leans against the fireplace. Arslan remembered the instrument at once. He had picked it up and played it, first some bittersweet folk tune and then the theme from *Doctor Zhivago*. Who knew he could actually play? He turned to Chloe and said, 'Tonya, can you play the balalaika?'

Elaine had thought the reference would go over Chloe's young head, but the girl replied, 'Can she play? She's an artist!'

'Ah, then it's a gift,' Arslan said.

And they laughed. Elaine wasn't sure she had ever seen a woman make Arslan laugh before Chloe. Certainly she had never seen him toss off a movie quote.

They are a puzzling couple. On the surface they make perfect, if scornworthy, sense: the older, famous, wealthy man, and the young, slender, beautiful blond girl. And yet Chloe mothers Arslan, who is almost thirty years her senior, scolds and teases him, hectors him to drink less, drive more carefully, go away once in a while and give her some peace and quiet. (Elaine has never seen Arslan endure being teased, either.) Chloe is not possessive, but for the first time since Elaine has known him, Arslan appears to be faithful. He has to cajole Chloe into appearing with him in public. She returns most of the presents he buys for her. She will spend weeks holed up with him at his place in Maine, but she has an apartment of her own in New York, a tiny studio in Chelsea, ten blocks from his place. She will not live with him unless he marries her, and she seems to offer the caveat without resentment, even though he says he will never marry again. Perhaps she is untroubled because she has plenty of time, time to change her mind and move in with him or time to leave him.

The task of telling Joan about Chloe and Arslan's involvement had fallen to Elaine. It had not been a pleasant conversation. First Joan had giggled like a lunatic. Then she had issued a series of sarcastic warnings for Elaine to pass along to Chloe, followed by serious ones. She had been worried for Harry. She had been disgusted with Arslan. She had gone silent. *The father-and-son thing is incredibly strange,* Elaine had said, wanting Joan to know she grasped the epic weirdness at work, even more than Harry could. *Jacob is Harry's father,* Joan said. Then Elaine was silent until Joan said, *Like you used to say, control is everything,* and Elaine said, *Okay.*

But time has soothed everyone. Two years without implosion have made Arslan and Chloe seem borderline viable.

'This thing with Chloe isn't about Harry, is it?' Elaine had asked him at the beginning. 'Or Joan?' Although it wasn't really at the beginning when she asked him because Chloe had resisted sleeping with him for six months and refused to be seen publicly with him for another six months after that, so by the time anyone knew about their romance, it was a year old.

'It is only about Chloe,' he said. 'But I needed to be sure of that, in myself, so I told her about Harry.'

329

'Jesus,' said Elaine. 'Really?' If Arslan had not seen for himself, she would not have told him, as Joan had never told her. She had suspected the truth when Joan was pregnant, and had been certain as soon as she saw Harry. Even when he was six years old it was obvious. Elaine suspects that Joan suspected she knew the truth all along, as though they were a pair of double-crossing spies.

'That is why it took six months for her to sleep with me,' Arslan says matter-of-factly. 'But now we have trust.'

'I didn't know you had it in you to be so patient.'

'Well,' he says, 'I had other friends I saw sometimes while I waited.'

'Of course you did.'

'But not anymore.'

'I'm impressed. Honestly.'

'I always used to say I would like being old, and it's true. I do. Although I am less of a eunuch than I thought I would be, thank God.'

'Maybe someday,' Elaine said. 'You're really not old. Just older.'

She had been the one to suggest Chloe audition for Rusakov Dance Project when she could no longer in good conscience keep her on as an apprentice, and Arslan and Chloe had put on a convincing deception, acting like friendly acquaintances when really they were already wrapped up in each other. But even if he hadn't been in love with her, Arslan would have asked

Chloe to join his company. Elaine's great strength as an artistic director is her generosity, something that sprouted in her only after she stopped dancing. She is not a gifted choreographer, but she nurtures those who are, granting them access to her company, giving them freedom, a large stage, nice posters, the chance for prominent reviews. She has an eye for artists who should work together, and Chloe is perfectly suited to Arslan's choreography, which is too technically demanding for dancers without heavy ballet training but so modern and strange that most ballet dancers, male or female, can't shed enough of their refinement to satisfy him. But Arslan likes the ferocity that emanates from Chloe when she dances, and together they have trained it in a way Elaine never could, working its angles so sometimes it looks like anger and other times grief or lust or even joy or stillness. They shared credit for the choreography of *Emma Livry,* in which Chloe metamorphosed from ethereal ballerina to fireball to ghost. She made the audience see the flames as she clutched her costume's bodice to her chest, trying to preserve her modesty even in the face of death. Elaine thinks that what Arslan has really taught Chloe is how to forgive.

They reach the far end of the field and turn back toward the house. So far, for two days, they have been secretive about whatever they have come to discuss, preferring to gossip and drink tea and smoke a little pot and swim in the pool she put in three years ago when her joints had gotten serious about aching. Arslan seems to be dancing more than he has for years, stretching and doing barre in the mornings with Chloe on the porch while Elaine sits and works the crossword.

Elaine goes downstairs and out to the porch and is waiting, legs crossed and fingers steepled, in her favorite chair when they come in, Arslan holding the screen door open for Chloe. 'Okay,' she says. 'Enough. Tell me.'

They pause, exchange a glance. 'It's just an idea,' Chloe says warily.

'For a ballet?'

'Yes. Full-length, abstract, but also with a narrative.'

'And you want to use my company.'

'And your theater and your orchestra,' Arslan says with an air of coming clean. 'And some of your money. But, if you do it the way we want, you will make it all back, and then some.'

Elaine works along the fingers of her left hand with her right thumb and forefinger, pinching the bones tenderly. 'What's the catch?'

'It's Harry,' says Chloe.

'What about him? You don't want to use him? You should. He sells tickets.'

Arslan sits in the chair opposite, hands between his knees. 'No. We do want to use him. Actually, we need to use him. It is essential.'

Elaine's confusion feels ominous. 'But?' she says.

Chloe is standing several feet away from Arslan, looking like she has come to inform Elaine of a death. 'He would have to know the truth.'

Elaine laughs, appalled. 'No. Absolutely not.'

Arslan leans forward. 'Don't you think he deserves to know? Wouldn't you want to know? He's not a little boy anymore.'

'But Joan. And Jacob. This would kill Jacob. You would be destroying a family. And *why*? Why would he have to know? What is this ballet?'

They explain, and at first she can only stare, dumbstruck. Then she laughs again.

Arslan sits back. 'It's not so funny. Stop and think.'

'It's just, I was watching you this morning in the field and thinking how you'd finally grown up. I thought, Chloe has made Arslan a man. After all this time, Arslan is a man. But this is the worst kind of selfishness, and I think it's disturbing – deeply disturbing – that you don't see that. It's so *obvious*, so *basic*. And I'm not some altruistic goddess, so if *I'm* disturbed, something's really wrong.'

'It was my idea,' Chloe says. Arslan holds out a hand, and she comes, slowly, to lean against him.

Elaine is still addressing Arslan. 'You said this wasn't about Harry or Joan.'

'What isn't?'

Elaine frames them with her hands. 'This! You! You said it wasn't about getting back at them.'

333

Now he is angry. 'It isn't! I love Chloe because I love Chloe. We're talking about dance.'

'I know why you laughed,' Chloe says. 'I get it. But just stop and think for a minute. Imagine what it could look like. There's never been anything like it.'

Elaine's mind quiets. Once she starts to think about dance, she doesn't think about Joan or Jacob or Harry. She imagines a stage, people moving on it. 'Ballet about ballet has been done,' she muses. 'Like *Le Conservatoire*.'

Arslan flicks his fingers. 'That doesn't have the same scope. That's vaudeville, not personal.'

'Elaine, think' – Chloe hesitates, then plunges – 'think about the commercial possibilities, too. It's an incredible story. It's a ballet about a person who was part of a bigger story. People are nostalgic for the cold war already. This ballet is historical, and it's personal. The media would be all over it. Arslan is still famous.'

For a moment, all three are silent. Cicadas grind away in the trees. 'Harry couldn't do every performance,' Elaine says. 'Neither could you. Would it work with other dancers? Is it a circus with you in it?'

'People will come,' says Chloe. 'We'll make a good ballet. You know we will.'

'Every performance will sell out,' Arslan concurs.

'So you're just going to call up Harry and tell him? He'll hate you. He won't want to be in your ballet after you detonate his family.'

The look Arslan and Chloe give each other is full of the kind of solidarity that can only come from love and conspiracy, if those are two things and not one. She sees they have already thought of a solution to this problem.

The next month, at 4:00 a.m. on a Tuesday in New York, Harry's phone rings and he answers, still half asleep. Five minutes later, Jacob answers a different phone in California, his voice tight with fatherly fear. She says the same thing to both of them, and when they ask, *Who is this,* she tells them gladly, defiantly. She says she thought they should know, and she hangs up, sets her heavy, old-fashioned white and gold phone down on the floor, lies back on her green velvet sofa, marred here and there with cigarette burns, and looks out into the same urban half-light that the boy must be looking at. Neither of them will be sleeping for quite some time, Ludmilla is certain. Maybe days. The dachshund by her feet stirs and groans. She wonders what they are doing, if they have called each other yet. Perhaps the man is waking up that witch, perhaps he will strike her. They must know it is true. Neither had laughed. The man had said *No,* but more like someone who sees the reaper sliding in under the door than someone who disbelieves.

Poor darling Arslan, so distraught when he came over. Yes, she had screamed at him and smashed one of the precious Chinese vases he had given her years ago in apology for some forgotten transgression, but really her heart broke for him. She was a witch, that silly, moony girl from the corps, a temptress and a cheat and a thief and a slut. Arslan had come to Ludmilla willingly; it had been his idea to get married; she had not needed any black magic to lure him from the silly girl who was so impressed with herself for driving him from Canada. So she could drive a car. So what. From the beginning Ludmilla had known he would not be faithful, but when it got to be too much, she would smash something to make him behave for a while. He had not known about the boy, could not have known – the witch had seen to that – and he had always wanted children, poor lamb. He called and said he needed to talk, that only she could understand his suffering. *But you must tell him,* she had insisted, holding his hands on this very sofa. *He must know that you are his father.* But he only sat there, looking tired and old and slumped, and said that *he* could not tell the boy. *He* could not be the one to do it. And she patted his hands and told him not to worry, everything would be fine. She had wanted to make love, for old times' sake, but he pretended to be too sad, when really the impediment was the new little witch, the little blond one with the fat hips.

She wants to smash something else, but she doesn't want to clean up the mess, and the maid only comes every other week now. The room is cluttered with gifts from her husbands and lovers and self: shiny, valuable, breakable things. She should sell them, not smash them; she keeps meaning to find someone who will do it. Rising, she pulls her shawl around her shoulders and crosses to her piano, a white baby grand inlaid with mother-of-pearl. Two more dachshunds sleep beneath it, curled up together on a cushion behind the pedals. The instrument was sent to her by one of her countrymen who had admired and seduced her when she returned to St Petersburg for a time after the government fell, full of patriotism, unprepared for the inconveniences and slights of national transition. He only became wealthy (nickel? tungsten?) after she fled back to New York, stunned by the discovery that she had turned into an American. The note that came with the piano was an attempt to convince her to try Russia again, one last time. Why you would give someone an unmovable piece of musical furniture as an enticement to change continents was something Ludmilla had never understood.

Sitting on the bench beside a floor-to-ceiling window, she is up among the water tanks. The city spreads out below, purple-orange and silent. Taxis glide along the dim streets like lonely yellow beetles. She lights a cigarette, clamping her teeth down on the long white holder. For a moment she sits and smokes, considering what to play. Dawn won't break for another hour. The neighbors are sleeping. She lifts her hands high and then drops them hard on the keys, releasing a torrent of Rachmaninoff.

APRIL 2002 – NEW YORK CITY

In the morning, there is company class. Then there won't be any rehearsal, just the premiere at night. They are ready, Arslan says. He wants the cast to be fresh. Standing behind him at the barre, Chloe studies the grey hairs scattered around the back of his head, the creases in his neck, the freckled edges of his ears, the butterfly-shaped patch of sweat coming through his grey Mariinsky Ballet T-shirt. She had convinced him, finally, the year before, to go back to St Petersburg with Rusakov Dance Project. They had taken a boat tour of the canals, had wandered through the Hermitage with ungainly slippers over their shoes, had lit candles in the Peter and Paul Cathedral. Then he had taken her to see the grand building where he once had an apartment, the Vaganova Academy where he had learned to dance, the fashionable boutique that had once been a café where he had boldly sat and written letters to Joan. At the Mariinsky, he walked onstage alone and looked out at the empty chairs, the imperial box. Then he had turned and held out his hands for her.

'And back back back, plié, reverse,' Elaine says, moving among them.

Chloe feels the presence of Arslan's body as if it were her own ghost. She won't disrupt her form to look down, but she is peripherally aware of his leg in black sweats sliding out and in, out and in. When they turn to face the other way, she listens to him breathing behind her, the scrape of his slippers on the floor. In the mirror on the far wall, she sees his face over her shoulder and knows from his inward look that he is not aware of her in the same way. He focuses on his dancing so completely that there is no room for anything else. He's lucky he's not the pregnant one; he's not the one making space for something to grow.

The timing is not ideal, but she thinks she will be able to dance through the run of *Rodina,* which is planned as three weeks. She's only five weeks in, but she is having to fight her instinct to be tentative, protective of her body in a way she never was before. Once, Joan had told her that she danced her best ever while pregnant, that it had liberated her, but Chloe feels she is dancing around those new cells, not with them. She imagines they are as delicate as a bit of sea foam.

'Fully stretching, Harry,' Elaine says. 'Yes. Okay. Reach, stay, stay, stay, and fifth.'

Chloe finds Harry in the mirror. He has a bandanna tied around his head. His eyes bore holes in space. If she didn't dance with Harry, she would not know him anymore. The situation is beyond unusual, no denying it. When she started seeing Arslan, he had been jealous of both of them, certain there was some revenge plot at work. After Ludmilla told him the truth, and again after she and Arslan married, he distanced himself from her for a while, but he came back. She knows sometimes he wanted never to see her again, as, when she was younger, she had wished he would disappear, but they have accepted that they are yoked together. They were in dress rehearsals when she told him she was pregnant; he had no time to pull away. He had been forced to endure and to accept. The choreography includes the daredevil fish dive they had so clumsily attempted in the basement studio the night they first had sex, and she told him so he would not drop her and also so the audience would see his fear. She wonders if their shared childhood, spent hearing bizarre stories of love and devastation and enchantment, women dying from heartbreak, women turning into birds, prepared them for the tangling of their lives, if this ballet is a form of therapy.

When they go to center floor, Arslan retreats to the back. He will not do the whole class, not the allégro. Age has humbled him, Chloe gathers. She is glad she did not know him when he was young.

Harry drinks from his water bottle, wipes his face, comes to the front. She catches his eye, sees his preoccupation. He is probably thinking of his father. Jacob has promised to come, but his flight won't land until the afternoon. Harry thinks he's cutting it close on purpose, so he can pretend something went wrong and stopped him from showing up. But only if Jacob sees the performance and still loves Harry afterward will Harry forgive himself for dancing the role.

'. . . and one, croisé. And two, open,' Elaine is saying. 'Lift three, full ronde de jambe to the back, promenade, six, seven. You hold the eight. Like this. Okay? Clear? Then prepare.'

Side by side in the mirror, Chloe and Harry cross their legs in fifth position, lift their arms.

Jacob sits in front of the TV in boxers and a T-shirt. Dawn has barely broken. A morning talk show is on. Behind the hosts, outside their fishbowl studio, New York is green with spring. He stands and looks out the window at the driveway of his rented townhouse, goes and looks out the other window, looks in the refrigerator, snaps his fingers, swings his arms, sits down again. He has decided not to go. The time when he should have left for the airport has come and gone. But he still might make the flight if he leaves now. He will feel better after it is really too late. Or he will feel worse. He doesn't know. How can they ask him to do this? How can they ask him to do anything? But it's not really *them* asking. Joan hasn't tried to contact him in months. It's Harry. But Joan would want him to go, too, he knows.

He gazes at the TV and wills it to give him a sign. A commercial for frozen pizza comes on.

Jacob turns off the TV. It is not a sign, but to have asked for one is enough. He has not packed a suitcase. He grabs the garment bag that holds his tuxedo from his closet and tosses some random clothes, his toothbrush, and a book in another bag. He will buy whatever else he needs.

At the airport, while he panics that he might miss the flight he has been contriving to miss all along, his agitation and lack of luggage attract some attention from security. Eventually, after Jacob's urgent explanations, the guard gives him a slow up and down and says, 'All right, you seem harmless.' *Harmless,* Jacob repeats to himself as he hurries down the terminal, emasculated but giddy. *I am harmless.* Only when the plane is airborne, swinging out over the Pacific, gathering speed for its long arc back over the continent, does the dread return and wrap around him. He peers out of it into an oval of pale sky and morning sun. He will not disappoint Harry, but he will pay a price of whispers and pity.

The plane's engine is the audible rush of hours passing, time pushing him to New York even as he braces against it. He tries not to think, only to surrender to the flow of obligation. He is on the wrong side of the plane to see the missing twin towers. He sees the Rockaways and the ocean instead. Then he is through the airport, and a taxi is pulling him past the deteriorating flying saucers of the World's Fair, past row houses and a cemetery and neighborhoods that mean nothing to him, over

343

the Queensboro Bridge among secretive Town Cars, Midtown standing up like a waiting bully. Then a rushed shower, three attempts before his bow tie is tied, cursing his clumsy fingers and his sweating, miserable face in the mirror, wishing for Joan to help him, remembering not to wish for Joan. A minibar bottle of Jim Beam. He hurries through the city with all the other hurrying people, and then he has crossed the plaza and given his ticket to the usher and climbed the stairs, looking down so as not to see the posters of Harry and Chloe and Arslan, not to see anyone he might recognize. He is exposed and alone but surviving, and he is in his seat.

Joan is somewhere in the theater. Jacob does not see her, does not look for her. He had asked Harry to get them seats as far apart as possible, and it seems his request was honored. Audience chatter rises as a movie star in a spangled gown finds her seat near the front. Other famous people are here, politicians and pop stars and moguls, all of Arslan's dazzling friends. Jacob sees Sandy Wheelock making her way down the aisle in emerald moiré silk, on the arm of a grey-haired man.

At first Jacob had told Harry no, under no circumstances would he attend the premiere of *Rodina,* the monstrous ego trip of a ballet about the man who had pulled Jacob's life out from under him like a cheap rug. But Harry had made the point that Jacob would otherwise spend the night alone getting very drunk, and so he should probably just come and support his son instead. *Son.* Harry uses the word a lot these days, more than is necessary, and Jacob knows he is being reassured, something he finds both irritating and, truthfully, reassuring.

Tired of craning his neck for celebrities and unwilling to be impressed by their abundance, he opens his program. The advertisements in ballet programs are always for expensive things, watches and fancy hotels and, toward the back, private schools and dance academies and barge trips down the Danube. Usually there is an insert on colored paper with that night's cast, but because this is a premiere and because Arslan is the most important being in the universe, the usher had handed Jacob a stiff sheet of embossed card stock. Beneath *Rodina* stamped in red at the top along with the date and above the names of the dancers in the company and the list of scenes and acts, there is printed the following:

YOUNG DANCER . . . . . . Harold Bintz
THE AMERICANS . . . . . . Chloe Rusakov
THE RUSSIAN . . . . . . Tatiana Nikulina
THE HUSBAND . . . . . . Georges Lazaresco
OLD DANCER . . . . . . Arslan Rusakov

Harry's name is indeed terrible for a dancer, as its bearer had whined throughout his adolescence, but Jacob is unexpectedly and absurdly moved to tears at the sight of it. Harry could have changed it, taken a stage name or, horrifically, Rusakov's name, but he had kept the name Jacob gave him. *I want you to name him,* Joan had said. *I don't want to choose.* Jacob closes the program without reading the synopsis. He knows the ballet is the story of Arslan's life ('But abstract,' Harry says), and that is enough.

He hears a small, anxious laugh and looks up at Joan. She is standing awkwardly in front of the person on Jacob's left, a tall man who has opted not to get up to let her through but instead to swivel his knees as far over as he can and brace his torso backward as though trying to evade a searchlight. Joan points at the empty seat next to Jacob and cringes an apology. He has not seen her in a year, nor has he spoken to her or replied to her e-mails or given in to any of Harry's suggestions for friendly dinners or holiday reunions. But he has not been to see a lawyer, either. He has dated a few women without much enthusiasm. Joan looks thinner than ever, a little drawn in the face and, under tight sleeves of sheer black chiffon, withered in the arms, but the sight of her is not unpleasant. Really, he could almost laugh at how uncomfortable she looks, trapped against the shins of a stranger. The lights dim.

'Jacob?' she whispers. 'There's nowhere else.'

He swings his legs to one side, letting her pass. The conductor's solemn face, flowing hair, white tie, and black shoulders pop up from the orchestra pit like the bust of an Asian Beethoven. He nods in acknowledgment of the applause and descends again. Only the tip of his baton and the uppermost waves of his hair are visible. The baton jerks once; the overture begins. Jacob's pulse speeds up so much that he feels he is blurring around his edges. If he gets through the evening without having a heart attack, he will consider it a victory. He dips into his pocket and finds the other minibar bottle of Jim Beam. He unscrews the cap and drinks half of it. He pauses, considers offering some to Joan, swallows the other half. Joan's hand alights on his forearm and then springs away like a grasshopper. 'It's only a ballet,' she whispers. 'The worst is over.'

This calms him a little. Maybe she is right. All the things that will happen onstage have, in fact, already happened. The performance is an illusion, but the past twenty-four years have also been an illusion. After Ludmilla's call, he had gone back to bed, telling Joan, who barely stirred, that it was a wrong number. For five and a half hours he lay paralyzed, packed so closely inside his thoughts that they absorbed him, sucked him out of his body. A series of revelations exploded, bringing a blinding, excruciating pain that felt almost ecstatic. As dawn broke, his visions faded into the dull whir and flicker of a film projector replaying his life, the life of a fool, until the alarm clock finally beeped his release. He got up and called in sick. Then he called the ballet studio and left a message that Joan would not be teaching, and while Joan showered, he sat at the kitchen table and readied himself for battle, preparing his arsenal of accusations, arranging them into a neat line, stroking and polishing them.

'I know why you married me,' he told her later, following her up the stairs. 'Because I have dark eyes. Because I'm not tall. Because you knew you could pass his son off as mine.'

Joan stopped and turned, slowly, deliberately, her elegant head swiveling on her slender neck, and the grace that had once made him proud now made him want to sweep her feet violently out from under her. 'I married you,' she said, 'because I wanted a life with you.'

'Clearly not. Clearly not because you've been using our family as a ballet sleeper cell while you tinkered around in your studio and perfected this Frankenstein monster that you *bred*. You *made* him. I was just the patsy who gave you the time and money to do it.'

'Harry is your *son*.'

They had not known then that Ludmilla had called Harry, too.

'He's your *experiment*,' Jacob spluttered. 'Your championship pedigree science project.'

She retreated up the stairs, down the hall, past Harry's room. 'That's not what I wanted. It's not what I was doing.'

'What were you doing? Tell me what you were doing. Explain to me what you were doing. I'm listening. Tell me. Tell me. Tell me.'

He followed her into their bedroom, and they

faced off across the bed like actors in a play. 'I wanted you!' she said. 'I wanted a family! I wanted to be important. I had no idea what it meant to be content. I'd spent my whole life laboring away for something that's impossible, but you – this family was possible.'

'This family is a lie.'

'No. The secret is nothing compared to everything else. You can have a secret that stops *mattering.*'

'Oh, sure. Sure. Like a Nazi war criminal, going about his business in Buenos Aires, doing some errands, taking the kids to school. Nothing matters but the present. Clean slate. All you're saying is that it didn't matter *to you,* and I don't even buy that.'

'You're the one who says things can be true without actually being true. This is true, Jacob. You gave me a life. What we are is true. You know me. It's been twenty-two *years.* No one knows me like you do. You know the truth about me.'

'Do I? That's great – I'm glad I know the truth about somebody, because I don't know the truth about my own fucking self.'

'You are Harry's *father*!'

Jacob had wanted to deny and to agree with equal fervency. 'You didn't want more children. You would have his child, but you didn't want mine.' He mimicked her: ' "Let's just count ourselves lucky we had Harry." You wanted his child, but you wanted me to raise it. I don't have any children, Joan. You took that away from me. Unless I'm infertile, which seems possible now, and I never knew. In which case, *thank you*, Joan. Thank you for loaning me a son. But I guess now I should step aside. What's behind door number one? It's Arslan Rusakov! The father you've always dreamed of! The greatest ballet dancer in the world and – now that I think about it – genetic material that makes a whole *lot* of *sense*.'

'Don't say that,' she said, crying. 'Please don't.'

'Would you have come to Chicago if he hadn't gotten you pregnant?' he demanded. 'Would you have married me?'

The helplessness on her face had launched the silence. It had not taken hold right away – there were more battles to be had – but he had seen the truth, nodded curtly, turned away from her and their bed, and said nothing else for the rest of that day. Gradually more days were silent than not, and then whole weeks, and finally he had left the house and her, rented the townhouse close to school. Harry had recovered far more quickly from the news, or else he was determined not to show Jacob his true reaction. He said Arslan had always been so important to him, even before he knew him, that, in a way, there wasn't much room for him to take on any more significance. Maybe, he said, on a subconscious level he had already guessed and so was on his way to being used to the idea. 'Nothing has changed,' he told Jacob a thousand futile times. 'Please, Dad, don't let things

350

change. I'll never think of anyone but you as my father.'

'Please still be proud of me,' Harry had begged. 'Please.'

And that plea was why Jacob had endured the news that Arslan and Harry were going to appear together on *60 Minutes* to tell their story, why he had tried not to be demolished by Harry's participation in this ballet, why he had taken Harry to the Bahamas after Chloe and Arslan had gotten married and kept him company while he stared at the ocean in silence, why he didn't miss his flight, and why he is now sitting in the dark with thousands of glittering people waiting to see his own life be danced by a man named Georges Lazaresco. Things have changed. If he hopes for one thing, he hopes that someday he will be able to look at Harry and not immediately be reminded that his son is not his son. He is still proud of Harry, but the pride is different than it used to be: it has been cut away from his pride in himself and left to stand on its own.

At first the music is sharp, jangly, modern, and then a melody swells up, strong but melancholy, Russian in flavor. Jacob remembers Harry's Russian music phase, triggered by *The Hunt for Red October.* He can smell Joan's perfume. He has sat beside her in so many dark theaters, smelling that smell, waiting to watch Harry. He leans toward her and whispers, 'We've been parent trapped.' After all the months of silence he would not have expected

351

his first words to her to be a joke, but he is glad not to want to heap more recriminations on her and surprised to be grateful for her presence beside him as the curtain goes up, revealing a bare stage and, at its center, Harry in fifth position, arms low, dressed like a student in black tights and white T-shirt. His hair is longer than usual and has been lightened and cut in a feathered seventies style. The resemblance to Rusakov is unmistakable. A murmur ripples through the audience.

The first act is about Russia and the Kirov; the second act is about the defection and America and fame; the third act is about age and youth. There is a story, but it's not complicated. Most of Harry's role, the Young Dancer, is based in ballet, but Arslan has forced him to loosen up, to let his hands flail, to push his movements slightly off balance and do some ugly, turned-in steps. Harry watches the beginning of the second act from the wings, as Chloe dances with the corps and then, subtly, against it. Besides Arslan and Elaine, only he knows she is pregnant, and he thinks he can see the change in her, even though her stomach is perfectly flat, her breasts still minuscule.

The first act ended with a pas de deux between Harry and Chloe that Arslan had said must be passionate but not romantic, two strangers grasping each other only as bodies but also, somehow, with a sense of destiny, of purpose. An image of the ceiling of the Paris Opéra was projected onto the blank drop cloth behind them, Chagall's angels and goats. *Why did you choose Mom?* he had asked Arslan without receiving an answer. He had asked his mother too, and she claimed to have no idea. She said she wasted years wondering but eventually concluded there might not have been a reason.

Chloe hurled herself at him, and he caught her in the fish dive, his arm around her belly, around what is beginning there. When Harry thinks it through, that he is dancing the role of his biological father while his exgirlfriend plays his mother while pregnant in real life with his half sibling, he becomes disoriented and troubled, and so he prefers not to think but to simply inhabit the role.

He has done a lot of simply inhabiting lately. He uses his old trick of closing his eyes and driving everything away, then dropping back into his body. If he could be only his physical self, he would be happy. You can be happy with only your body, he thinks. But Elaine says that he is incomplete unless he inhabits his body and his mind and the reality around him. He has inhabited the knowledge that Arslan is his father, that his parents are not speaking, that Chloe is a marvelous, stunning dancer and he had been a blind, conceited little idiot when he dumped her. As he watches from the wings, she turns a horrendously difficult double pirouette, the heel of her supporting leg just off the ground, the toe of her other shoe barely brushing the stage, as though drawing a circle in the snow. Arslan was the one to recognize her for

353

what she is, to turn her strangeness into power. Harry has inhabited his regret.

The corps disperses, scattering into the wings, their pointe shoes making a hollow galloping sound. Chloe is alone onstage, and Harry lifts his arms, prepares, and goes out to meet her. They dance together victoriously at first, full of freedom, and then awkwardly, misunderstanding each other, moving to conflicting tempos. The dance breaks down. Other dancers come and go around them. The Russian is always sliding in between them, a delicate, sinister ballerina who snuffs out the American's wildness, makes her ordinary by over-powering her with impossible challenges to her technique. Harry lifts one and then the other, and soon they are only bodies, only weight and move-ment. The ballet is the result of endless repetitions: uncounted rehearsals of acts, of scenes, of combin-ations, of steps. The steps themselves are only the most recent repetitions of movements he has done thousands, probably millions, of times in different rooms, on different stages, with different partners. He dances through a confusion of echoes. There are echoes of echoes, of other people, other places, other lives, other times and places. He wants to drive the echoes away, to be unobscured by their expanding, bouncing rings of memory.

At the end of the act, he dances alone, the speed and difficulty of his steps increasing as he goes. His concentration is so absolute, his body so close to the breaking point, that darkness contracts around him. There is nothing outside himself. He turns grandes pirouettes à la seconde at center stage, spotting off a red light at the back of the theater. Somewhere his parents are sitting together, watching him. His head whips around and around. Sweat flies from him like spray from a fountain. He can't turn anymore, but he does, his stomach and back aching, his leg burning. His lungs, which have always looked after themselves, now need to be reminded – ordered – to fill with air, then begged to fill again, one more time. What confusion of fate and electricity will one day tell his heart to stop? Could you live forever if you had enough will? He turns and turns until his leg drops of its own accord to retiré and he is spun through two final rotations before he falls to his knees and the lights go off. The fall is planned, but he would not be able to stay on his feet anyway. A breath, and then the applause crashes onto his back as the curtain comes down. He gets to his feet; the curtain flies up, and he bows. He can see the conductor, a few rows of faces, and then nothing, a roaring emptiness. He bows again.

As the houselights come up for intermission, Joan and Jacob sit stunned, like two people picked up by a tornado and then set down again. Jacob says something Joan doesn't quite catch. 'Sorry?' she says.

'I said, what happens now?'

Joan pages needlessly through her program.

355

'Now it's mostly Arslan and Chloe. Harry says it's good. He said the dance is about age and also the contrast between the limitations of the body and the way love makes you' – she gives an embarrassed flip of one hand – 'free.'

'Free,' says Jacob. 'No, it doesn't.' They sit, knees twisted sideways to let people pass. 'Are you in it again?'

'No, in the third act "The American" means Chloe. Chloe as Chloe.' Joan has seen a dress rehearsal.

'Is Harry in it again?'

'At the very end, he and Arslan and Chloe dance a pas de trois.'

Jacob blows out a breath. 'I might have to get out of here.'

The thought of sitting beside an empty seat for the rest of the performance distresses Joan. She is alone so much now, she should be used to empty seats. But she touches her fingertips to her temple, shielding her face from him.

'I'll come back another day,' he says gently. 'I promised Harry I would see the whole thing.'

She digs in her purse for a tissue and nods, pressing the back of her hand to her dripping nose. She will not beg him. She has already said everything that can be said.

'Joan.' Jacob rests a hand on her shoulder. 'Don't cry.'

'I'm sorry,' she says. 'I'm trying not to. I just don't want you to go.'

Pressure from his fingers. She looks up. He is watching her intently. He says, 'You could leave, too. We could get a drink.'

A tiny, foolish tendril of hope unfurls.

'Please stay,' she says. 'Stay until the end.'

PART V

FEBRUARY 1973 – PARIS

Arslan studies himself in the mirror, surrounded on three sides by lightbulbs. The girl had written her name and address in kohl pencil on a scrap of paper before she left. What kind of place is Virginia? He folds the paper carefully, places it inside an eye shadow compact, and pushes the compact to the bottom of his makeup bag. She must be a real dancer, this girl. She had the cursedness, the insatiability, the doom. Other girls, many girls, have wanted him, but their desire was always playful or sultry. Her desire was like a whip at her back. When he looked into her eyes, he could see she was suffering from it, the wanting, and for a moment, they understood each other. *Tu m'étonnes,* she said. You astonish me.

So there are real dancers in America. He had not been sure before. Now he will go. He will find this girl again and dance with her. When he is homesick or uncertain, she will remind him of this, the moment when he decided.